THE ELVEN APOSTATE

THE MOONSTONE CHRONICLES - BOOK THREE

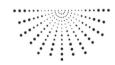

SARA C. ROETHLE

CHAPTER ONE

Alluin

"Why is she still here?" The hurled vase barely missed Alluin's head just moments after Elmerah spoke.

He looked down at the shattered vase, then stepped further into the room, suddenly regretting the visit. Even so, he couldn't help it. He, like Elmerah, felt pent up biding time while Faerune was rebuilt. They needed to move on with their plan, and it was quite apparent that Elmerah expected her sister to do the same.

Elmerah paced across her chamber, then slumped into a cushioned chair atop an ornate rug from the Helshone Desert. They truly could not complain about the accommodations. Not only had Saida's father, Ivran, insisted they stay within the High Temple, but Immril and Cornaith too. The latter pair, Alluin suspected, with motives concerning their own protection. Elmerah might be a pain in the rump, but she was also a destructive force to be reckoned with.

After a moment of debate, he shut the door behind him, then approached the sulking witch, who was now glaring at the cold hearth. He half expected the untouched kindling to burst into flames at her thoughts.

He crossed his arms, feeling stiff and uncomfortable in the new charcoal gray linen tunic and wool breeches. "Rissine will go when she's ready. The sea has been choppy. Too many storms."

She glared up at him through a lock of black hair. "The Winter Isles clan can control the winds. She has several of them who will sail with her. Storms are not an issue."

He sighed. In truth, he did not know why Rissine hadn't left yet. It had been her intent all along to sail far north on the Kalwey Sea in search of more Arthali, yet she hadn't even begun to prepare her ship for the journey. "Maybe she's worried about you."

Her gaze drifted to her crossed arms, clad in her new black coat. "Rissine only worries about herself."

This is going nowhere, he thought. "I came to see if you wanted to travel to Skaristead with me. It would be good too if Saida came along, so the High Council might actually provide us with horses. Several small Valeroot clans are to arrive there either late this evening, or tomorrow morning. They refuse to travel to Faerune without an escort."

She looked up, a bit of the anger fading from her expression. "Even with the city half in ruins?"

He shrugged a shoulder. "My people have been shunned by Faerune for generations. Can you blame them for lacking faith?"

Despite his words, he too lacked faith at times. While some Faerune elves were grateful for the Valeroot and Arthali presence, he did not miss the wary glances— some filled with darker emotions than distrust—often cast at his kinfolk's backs . . . though they were mild compared to the looks the Arthali received.

Elmerah was watching him, and he realized he was now the one glaring at the hearth like a petulant child. She grinned at his silent realization. "Yes, let us be off to Skaristead. I tire of all this flowery burrberry brandy. I could use a hearty ale."

He rolled his eyes. "We're not going there to drink."

She stood, fetched her new leather-sheathed silver cutlass leaning against her chair, then turned to him as she belted it around her waist over her coat. "No, *you're* not going there to drink. I will do as I please."

"Fine," he muttered, heading for the door. "If you're going to be a total nuisance, at least go find Saida for me."

"What's the point? All she'll do is wallow about what's happened."

The door partially ajar, he looked over his shoulder at her. "If you were a true friend, you'd try to talk her through her pain."

"Good thing no one has ever accused me of being a true friend. You find Saida. I'll meet you at the gates."

With a huff, he stepped outside, then shut the door for Elmerah to finish getting ready. Now that she couldn't see him, he smiled. She might spew bluster every chance she got, but he knew without a doubt she'd eventually talk to Saida and shake the sadness from her. What they all needed was a bit of adventure, and a bit of space from the cracked and shattered crystal walls, towering over them like a grim reminder of what had transpired, and what was still to come.

Elmerah

With a freshly packed satchel slung over her shoulder, and her cutlass at her hip, partially hidden within the folds of her coat, Elmerah ventured across the main thoroughfare toward the edge of the city. A crisp spring breeze blew through her loose hair, promising warm days and green growing things soon to come. As her boots echoed across the cracked cobblestones, she wondered how different this spring would be without the elves magical moonstones. She knew their magic could amplify the sun's effects, and could nurture weak saplings into full fruition within a single season. Just how dire would things become now without that power?

She glanced at the elves working hard to rebuild this part of the city as she continued walking. Others were busy in the new smithies, making tempered silver steel weapons like the one at her hip. The silver steel was imbued with moonstone dust, giving the blade just a hint of the magical properties for which the greater Faerune artifacts were known.

She reached the shattered crystal walls, and the warped iron gate that had been repaired back into usefulness, if not as grand as before. Before that gate stood Alluin, Saida, *and* Rissine.

Elmerah stepped up to the group, looking her sister up and down. "Finally setting sail then?" She knew it wasn't the case. Rissine carried but a single satchel, and none of the other Arthali were to be seen.

Rissine pursed her plump lips. "I hear you're traveling to Skaristead. The ship needs more flour and grain stores for our long journey, so I thought this a prime opportunity to obtain some."

"Why not send your underlings?"

"I like to do things myself." Rissine turned with a flourish of her hips, jingling the little coins and jewels sewn onto the red sash which hugged them.

Alluin shrugged apologetically, while Saida just stared at her feet. What a joyous journey this would be.

The trio followed Rissine toward four horses tethered off to the right by the ruined inn. Odd, that Rissine could find a horse so quickly in a city sorely lacking in mounts . . .

Elmerah grabbed Alluin's arm before they could reach the horses. "You told her we were going before you even asked me," she hissed.

He shrugged. "She asked me to let her know if you were to depart. She worries."

She lowered her voice, glancing at Rissine, who was stroking the largest horse. "She has no right to worry."

"That doesn't stop her from doing so," he sighed, then pulled away.

Hands on hips, she watched him go. Saida had remained silently by her side. She wore crisp priestess white, with little silver moons embroidered along the edge of her tunic. Not exactly travel clothes—except for the light gray cloak slung over her shoulder—but what remained of the High Council was doing its best to keep order, and Saida would need to take her mother's place soon. It was important to them that Saida show her status.

A few elves glanced their way, but seemed to pay them little mind. Elmerah turned her sights back to her sister, deciding she couldn't blame Alluin for the betrayal. He didn't know her full history with Rissine. The only person she'd told in recent times was Solana, and she was dead.

She had to shield her eyes from the reflected sunlight as she looked up at the massive cracked and shattered crystals. "Let's go, princess," she said to Saida. "A little fresh air will do us both good."

"Yes," was all Saida said as she walked past her toward

the horses, her long, white-blonde hair flying free in the breeze.

Her mood souring by the moment, Elmerah followed. She knew she'd need to have an important conversation with the elven priestess soon. This malaise could not continue. It was selfish to avoid it, but she'd struggled to find the time . . . No, that wasn't right. She'd struggled to find the motivation, for speaking of Saida's murdered mother would surely lead to talk of her own.

They reached the horses. Rissine had already chosen the horse she'd been stroking, a sleek silver beast with wild eyes. The other three were varying shades of brown, tamer, the depths of their eyes more serene. Alluin had untethered them, and handed one set of reins to Saida.

"Where'd you find the horse?" Elmerah asked Rissine. She took the remaining set of reins from Alluin and mounted the darkest mare.

"The stables. The elves have been too afraid to saddle her."

Elmerah smirked, then tapped her heels, guiding her horse toward the gates. As far as she could remember, Rissine didn't get along with animals. She looked back. "And you're a beast charmer now?"

Her sister's silver mare fell into step beside hers. Rissine lifted her nose. "Mireldah helped."

Elmerah sucked her teeth. She'd briefly met Mireldah, but had not been informed from which clan she hailed. Now she knew. The Silver Leaf clan could charm any manner of beast. She'd long wondered if they'd been a part of her mother's murder. On that fateful day when Rissine took her out in their small boat, the fish had been plentiful, swarming and splashing in the waters around them—almost as if they'd been summoned. The excitement had kept her and Rissine out past nightfall, leaving ample time for their mother's murder.

A horse's snort brought Elmerah back to the moment. They were already riding through the opened gate, past glaring elven sentries. Soon they were on the road heading east toward Skaristead. It was early enough they'd make it there by nightfall . . . if they didn't encounter any dangers along the way.

She almost wished for a bit of danger. If they ran afoul of witch hunters, she could give Rissine to them.

She tilted her eyes up toward the sky, letting the faint surrounding birdsong wash over her. No, she could not sacrifice her sister just yet. Not until she rallied more Arthali to aid the elves.

And not until she finally admitted out loud what she'd done.

The tavern attached to Skaristead's small inn bustled with activity, but the Valeroot elves had not yet arrived. After stabling the horses, they'd been met by Alluin's sister, Vessa, a concerned expression wrinkling her narrow brow. Now they waited at a round wooden table in the tavern, considering there was nothing better to do. Rissine sat to Elmerah's left—yet to go off in search of flour and grain—and Alluin to her right. Across the table were Vessa and Saida. If Saida sensed the mass amounts of sibling tension at the table, she did not show it. Perhaps she just didn't understand, being an only child herself.

The elven barmaid arrived with a tray of boiled leather mugs, the honey-scent of the mead almost overwhelming. The elves loved their flowery and sweet drinks. Elmerah didn't really care about flavors, as long as they were alcoholic. If she were to survive a full evening with Rissine, she'd need to be at least a little bit fuddled by spirits.

"You're worried," Alluin said to his sister as the barmaid placed a mug in front of each of them.

The barmaid cast a final wary glance at Rissine and Elmerah, then hurried away without waiting for payment. Perhaps she was leaving it up to the witches whether they would pay, or destroy the inn with their Arthali magic.

Vessa glanced at Rissine, then turned her green eyes back to her brother, raking nimble fingers through her brown shoulder-length hair. "Even if the clans were delayed, they should have at least sent scouts ahead by now. *Someone* should have been here. I'm worried they were attacked."

It was a sensible worry. With Dreilore, Nokken, and Akkeri roaming about, the dangers for a few small clans of Valeroot elves were countless.

Alluin's jaw tensed. He took a long breath, then answered, "All we can do now is wait. If they do not arrive by morning, we will return to Faerune and send trackers to find them."

"You and I are the best trackers around," Vessa pressed.

Alluin didn't reply right away, but Elmerah knew he was warring with that fact. If he didn't have other responsibilities, he'd search for the missing elves that night. But the demon emperor had to be their primary objective, and they'd already wasted too much time. Time they no longer had. The High Council had to be convinced to act now.

Elmerah swilled half her drink in one go, and was about to ask Saida for a talk—*the* talk—when the inn's double doors burst inward, rattling with a gust of cool wind. A panting, sopping wet Valeroot elf fell to his knees on the floorboards just a few paces from their table.

"Demons!" he rasped, then his eyes rolled back in his head, and he promptly fell over.

CHAPTER TWO

Elmerah was the first to reach the elf, with Alluin right behind, followed by Saida and Vessa. The entire tavern had fallen silent, except for short bursts of frightened whispers. Elmerah peered out the doorway into the still dusk, then down at the elf, face down. The poor sod had a sleek black spike sticking out of his back, impaling him.

She knelt by his side, checked his pulse—or lack thereof—then turned her attention to the strange weapon, stretching her fingers toward it.

"Don't touch it!" Rissine hissed.

Elmerah stopped mid-motion to glare up at her sister. "Why not?"

Rissine knelt beside her, too close. Elmerah shuffled away as her sister replied, "The elf said demons. If this is a demonic weapon, it may contain a . . . residue."

"It looks like a spine from a bristlepig," Alluin observed, "only larger."

The whispers were growing louder in the tavern. There would be limited time to observe the body before the patrons started cutting past them to escape into the night.

Only the night might hide demons, Elmerah's thoughts whispered. *Demons like the Ayperos, and like Egrin Dinoba.*

"I don't know him," Vessa blurted, her eyes wide and features tense. "But he must be from one of the three clans meant to arrive here. We need to search for the others."

Rissine stood, done observing the victim, then turned her back to Elmerah to face Alluin, Saida, and Vessa. "You three search his pockets, see if you can find any other clues of who he is and from whence he came. Elmerah and I will check outside."

Her voice was loud enough for the entire tavern to hear, and no one was fool enough to argue with an Arthali witch.

Elmerah rose with a sigh, nodded to Alluin that she agreed with this plan, then turned to follow Rissine as she led the way outside.

Fingers on her shoulder stopped her. She looked back at Saida, for the first time in a while seeing true fear in the priestess' eyes.

"Be careful. I cannot—"

Elmerah patted the small hand on her shoulder. "I know. It will be alright."

She hurried out the doorway before the moment could grow more emotional. She knew Saida could not bear to lose anyone else so soon after her mother. She understood. But she still had to venture out into the night in search of demons.

Her breath fogged the dark air outside, still crisp though the growing season had arrived. Soon the final frost would come and go, and the more delicate crops would begin to sprout. She wondered if she'd live to see it. Rissine's tall form was little more than a shadow walking down the quiet dirt road bisecting the small settlement.

Elmerah hurried after her, eyes on her surroundings, keeping her senses open for any signs of demonic magic. The dark road, the surrounding hills, and the sparse forests beyond were quiet—too quiet. No chirping insects nor hooting owls. *Something* was out there.

She sensed *them* a moment before they crested the hill overlooking the northern end of the settlement, but it took her eyes far longer to make sense of things. *Spiders.* The Ayperos. She had battled the massive creatures once before, but this time, there were more. Their hairy legs carried them over rough terrain like they were floating. She narrowed her eyes, trying to make out the other demon creatures in the distance. They were most certainly not timid little bristlepigs. They were wild boars, even larger than the Ayperos, black tusks catching moonlight, the slivers of light echoing on the quills coating their bodies. Now she knew where the spike piercing the elf's back had come from. How he'd managed to get one of those quills in his back was anyone's guess, and it was the last thing on her mind now. The demons charged down the steep hill toward the settlement. In a heartbeat, they were at the first of the buildings.

Suddenly Rissine was at her side. "Summon your storm, Elmerah, we must strike while they are still gathered closely together."

She blinked, nodded, then unsheathed her cutlass and raised it skyward with a shudder. There were so many of them, so many *demons* heading right their way. They'd never be able to overcome them all.

Thunder rattled the earth beneath her boots, echoing her call. Rissine had unsheathed her rapier, mimicking Elmerah's stance.

Elmerah dared a glance at her, surprised since Rissine felt using a weapon to guide one's magic was amateur.

"We must be precise," Rissine explained.

The demons reached the street in a cacophony of swishing hairy legs and pointed hooves the size of Elmerah's head.

"Now!" Rissine shouted.

Rain burst from the sky, pelleting Elmerah's face as she directed her lightning toward the front line of demons. Screams and shouts sounded behind her. The tavern patrons must have emerged at the sound of thunder.

They were just in time to see brilliant lightning surging forth from two directions—each summoned by a single witch—zinging across the first long row of demons. The strikes collided, erupting in a blinding explosion of light.

The boar demons shrieked, the spiders hissed, flesh and hair sizzled, but still more came, trampling the corpses of their fallen brethren. They didn't veer toward Elmerah and Rissine further down the street as expected. Instead, they ignored their sole threat and headed right toward the tavern, where Saida and Alluin now stood framed in the outpouring light from the door amongst a crowd of elves and humans. Some patrons screamed and ran back inside. Others fled in different directions into the night.

Elmerah lowered her cutlass. Sick realization dawned on her as Alluin stepped in front of Saida and lifted his bow. Hotrath, High King of the Akkeri, could summon demons, and he wanted Saida.

"Get to Saida!" she screamed to Rissine. "It is her they want!"

But Rissine wasn't listening. She directed bolt after bolt of lightning into the oncoming horde, thinning their ranks but only by half.

Elmerah lit her blade with flames, then ran toward Saida and Alluin into the fray of demons. The sharp hiss of raindrops hitting her cutlass was deafening, but her fire burned strong. The cumbersome boars were struggling to climb over demon corpses, but too many spiders were ahead of her, behind her, and all around. If they changed targets, she would die. But she had to risk it. Once the spiders reached Saida and Alluin, they would be overcome in an instant.

She squinted her eyes against rain and darkness as she ran, racing breathlessly toward the guiding light of the tavern. Closer now, her vision cleared. They were already overcome! The spiders moved too quickly for her to keep track of them. She reached the opened tavern doors and moved past, launching herself into the chaos of spindly legs and plump black abdomens. The boars squealed far off behind her, more frightened of the lightning than their spider kin.

Fortunately, Elmerah knew exactly what the Ayperos feared. She forced more energy into her burning blade until it shone like a tiny sun. Spiders hissed all around her, trying to leap away, but she showed no mercy, slashing their limbs off to land in sizzling, twitching heaps.

"Saida!" she called, slashing her way through spider limbs. She glimpsed all the frightened patrons hovering inside the tavern—too frightened to shut the damn doors —but no Alluin nor Saida.

Rain soaked her hair and clothes, plastering her coat to her body. "Alluin!" she screamed, turning back toward the spiders. They weren't even attacking her, entirely intent on their purpose.

"Here!" Alluin's voice could barely be heard over thunder peals, pounding rain, and hissing spiders.

She flicked her sopping wet locks out of her face, then starting cutting her way back through the demons. She didn't understand what they were doing, swarming but not attacking. She realized it too late as she reached Alluin, trapped in the midst of the spiders, his bow nowhere to be seen.

He lifted slime-coated daggers in each of his hands. "Find Saida!" he urged. "They carried her off!"

The spiders' intent clicked into place. They were swarming in this mind-boggling manner to prevent her and Alluin from going after Saida. They might not be intelligent beasts, but whoever was directing them was.

"Son of a muckdwelling bristlepig!" she cursed, stepping a safe distance from Alluin. She lifted her cutlass, pumping so much magic into it that she was on the brink of burning out. Flames whipped around her, forcing the spiders back.

In flashes of crackling lightning, she spotted two figures far beyond, standing atop the hill opposite the one the demons had descended. A man's silver hair whipped in the storm winds, and a gleaming circlet was upon his brow. She'd never seen the circlet in person—only the velvet box which had contained it—but she knew what it was. Malon was wearing the Crown of Arcale, and he'd used its magic to summon demons. All so he could kidnap the elven priestess now grasped in his arms.

Saida sagged in his grip. Elmerah could only pray she was not dead. Even from the distance, with lightning flashing, Malon's eyes met hers. She watched him through gaps of hairy spider legs, growing thicker around her, blocking her way to Saida. She'd never break through their ranks in time. Malon smiled, then turned away.

"Saida!" Elmerah screamed, slashing her burning blade through the Ayperos. Her arms throbbed, and cold rain chilled her to the bone. She could sense Alluin at her back protecting her as she made way through the spiders. Rissine's lightning crashed closer and closer, but she could not wipe out many of the spiders at once, lest she hit her trapped allies.

Elmerah screamed again, a hot cry of rage as she continued to slash through the spiders. Blood and other fluids coated her face and hair, too thick to be washed away by the rain.

She barely felt any of it. Barely recognized the danger she was still in. She had promised to protect Saida, and she had failed.

Saida

Saida fought every moment for wakefulness. She remembered the spiders, so many spiders rushing toward her. Then . . . nothing. But her head ached horribly, someone was carrying her, and she needed to wake up. *Blessed Arcale, please let me wake up*, she thought, but the sky god did not answer.

The person carrying her slowed, then she was handed off to someone else. Finally, she managed to open her eyes, but the night was so dark she couldn't see who now held her like a child in their arms.

"Don't worry, priestess," a young man's voice soothed. "You are safe."

She'd feel a lot safer if she actually recognized the man's voice. Where were Alluin and Elmerah? Where were the spiders?

"Open the door," a woman said somewhere to her left, another unrecognized voice.

She heard the creaking of a door, then felt a soft cushion beneath her. The arms of the man carrying her pulled away.

Boots stomping. More people getting into the . . . carriage. That's what it was, she was in a carriage. She groaned, regaining a bit of control over her body. She rubbed her head and tried to sit up.

"Should we give her more?" the woman asked. "She woke more quickly than we expected."

"No, let her wake," a new man's voice replied, this time, one she recognized. "She must have worked at building up a tolerance to bloodflower extraction since we last met. Clever girl." Silence for a moment, then, "Help her sit up."

Hands grasped her arms just as the carriage started

moving. She weakly shoved them away. He was right, she'd dosed herself many times with weak concoctions of bloodflower extraction to build up a tolerance, though it seemed it hadn't been enough. The spiders must have knocked her unconscious, then she'd been dosed to keep her that way. Just how long had she been out? How far from Skaristead was she now? For surely, with that voice she recognized, she was no longer in the care of friends.

She rubbed her eyes, leaning heavily against the carriage cushion, then opened them, but it was black as night in the carriage. Even with her superior night vision, it was difficult to make out the shadowy forms—two sitting across from her and one beside. She could see their reflective eyes though. They were all Faerune elves.

A small light came into existence, temporarily blinding her. Slowly, her eyes adjusted and landed on Malon, a small white wisplight hovering over his outstretched palm, swaying gently with the movement of the carriage.

"Hello, Saida."

She glared at him, not missing the Crown of Arcale upon his brow. "How dare you wear that," she rasped, her words feeling sluggish. "You are a traitor to our people."

"Saviors often begin as traitors, in one way or another."

She glanced at the other elves, the male beside Malon, and the female beside her, though she did not recognize them. They were either exiles, or those who Malon convinced to stand down when the Dreilore attacked.

"Where are Alluin and Elmerah?" she snapped, then reflexively raised a hand to her aching brow.

"They are unharmed," Malon explained. "As I told you before, I hope that you will not hate me. I would not harm your closest friends, though they are my enemies."

Tears stung her eyes. The last thing she wanted to do was cry, but she'd been holding in these tears far too long. She could not force down the swelling of emotion. "You killed my mother!" she shrieked, lunging for him. "You killed her!" Her voice cracked as the two unnamed elves shoved her back, then pinned her shoulders against her seat. "How dare you?" she gasped. "How dare you ask me not to hate you?"

Malon's brow furrowed. "I did not kill your mother, Saida. I was not present when that happened. She was supposed to be safe in one of the High Temple's hidden rooms."

Unable to use her hands, she bit the inside of her cheek hard enough to make it bleed. The sharp pain helped steady her. "You may not have held the blade, Malon, but *you* killed her. You killed every elf that died that day, and I will never forgive you. I will not rest until you pay for your crimes."

He leaned back against his seat with a huff. He wore a blue tunic embroidered with silver, the designs evident in the wisplight now hovering freely at his shoulder. Fine clothes for a rebel, she thought, far finer than those worn by his two comrades still pinning her, because knowing him, he believed he was better than them all.

"Why did you enlist into the guard?" she asked bitterly. "With your magic, you could have been of higher station."

"Not high enough." He looked to the elves on either side of her. "Let her go. If she attacks again, let me handle it."

They released her and returned to their seats, neither saying a word. The carriage ambled onward, carrying her farther and farther from her friends, and from her father in Faerune. This loss would be unbearable to him. He'd already lost his wife, she could not abandon him. She just needed to find a way to escape.

"Where are we going?"

Malon lifted a brow. "Does it matter?"

She stared, hoping her eyes conveyed exactly what she thought of him.

"We're going to our temporary home. You'll be safe from the Akkeri there, and from Egrin Dinoba."

He must think her an utter fool to believe he would shelter her from Egrin. "You are working with Dinoba. Could you not barter for my safety another way?"

The first bit of emotion she'd seen from him tugged his lips into a bitter smile. "Dinoba is no better than the High Council. I worked with him as long as I needed, and now with this," he tapped the circlet, "I need him no longer. You are right, I could have easily attained a higher station within Faerune, but I would not waste my gifts on making the plants grow."

Just how much magic did he have? If he was able to

use the Crown of Arcale to summon demons, what else could he do?

"I see you're beginning to understand," he said. "I am stronger than any guessed, and with my new allies, I will create a new Faerune."

The rocking of the carriage increased. A more primitive road now than before. "What new allies?"

"The Makali of the Helshone Desert."

Her jaw dropped. Nothing could have shocked her more. The Capital of the Helshone Desert was ruled by the Lukali, a civilized race. They held trade treaties with both Faerune and Galterra. The Makali, however, were wild barbarians, long separated from their civilized kin.

Malon smiled while she processed his words.

The mention of the Makali led her to a single, terrifying thought. "You're taking me to the Helshone Desert."

His smile broadened, though the other two elves seemed uneasy with this talk. "Yes, Saida. I daresay, your friends will never find you there. And you will not escape me, for to travel across the desert alone is a death sentence. So you may as well sit back and listen to what I have to say."

Saida dove from her seat, evading the female elf's grasp as she landed hard on the floor. She rolled onto her back. The male elf stood as much as the carriage would allow and she lashed out, kicking him in the knee. He fell away with a shout, then she rolled away from the female elf and reached for the carriage door.

Hands grabbed her shoulders, pulling her back. She

screamed at the top of her lungs. She thrashed against that grip. If she could escape this carriage, she might be able to disappear into the darkness.

The grip tightened, and Malon pulled her back against his chest. One strong hand grasped her jaw, his elbow pinning her against him. With his other hand, he lifted a vial of red liquid and lifted it to her nose. The bloodflower extraction wouldn't knock her out for long, but if they kept dosing her, she'd be asleep all the way to the Helshone. She had to escape. She had to—

Her eyes fluttered shut. The grip on her jaw became less painful.

"You will understand in time, Saida," Malon's voice was soft in her ear. "You will understand that I never meant to harm you. You will be our people's savior, Saida. The crown of Cindra is meant to rest upon your brow."

Blackness took her, and the carriage continued on, carrying her far away from anything she had ever known, and everything she had ever loved.

Elmerah

Morning had come. With the help of Elmerah's fire, the townsfolk had piled and burned the demon corpses. No one else had a better idea of what to do with them. They couldn't leave them to rot in the streets. Mostly Ayperos had been killed, but the few dead massive boars stunk more than twenty spiders. The rays of dawn over Skaristead barely pushed through the smoke.

Elmerah hadn't wanted to stay to help. She'd wanted to drown her failure in ale, but there hadn't been time. After a fruitless search for Saida, she, Alluin, and Vessa sought the missing Valeroot clans, while Rissine searched for where the demons had gone.

Rissine had come back with no further information. Elmerah wished it had been the same for her. Fifteen elves had been killed by the passing demons. They'd found the rest of the traveling clans preparing the bodies for burial rites. Alluin had sent those still living on ahead to Faerune, assuring them he'd see to the bodies. Those dead had simply been in the wrong place at the wrong time, directly in the path of the charging demons.

Elmerah, Alluin, and Vessa had piled the bodies and burned them, just like they'd been doing with the demons all morning. Good and evil, all going back to the earth and sky in the same way.

Exhausted, she flicked her flaming blade at the last of the spiders that had been dragged far off from the settlement in horse-drawn wagons. She wrinkled her nose at the acrid scent, commingling with wet soil and wood from last night's rain. How was she going to face Ivran? She knew it was upon her to tell him. She was the one who was supposed to protect Saida.

Well her, and the elf now standing at her side. Alluin

looked even more tired than she felt. His face when they'd found his slaughtered kin . . . she could have sworn they were back in Galterra on that rainy night where he'd found her, his hands stained with the blood of fallen elves. Even finding the rest alive had not chased the shadows from his eyes.

Those haunted green eyes landed on the burning pile of spiders. "What do we do now?" he muttered. "How do we find her?"

She let the flame die from her blade. "We don't. She could be anywhere."

He blinked at her. His tunic was still damp from the night before. "We at least have to try."

She turned to fully face him. "What we have to do is kill Egrin Dinoba and his pompous little cousin." She flourished her cutlass with her words. "We have to end this, Alluin. We can only hope that end will return Saida to us."

He shook his head. "She was taken by Malon. She might not be with the emperor when we find him."

Ice shot through her heart. *Malon.* They should have never trusted him. She didn't think for a second he would give Saida to the Akkeri. He was too proud an elf to stoop so low, but he might give her to Egrin. The question was, why? The only reason Egrin had wanted her was to give her to the Akkeri, and he'd already used them as much as he needed. He might want her gift of seeing through illusions and magic, but he already had Thera for that . . .

Unless Thera was dead. A death for which she'd not spare even a heartbeat of mourning.

Alluin watched her, waiting for her to speak, but there were no words. She felt in her heart that Malon wanted Saida for himself, she just didn't understand why.

Her shoulders slumped as her anger leaked away, replaced by fear. "We don't know him at all. Malon might as well be a stranger to us. There is no telling where he would take Saida, and the tracks we followed ended at a stream not far off, so we don't even know which direction to search. All we can say is that he is unlikely to kill her. He wants her alive, so for now, she is safe. Perhaps safer than any of the rest of us."

Alluin glanced over his shoulder at the sound of voices. Rissine and Vessa were approaching from the direction of town, leading their four horses. With Saida gone, there was now a mount for Vessa. It was time to return to Faerune. "You're right," Alluin breathed. "I hate it, but you're right. We need to focus on Egrin, but we can hardly call our gathering in Faerune an army. If we march on Galterra, we'll be slaughtered."

She glanced back toward Rissine, now not far off, and lowered her voice. "That's why just you and I will find him. We'll bring Isara, and that's it. We will not tell any of the others we're leaving. We cannot risk that there are yet spies within Faerune, and we cannot risk that the High Council will keep us locked within the city."

Rissine and Vessa reached them before Alluin could reply. Rissine looked at her like she knew exactly what

Elmerah was hiding, but said, "They won't sell me any grain. They want us out of their town."

Elmerah sheathed her cutlass, slamming it hard enough to make a thud. "We saved their lives! What do you mean they want us to leave?" No grain meant Rissine could delay her journey even longer.

Rissine narrowed her dark eyes, tugging the two horses she led into submission as they strained against their leads for a chance at dry grass. Her black hair had dried into a curly mass, the waves brought out by the moisture. "You should be used to this treatment by now, sister. They will always hate us."

Bloody stupid elves. How many times did she have to prove herself? Would she always be a monster in their eyes? She accepted the set of offered reins from her sister. "Let's get out of this rotten hole of a town." She glanced at the spiders, some half-burned, some little more than ash. "The elves can finish cleaning up the mess on their own."

Rissine nodded sharply in agreement. Alluin stood silently by Vessa, each now holding their own reins, not making eye contact. Would they speak about their fallen kin when they were alone, or did they not have that kind of relationship? She thought it likely Alluin had not yet spoken of his uncle or the others slain back in Galterra to anyone, at least not beyond relaying the tangible details of the event.

She squeezed her reins, then climbed atop her saddle as the others did the same. Part of her wanted to ride away from her companions, far away from Faerune and the burdens on her heart. But she did not. She did not give in to her fear. She would charge right toward her challenges. She would defeat Egrin Dinoba, and she would find Saida, even if it killed her.

CHAPTER THREE

Saida

The heat in the carriage woke her. They were still moving. She couldn't be sure how much time had passed, but imagined they had traveled through the night and half the next day if it was this hot. Fourteen, perhaps fifteen hours lost. They must have reached the edge of the desert.

She had blurry memories of being given food, and being assisted by the female elf to relieve herself outside. She'd remained under the constant influence of the bloodflower extraction, so much so that she'd been barely able to move her limbs and swallow the water that was offered to her. If she'd seen Malon during this time, she could not recall, but she knew he had to be near.

She cracked her eyes open, just barely, not wanting to let her captors know she was awake lest they dose her again. She lay on her side across one full cushion, her legs short enough to fit curled up as she was. Across from her sat the male and female elves, no Malon. Were there other elves in their entourage, or just these two?

A bead of sweat dripped down her brow and she reflexively wiped it away, then cringed. Both elves looked down at her.

"Don't worry, priestess," the female said. "You're not to be dosed again. We've reached the desert now. If you escape us, you will not get far. We'll need to abandon the carriage soon before the sand gets too deep, so you'll need to be conscious enough to ride."

They were going to ride out in the open in this heat? Were they mad?

The carriage slowed, then stopped. She fumbled to sit up, her limbs stiff and sore. When she finally managed it, she could do little more than lean back against the cushions and cross her legs against her full bladder.

The female elf seemed to read her thoughts. "Don't worry, priestess. I will aid you as soon as we are told it is safe."

She could hear people walking outside the carriage, and several voices. Mostly just talking about the heat, and readying their mounts. So it wasn't just her, the two elves, and Malon. They had a full entourage. In her weakened state, there was no way she would be able to escape.

The carriage door opened, revealing Malon, now dressed in a flowing tan robe, and another older male elf dressed the same. At least, she assumed he was an elf. The older man had more of the tan fabric wrapped around his head and face, revealing only the soft lines around his sky blue eyes. In his hand, he held a neatly folded pile of the same fabric.

His gaze on Saida, Malon stepped aside for the older elf to hand the fabric to the female inside the carriage. All she could see beyond them was golden sand.

"Phaerille, help her get dressed," Malon instructed. He looked to the male elf in the carriage. "Luc, you'll get dressed out here."

Soon Saida was alone in the carriage with the female elf, who now had a name, not that it really mattered. To Saida, all her captors were almost as bad as Malon.

Phaerille helped her into the robe, far too long for her small frame. Then she braided back Saida's hair and wrapped the fabric around her head, struggling to achieve the same effect the older elf had.

"I apologize, priestess," she said, kneeling on the carriage seat at her back, "this way of dress is foreign to me. I'm sure I'll become more adept at it soon."

Saida licked her cracked lips beneath the soft fabric. She needed water, but couldn't think about it until she was allowed to relieve herself. "Why are you doing this? Why are you helping Malon?"

"I believe in him. You did not grow up as many of us do. We cannot blame you for not understanding."

Saida's face felt hot, and not just from the growing warmth in the carriage. "Did Malon tell you that?"

Her lack of reply was answer enough.

Once they were both dressed in the flowing robes, heads wrapped with only their eyes showing, they exited the carriage. Saida tried to walk down the two steps on her own, but her robe was too long and her joints too stiff. She stumbled, and would have planted her face in the sand had Malon not caught her.

She wanted to shrug off his grip, but she couldn't tear her eyes away from the landscape, now in full view. The golden sand stretched on endlessly in all directions. She was shocked the carriage had made it this far, its wheels now sunken a hand's width into the sand. There were ten more in their party, all dressed in robes with features obscured. She could not tell for sure whether they were male or female, unless she tried to judge by height alone, but most female elves were nearly as tall as the men. While two horses were being freed from the front of the carriage, she noticed a group of saddled antlioch, their heavy wool shaved down to almost nothing.

She found herself staring at them instead of the strange landscape, lest she become entirely overwhelmed.

"They fare better in the desert than horses," Malon explained, his hands still resting lightly on her arms as he stood behind her. "We leave the wool just long enough to protect their skin from the sun."

She pulled away from him, then looked for Phaerille, but could no longer tell her apart from the other elves. Fortunately, Phaerille stepped forward, identifying herself by stating, "The priestess and I need a moment of privacy."

Malon stepped away from her and nodded. "Be quick about it." He moved in front of Saida and peered down at her. "Please, do not run. I much prefer you conscious, even with your sharp tongue."

She glared at him, but allowed herself to be led away by Phaerille, her attention once again turning toward her surroundings. Now that they'd stepped away from the carriage she could see different terrain in the far distance. Judging by the direction of their tracks, that was from whence they'd come, and it was too far for her to reach on foot in this heat.

She turned her gaze back ahead of her. Empty sands, sands so warm her feet sweated heavily within her boots. "There is no privacy to be had."

"I will hold my robe open to shield you," Phaerille explained. After a moment of hesitation, she added, "I hope you will do the same for me. We are the only women in our party."

"Of course," Saida replied, an alliance seeming her only hope in the world. If she could convince Phaerille to help her escape . . . then they'd both die in the desert together. Perhaps if they neared a settlement, she could hide until a messenger could be found to send word to Faerune. Her father could send guards to rescue her.

By the time they stopped walking, her body was drenched with sweat, and she could still see the men in the distance when she looked over her shoulder. Phaerille shielded her, then she took her turn, and soon they were headed back toward the waiting elves and antlioch.

She spoke no more, her throat too dry anyhow. There would be ample time to build upon this alliance. For now, she would cooperate, if only to remain conscious.

She even allowed Malon, his head now wrapped like the others, to help her atop her antlioch. Let him think she'd been cowed. She'd stick a dagger in his back the first chance she got.

She tried not to let her disappointment show as she realized her antlioch was the only one with a tether. The others only needed their riders' feet to guide them, and the extra mounts would follow the herd willingly. Only hers had a tether, to keep her from galloping away.

Malon looped that tether around his saddle before mounting, then pulled her antlioch forward to ride beside him. She glanced back at the carriage as they left it behind, noting that the horses were not to be seen.

"You let the horses go," she observed softly.

Malon nodded, his silver eyes on the distant horizon. "They will journey back to Fallshire on their own. They would not survive if we tried to take them with us."

The heat was beginning to make her dizzy. The sun seemed to physically pellet her shoulders and head. "And *we'll* survive?"

She couldn't see his face, but the crinkle of his eyes said he was smiling. "Yes, Saida. We have plenty of water and food. And I know the way."

"You've traveled the Helshone before?"

"Yes, I have the High Council to thank for my knowledge of the desert. I've escorted many trade caravans."

She tugged her head wrap a little further over her eyes. The sun was so blasted bright. Not for the first time, she wished her parents hadn't kept her so sheltered. Perhaps if she'd been able to join one of these caravans, she could have learned something that would be useful now. Perhaps if she'd managed to find Malon back then, she could have helped him choose a different path.

Instead, she would have to depend on him now to keep her alive. From one keeper to another—though she by far preferred Elmerah's care. She kept having to rely on others to guide and protect her.

And she was bloody tired of it.

Rissine

It was nearly midnight by the time Rissine returned to her lodgings in Faerune. The building used to be an inn for foreign caravans visiting the city for negotiations, but now housed Arthali. Her crew were all in neighboring rooms, and Celen's mishmash halfblood clan was in the northern wing.

And yet, here Celen was, in her side of the inn, leaning against her door as she reached it. Tattooed, scarred arms crossed over his broad chest. His furrowed brow tugged at the heavy scarring on one side of his face, some marks reaching up into his short dark hair.

She slung her satchel from her shoulder, irritated, and ready to rest. She'd not mind a pipe of bitterroot either. "Kindly remove yourself from my door, lest I remove you."

"You need to leave Elmerah alone. She doesn't want your help."

She sucked her teeth, eyeing him up and down. He was a big man, taller than her, but she could drop him like a sack of grain where he stood with hardly a thought. "My sister is none of your concern. Do not poke your head where it doesn't belong." *Again*, she thought. She'd heard whispers that Celen was the one who'd helped Elmerah flee, and it had been no coincidence that Celen's ship had run afoul of a reef shortly after.

Unfortunately, he had survived.

He watched her, the flicking of his eyes giving away how carefully he was choosing his words. "She knows what you did. She knows why you took her fishing that day. You do realize that, don't you?"

A shiver went down her spine. Yes, she suspected that Elmerah knew, but she wasn't about to discuss it with anyone but her. "You were not there that day. You know nothing of the matter. I have always done what I must to keep Elmerah safe, and I will continue to do so. She is too headstrong for her own good."

Another moment of silence.

She was tired, hungry, and her rump ached from the

saddle. She lowered her voice to a growl, "Get out of my way, Celen."

With a sigh, he straightened, then stepped out of the way.

She walked past him and opened the door.

"You know," he said to her back, "if you continue to watch her steps, she will flee from you. She has entered into this alliance grudgingly. I would not push her too far."

Her hand still on the knob, she flipped her hair over her shoulder and eyed him dangerously. "Out of the two of us, *I* am the witch you don't want to push. You and your clan of halfbloods should sleep with one eye open."

He lifted a scarred brow. "You would threaten us here and now?"

"Consider it a warning. I *will* keep my sister safe, but I do not care who else dies along the way. She is all that matters."

He narrowed an eye. "I was led to believe your goal is to lift the Arthali exile. To gain respect for our people."

She sucked in her saliva, then spat on the floorboards. "I do not require respect from swine."

"Then what is your motive?"

Her anger finally got the better of her, and something she never planned to share with *anyone* spilled off her tongue. "Soren Dinoba, or as I've been led to believe, Egrin Dinoba, forced the clans to kill off Shadowmarsh witches. Elmerah blames me for our mother's death, but *he* took her from us both. *He* is truly the one who killed her. When faced with the choice of losing just my mother, or losing Elmerah too, I did what was needed. That does not mean I do not desire revenge for our mother's death."

He balked, and suddenly she didn't entirely regret her words. She enjoyed the stupid look on his face. "But you were working *with* the emperor. How can you claim to have wanted revenge from the start?"

She quirked a brow. "Dear Celen, the best way to crumble an empire, is from the inside."

She walked into her room, shut the door in his face, then leaned against it. Despite her calm words, her breath heaved. She hadn't lied. She wanted revenge on the emperor. She'd *love* to see his head on a pike.

The only issue was that she knew what he could do, and she was scared shitless of him.

Alluin

Alluin hadn't been prepared to return to his chambers, though his bones ached and his eyes drooped from their sleepless night, followed by a full day's ride. In fact, he never wanted to sleep again. He knew that once he closed his eyes, he'd see the mangled bodies of elves once more, and not just the clans killed by demons. He'd see his uncle Ured, and the clanmates he'd known all his life. He'd see his hands stained red with their blood, and he'd see Elmerah, the most unlikely of saviors, burning their bodies with her fire.

So instead, he was in Ivran's chamber with Elmerah. He'd stood by her side as she told him the news of Saida. They'd both watched the old elf's frantic tears. Elmerah had been so uncomfortable she'd practically forced several glasses of burberry brandy down Ivran's throat, and he was now in his chamber, fast asleep, muttering with fitful dreams.

Now he and Elmerah sat watching the dying embers of the fire, each occupying one of the closer chairs. They'd assured Ivran they'd find her, and Alluin hoped it wasn't a lie.

He dared a glance at Elmerah, watching the way the occasional gust of flamelight danced across her face.

Seeming to sense his gaze, she turned to him. "What is it?" Her words were short and clipped, but he could sense the emotion just beneath the surface.

"Maybe we should leave tonight."

She lowered her chin and lifted her brows. "I'm as eager as you to be rid of this place, but we should rest and supply first."

"If we gather too many supplies, Rissine will suspect what we plan." He hated using her sister against her, but knew this might be the only way to convince Elmerah to leave in the night.

She watched him for a long while. *Too* long. He was about to call off the whole idea when she spoke. "You see them when you close your eyes, don't you? That's why you don't want to return to your chamber."

"I never said I don't want to return to my chamber."

She snorted. "Don't play me for a fool. I'm bone-tired. The only reason I'm still sitting here is because you are."

He looked down at his clasped hands, unsure of what to say.

"You don't need to talk about it now," she continued, "but you will need to talk about it eventually."

Finally, he looked up. "Did you talk about it? When your mother—"

She lifted her hand to cut him off. "Only once, and probably not to the right person, for she has taken my words to the grave. Celen knows a bit . . . " she trailed off, then shook her head. "I hope that you are wiser than I, and will take my advice."

He inhaled a shaky breath, knowing he'd regret his next words as soon as he spoke them. "I'll talk when you do."

Her mouth fell open, then quickly shut. She raked her hair away from her eyes. "I didn't mean that you should talk to me, just *someone*. Perhaps your sister."

Her sudden discomfort made him smile. He eyed her more steadily. "I'll talk when you do, Elmerah. Take it or leave it."

She glared. "Leave it," she said, though he knew she'd think about it. Before he could say more, she stood. "Now let's fetch our things. I hope you're as sneaky as I remember. It's going to be quite a task to steal horses from the stables on our way out."

He blinked up at her. "Maybe you're right. We should rest for a day first. We've had no sleep."

She shook her head as she buttoned her long coat, cinching it tight around her waist. "No, you may have spoken for a veiled reason, but that does not make your words any less true. If we wait, Rissine or someone else will catch on. We should go tonight."

"What about Isara?"

She grinned. "We'll fetch her on the way. We might need her if Rissine catches us." She offered him her hand.

He took it, and stood, but held onto it for a moment. "Are you sure about this? I know you have issues with your sister, but I do believe she is trying to protect you."

She rolled her eyes, then removed her hand from his. "I don't need my sister to watch my back, and do you know why?"

She was already on her way to the door as he asked, "Why?"

She glanced back at him. "Because I have you."

He watched her, a bit stunned, as she veered from her course and began pawing through Ivran's cupboard, presumably for supplies. "What of Ivran?" he asked as he approached. "What will he think when he wakes and we have gone?"

"He'll understand. He knows we'll get Saida back if we can. He's far more rational than the rest."

He stared at her for a moment, rifling through the

cupboards like a wolf in a henhouse, then joined her. He knew he'd have to close his eyes eventually. They would sleep each night on the road. But perhaps it would be easier to face when he knew he had a purpose. When he knew he was on his way to enact vengeance for all his fallen kin.

CHAPTER FOUR

Elmerah

Elmerah cursed as she stubbed her toe through her knee-high boots. The cracked cobblestone streets proved treacherous in the dark of night. In the distance, glass lanterns flickered with light in the cool breeze along the main road. At one time, they would have been extinguished at midnight to save on oil, but since the attack, they burned through the night. You never knew when you might meet with a hidden blade in the dark.

Hopefully there were no blades in this darkness, save hers and Alluin's. Since leaving the High Temple, they kept to the shadows, out of sight of fogged windows and doorways. They'd collected Isara, who crept along quietly at her side. She had neither blade nor bow, yet was more dangerous than either of them. Being able to interrupt any magics was a skill Elmerah would pay ten coffers of pure gold to possess.

Elmerah shuffled her feet along between the dark expanse away from the lanterns, groping the wall of a vacant home as she led the way toward the stables. There should only be one or two guards present. Most were worried about threats coming from outside the cracked crystal walls, rather than from within. It would have been so much easier if the guards would just let them take the horses, but mounts were a precious commodity in these dire times, and would only be granted for purposes approved by the High Council. There was no way the Council would approve their mission without much deliberation, and perhaps not even then.

And so, they would sneak, but sneaking out presented one major issue. They could obtain horses easily enough —one or two guards wouldn't be difficult to distract— but how in Ilthune's name would they get the horses outside the city gates? She'd been wracking her brain from the moment she started gathering supplies, but an idea was yet to present itself.

Alluin stopped at her side as she peered out around the next building, the stables now in sight. "Someone is following us," he whispered in her ear.

"Rissine?" she hissed.

"No, someone bigger than Rissine, a man judging by the sound of the steps."

At the scuff of a heavy boot, she grabbed Isara and plastered both their backs against the wall. She glanced past Isara down the dark alley, but all seemed still and silent. She might have imagined the scuff, but she did not doubt Alluin's senses. Those pointy ears could pick up the sound of a single rodent scurrying across the street. She stifled a groan at her thoughts. If it was another elf following them, their abrupt stop would have already alerted them that she was aware of their presence. There would be no subtly drawing them out now.

Nothing moved. This was a waste of time.

With a heavy sigh, she gestured for Isara to stay back, then stepped into the middle of the alleyway. "Reveal yourself," she said, her voice low to not alert the distant stable guards.

"Damn elves hear way too well," a familiar voice replied, then Celen stepped out of his hiding place behind an adjacent home.

Her shoulders momentarily slumped in relief, then stiffened in irritation. "Celen, are you following us?"

"Why are you wandering around at this ungodly hour?" He wore his usual garb of leather and a bit of fur rather than something more concealing, so he hadn't planned on stalking her.

"I asked you first."

He closed the distance between them, then whispered, "I saw that your sister had returned, so I waited until I was sure you'd be in your chambers, then came to find you. Then I see you and your elf sneaking out of the High Temple with the little sparrow at your heels."

She sighed, sensing Alluin's presence at her back. He

didn't trust Celen, and wouldn't want her to tell the truth, but well, he wasn't her, and she trusted Celen with her life. "We're leaving. We're going after the emperor, and I don't want anyone following us, or knowing what we're doing. Any of these elves here could be Nokken in disguise. Without Saida, we have no way of telling. And without her—" she hesitated, "well, we need to end this now. I'm sick of waiting for the remnants of the High Council to decide on a plan."

Celen's expression softened. "I heard about Saida, I'm sorry. I'm sure you'll find her."

She waved him off, unable to talk about her failure just yet. "Well now that you know what we're doing, kindly watch our backs to ensure no one follows."

He swiped a hand over his scars and shook his head. "I can't let you go after the emperor on your own. I'm going with you, Ellie."

"I have Isara and Alluin. I'm not alone."

"A sparrow and an elf," Celen scoffed.

Still hiding in the dark against a wall, Isara made no move to defend herself.

"That sparrow can block your magic with a thought," Elmerah said. "If I have to face Egrin with anyone, it would be her." At a *harumph* behind her, she added, "And Alluin."

Celen crossed his arms, affixing her with a steely glare.

She sucked her teeth. "I'm not going to be able to get rid of you, am I?"

He shook his head.

"Fine, then at least help us procure four horses."

Celen grinned. "Not an issue, my people are on stable duty tonight."

"They cannot know where we're going," Alluin cut in. "They should not even see us leave."

"They won't see you," Celen said smugly. "They'll only see me, and nobody cares where I go."

Isara cleared her throat, a small meek sound in the shadows, her face visible by the slight reflection of moonlight on her round spectacles. "What about the guards at the gates?" she whispered.

"Always Faerune elves," Celen sighed. "No one else is trusted. I'll have to leave that part of the escape to you, Ellie. Leave the horses to me."

Already deep in thought, Elmerah stroked the hilt of her cutlass. She'd half-expected to be thwarted at the stables, now they were one step farther along than she expected to be at this point. "Just get the horses," she decided. "Meet us behind the old smithy."

With a nod that acknowledged her and completely ignored Alluin, he hurried away.

Alluin stepped up to her side. "What do you plan?"

"A distraction. I'll need you atop the guard tower to man the pulley when the time comes."

"Why me?" Alluin groaned.

She grinned. "The elves like you better. We only need the gate open enough to slip the horses out. You'll be fine."

"And what about me?" Isara asked, finally out of the shadows.

She turned toward her. "You and Celen will lead the horses, as I'll be a bit distracted, now let's go."

She led the way back into the shadows of the nearest building, then peered not toward the stables, but the distant gates. She trusted Celen to lead the horses there discreetly. So all she need do is be ready when he arrived.

Alluin

Alluin wasn't sure how Elmerah had convinced him to climb the ladder up to the guard tower, where three elves stood ready to man the gates below. There were more elves stationed further down in either direction on other guard towers, and on newly erected walkways bordering the massive cracked crystals.

The three Faerune elves who turned reflective eyes to him as he ascended the ladder were all young, blond, and stony-faced. They'd likely heard him the moment he set foot on the ladder, and would have peered down to see who approached. He was a bit surprised they'd allowed him to make it to the top.

"What are you doing here?" one asked, his hand hovering near the shortsword at his belt.

Alluin finished his ascent, placing his feet on the solid floorboards within a secure railing. His fingers itched for his bow, but he'd left it with Elmerah. He didn't need to give these elves any more reasons to view him as a threat.

He leaned casually against a beam supporting the guard tower roof. The wheel and pulley to open the gates was just to his left, he'd only need to give the wheel a few turns to open the gates a crack. Back up pulleys were on other towers, but he'd seen this one manned when they returned from Skaristead.

"I am unable to sleep after what happened last night," his words were a bit too true for comfort, "have there been any sightings of more spiders?" He knew word had spread of the event, and all would be on the lookout for demons. Even those who didn't believe demons existed.

Two of the young guards seemed uneasy, but the third maintained his annoyed expression, his hand now firmly resting on his sword hilt. "No one is allowed up here except the guard. You can request a report from the High Council in the morning."

Ignoring the young elf's words, Alluin stretched his arms over his head, maintaining a loose, unworried posture—though what he really wanted to do was pop this blustering elf in the nose. "Oh come now, we are all allies here." *What in Felan's name was Elmerah waiting for?*

Just as soon as he thought it, a nearby guard tower burst into flame, suddenly blinding in the dark of night. The three elves standing around him turned, shouting as the silhouettes of more guardsmen could be seen leaping down onto the adjacent walkway.

"What in Arcale's name is going on!" the most vocal of

Alluin's adversaries hissed. "Go see what started the fire," he said to the other two.

The two elves hurried toward the ladder, descending one after the other. Alluin had hoped all three would go. But it seemed he was out of luck.

The third guardsman narrowed his reflective eyes at Alluin. "Is this your doing? Why are you really up here? I'm taking you into custody."

The elf made a grab for him.

Alluin darted aside into a crouch, easily evading him. This elf was young and obviously inexperienced. He'd probably been promoted after over half the guard betrayed Faerune and fled.

The young elf drew his sword and whirled on Alluin, who was already coming up from his crouch with his palm poised outward. He drove it up into the young elf's nose, breaking it. The elf doubled over, holding his nose.

Alluin rushed to the wheel and gave three hard turns, the system of pulleys making the repaired gate light enough for anyone to open it. Another guard tower erupted in flames and he cursed. So much for escaping unnoticed.

At least he could place most of the blame on Elmerah. He hadn't expected her to light an entire guard tower on fire.

He turned back to the young guardsman, now standing upright with blood streaming from his nose and into the crevices of his mouth.

Alluin grinned, gave him a wave, then hopped over

the railing, falling straight down onto a walkway below. He tucked into a roll to absorb the impact, then came up running to shouts of "Traitor!" which grated on him, but there was no going back now. He ran along the walkway, soon reaching a massive crystal with its pointed tip sheared off. He hopped onto the slick surface, then half-ran half-slid to the outer edge.

A quick glance down showed a sheer drop, the surprise reeling him backward. He'd misjudged how far below the earth would be. He'd not survive a jump. Steadying himself, he glanced over his shoulder, spotting a bevy of guards approaching with bows raised.

He turned, raising his hands in surrender, then nearly lost his footing as the earth rumbled below the crystal. He looked over his shoulder and down. The earth near the base of the crystal rippled and shook in waves like water, rising up toward him.

Not questioning the sudden turn of events. He gave the guards a militia salute, then leapt.

A frantic heartbeat later, his feet hit the earth hard enough to buckle his knees. He tumbled backward, expecting a long fall, but more earth met his back, moving in waves which carried him downward. There was so much dust and soil clouding the night air he could see none of the guards above.

He rocked his body along with the waves of earth, using the momentum to launch himself to his feet just as he reached the bottom.

Someone reached out of clouds of dust, grabbed him, then forced a set of reins into his hands.

"Mount and ride toward the trees," Elmerah's voice said. "We must escape before the dust clears."

Dizzy and bruised, Alluin found a horse at the other end of the reins. His eyes open to mere slits against the powdery earth, he mounted, then rode in what he hoped was the right direction. He could already hear several sets of hooves going that way.

He had a moment to think as he rode, and pieced together that Celen must have raised the earth. He recalled Elmerah mentioning his brand of Arthali magic before.

He regretted Celen being the one to save him, because he had planned on begrudging his presence as soon as he had a chance. Now he'd have to thank him, and deal with him all the way to Galterra.

Elmerah

Elmerah coughed, coming up with globs of saliva, mucous, and dust. She slowed her horse to a walk, then spat the unsavory glob onto the ground. Alluin hacked and wheezed as he reached her side, but maintained slightly more noble manners. Isara and Celen had stopped their mounts ahead, deep in the forest shadows, both having missed the thickest layers of flying dirt.

Elmerah had ventured in to bring Alluin his mount on her own.

"So much for not making a spectacle," Alluin wheezed, his attention now on the surrounding woods. Woods where predators prowled night and day, but especially at night.

They'd be venturing further in before long, as they could not risk the road after the damage they'd done. Cornaith and Immril would be furious, and so would Rissine. But at least they'd escaped without anyone following them, and no one would guess them mad enough to go after the demon emperor on their own, when they could potentially have gone with an army at their backs.

"We should keep riding," Celen cautioned. "They may have sent trackers to follow us."

Elmerah snorted and turned to Alluin. "Fugitives from our only allies, are you quite content now?" She'd meant her words in jest, but Alluin looked absolutely miserable.

He wiped dirt turned to sweaty mud from his face. His normally deep brown hair shone almost white in the moonlight from the dusty coating. "The only thing that would content me now is a bath. When you said you'd cause a distraction, I didn't think you'd light an entire guard tower on fire. One of the guardsmen tried to arrest me."

"Regretting your decision to join us?" Celen whispered to Isara, loud enough for Elmerah to hear.

"Too late now," she cut in, not wanting to give Isara a moment to reconsider. No one had seen her leave, she could go back and say Elmerah had kidnapped her and forced her to flee the city.

She kicked her horse forward. "Keep your eyes wide open. Wyrms roam these woods, and things far worse than that."

Celen smirked at her as she rode up to him. "My clan has hidden deep in these woods for years. I'll keep you safe."

She could hear Alluin muttering under his breath behind her as the four of them rode on. Isara kept quiet, glancing warily around the forest. If Elmerah had thought before that she, Alluin, and Saida had made a strange group of companions, it was clear the gods were mocking her now.

CHAPTER FIVE

Saida

Riding across the Helshone long into the night had taken its toll on Saida. With her parents she had traveled through snows, heavy rains, and winds, but nothing compared to the overbearing heat, from which there was no reprieve. In the day, she could not shed any clothing lest the sun blister her pale skin. In the night, the heat remained, rising up through the hot sands beneath her antlioch's hooves.

Stopping to make camp had been an overwhelming relief. They had journeyed through the dark for so long, she feared they'd not make camp at all.

The weary animals seemed just as relieved to make camp as she. Even the spare mounts ambled through the sand with heads drooping, and the tired mounts from today would have to trail the fresh mounts tomorrow. She'd dismounted, waiting near her antlioch for one of the other elves to lead it away. Malon stood nearby, ignoring her. She didn't humor herself with contemplations of escape. Her legs were so stiff she could barely walk, her strength entirely consumed by the heat.

One of the elves came and took her and Malon's mounts away. Other antlioch were already drinking from lightweight boiled leather buckets of water. Nearby, the first fire flared to life, sheltered within a shallow pit dug into the sand.

Saida blinked until her eyes adjusted to the sudden light in the darkness.

Malon turned to her. "I recommend you sleep near one of the fires. I wouldn't want you to freeze."

She would have balked had she the energy. Instead, she tugged her head wrap from her mouth to hang loosely near her chin. "It's been dark for hours and it's still nearly as hot as day. I think I'll survive."

He stepped closer to her, loosening his head wrap to reveal the lower half of his face. She imagined the Crown of Arcale hidden underneath the remaining fabric upon his brow. "Trust me, Saida. Another hour and the air will shift. Travelers have frozen to death in the Helshone, even in the middle of the sun season."

She still thought he must be jesting, but she was too tired to argue. Her stomach growled, reminding her of another pressing need. They had not stopped for food all day.

"Come to the fire," he said. "We will eat, then we will rest."

His simple command sparked in her a deep resentment, fueled by hatred and loss. He had caused her mother's death and many others. He had kidnapped her and drugged her. Yet, he acted so casually.

He seemed to read her expression. "Phaerille can care for you, if that is your preference."

It was, but she bit her tongue and stuffed her anger back down. She would escape him eventually, and when she did, she would take with her the full knowledge of his plan. "Lead the way," she said through her clenched jaw.

Malon watched her a moment longer, then offered her his arm.

She stared at him. She was willing to play nice, but not *that* nice.

"Your legs are surely sore from the long ride," he explained, "and the sands tend to tug at your boots."

"And your legs are not in the same state as mine?"

"I am more accustomed to long rides than you." Despite his words, he had lowered his arm, and turned to lead the way.

She stumbled after him. The sand *did* tug at her boots, and her legs *were* almost unbearably sore. She dreaded climbing back in the saddle come morning.

By the time she made it to the first of three brightly burning fires, most of the elves had seated themselves around the farther two. She spotted Phaerille, her head wrap undone like Malon's, speaking lowly to two male elves. She suspected this third fire she had arrived at was reserved for her and Malon alone.

She turned her gaze anywhere but toward Malon, spotting the two elves who'd tended the antlioch, their hands now rifling through the plump saddlebags. She suspected that's where supper was coming from.

She plopped down in the sand near the fire, keeping two arm's lengths of distance between her and Malon. "Why three fires?"

Malon crossed his legs beneath him and looked into the flames. His silver eyes seemed to absorb the yellow light. "Scorpions the size of sheep come out at night. They fear the fire."

The thought of scorpions so large sent a shiver down her spine. "Demons?"

"No, just common denizens of the desert. There are far worse monsters out here, but fortunately they are far more rare."

They both fell silent as the two elves who'd tended the antlioch reached them with an offering of unleavened bread and cured silverfish. She accepted her share from a male elf who was perhaps as young as she. She tried to catch his eye, but he simply avoided her gaze and walked away.

"Eat and rest," Malon said. "We don't have long before the sun returns, and you'll want what sleep you can manage."

Though she was exhausted, sleep was the furthest

thing from her mind with the thought of giant scorpions lurking in the darkness. Although, she supposed Malon could summon demons to destroy them.

She took a bite of bread and swallowed, thinking upon what had happened at Skaristead. "You summoned those demons. How?"

Malon shrugged, already halfway done with his meal. "It is not difficult if you know the words, and possess the strength of mind. Would you like to learn?"

"Absolutely not!" she hissed. "And besides, I do not possess any magics."

"But you do, you know. It's why you are needed."

The flatbread crumbled as she clenched her fingertips around it too tightly. "I do not understand."

"You are a priestess of the moon. Your gifts may not have been appreciated by the High Council, but wiser elves know they should be treasured above all else."

She shook her head. Weariness tugged at her as she stared into the fire. "Do not lie to me, Malon. I may see through some illusions, but I know myself. I know of what I'm capable, and it is not much."

"You'll learn differently in time. I would not have gone to so much trouble for you otherwise."

Finally, she turned to him. "And you have believed this from the start? Is that why you rescued me that day in the snow?"

He leaned back and lifted his brows. "So you *do* remember?"

She stared at him.

He smiled softly. "No, I did not at that time possess the wisdom I do now. I simply saw a headstrong priestess wandering off, ready to get herself into trouble."

"So you rescued me out of the goodness of your heart?" she asked incredulously.

"Is that so difficult to believe?"

She fell silent. Perhaps he was a good man once, but it changed nothing. His ill deeds could not be revoked. She looked down at the dried fish and bread in her hands, having no desire to eat them, though she'd been starving moments before.

"The Crown of Cindra," she said abruptly, shifting in the sand for a more comfortable position, "you claim it belongs upon my brow. I'm surprised you left Faerune without it."

"The circlet is in your saddlebag, Saida. Check your mount if you do not believe me."

She went still, though soon her hands trembled around her forgotten food. It was not possible. After she'd revealed the circlet to her father, he'd hidden it in a locked trunk in his cellar. They'd all agreed its presence should remain a secret until any lingering traitors could be found out.

He watched her mull it over, the phantom of a patronizing smile on his lips. "I've known you had it since we were aboard the Arthali ship. You claimed the Akkeri kept the circlet, but my dear, you are a horrible liar."

"Then why didn't you take it while I was injured?"

"I didn't have much time. Not if I wanted to procure the Crown of Arcale before the Dreilore could give it to Dinoba. With the circlet in your keeping on the ship, it was safe for the time being."

She gritted her jaw. "Perhaps you speak the truth about why you left it, but I do not believe you have the circlet now. There is no way you could have found it."

He sighed. "Dear Saida, I turned half of Faerune against itself, did you think I would leave none behind to do my bidding?" He gestured to the accompanying elves. "Many left Faerune well after I did, and breaking into a cellar is not difficult. It would have been wiser of you to keep the circlet under heavy guard."

She dropped her food into the sand, then clutched her stomach, feeling overwhelmingly ill. A traitor had broken into her father's home, had gotten into his cellar, and into the trunk. They must have searched his chamber first, and hers. They'd been all over her home and she'd not even noticed. Neither had Alluin or Elmerah.

"When?" she rasped. "When was it taken?"

"The same night I found you in Skaristead. My spies knew to wait until your chambers were the least populated."

"My father—"

"He was not harmed, save for a small dosing of blood-flower extraction administered when he was already asleep."

The desert seemed to spin around her. He had both

the Crown of Arcale and the Crown of Cindra. Two of the most powerful artifacts ever known to her people.

"Why would the emperor let you keep them?" she asked, still trying to steady her swimming thoughts. "Doesn't he want the moonstones for himself?"

"Why do you think we're fleeing to the Helshone? He will not find us here."

Gods, she thought, *he's made himself an enemy of the demon emperor.* Perhaps he wasn't the coward she'd thought him. In truth, he was a madman.

"If you will not eat," he said, glancing down at her food forgotten in the sand, "then you should rest. You will regret staying up through the night come morning."

Her mind going numb and distant, she fetched her food from the sand and tossed it into the fire. She looked away from Malon, across the fires in search of Phaerille, and actually caught her already looking her way. Their eyes locked for a moment, then Phaerille quickly averted her gaze.

Saida decided that the next night, she would choose to eat and rest with Phaerille. She would have the entire unbearable ride the next day to drag more information from Malon. After that, she would set to the task of forming an alliance, one female elf to another. Ye gods, he had both circlets. What could he possibly be planning?

"You should rest," Malon said again. "I'll fetch you a bedroll."

"Have one of the others bring it. I don't want to be

anywhere near you." She'd gotten all the information she could stomach for a night.

He stood and left her without another word.

She watched his back as he approached the other elves, and suddenly felt like an idiot for sending him away. She should have learned what he intended with the circlets. She should have asked where the rest of the traitorous Faerune guard had gone. She should have made sure her father remained safe.

A male elf brought her a bedroll, but she barely noticed. She merely unfurled it far from the fire and crawled inside, wanting to be nowhere near the flames should Malon return to warm his hands.

She'd rather face a giant scorpion than rest with him watching over her, even for what little remained of the night.

※

Saida's uncontrollable shivers woke her before sunrise. Malon had been right, once the sand cooled, the Helshone turned into an icy wasteland. She lowered the top flap of her bedroll just enough to peek out, then looked through the fog of her breath at the still smoldering fire, too far away. The last she'd seen of Malon, he'd been sitting awake near the fire, allowing her to freeze if that was her choice.

Now he was missing, but she was not alone. In the firelight, she could see two male elves standing guard, reflective eyes turned away from her. She shifted under her bedding, uncomfortable in her boots, but she'd been too frightened to take them off—the idea of scorpions both large and small haunting her thoughts.

Footsteps shifted the sand behind her. She rolled over, then looked up at Malon, seeming impossibly tall from her viewpoint. His head wrap was missing, revealing the cool reflection of moonstones at his brow.

Though he stood just above her, his gaze was turned outward. "Curse it all," he muttered after a moment. He looked down at her. "Pack up your bedroll. We need to move, *now*." He took a step away and shouted to those standing guard. "Wake the others, ready the antlioch!"

It was the first true worry she'd heard in his voice since she'd met him, so she did not question the request. She scurried out into the shocking cold. Goosebumps erupted on her skin, sending her whole body back into shivers.

Malon knelt and hastily rolled up her bedding, placing it under one arm. His free hand grabbed her upper arm, then he tugged her along toward their waiting mounts. She was now glad she'd kept her boots, for she wouldn't have had time to don them.

"What is it!" she gasped, her eyes darting after hurrying elves.

"I did not think he'd track us past the border of the Helshone. I was wrong."

"Egrin?" she gasped. Her boots caught in the loose

sand, but Malon kept her standing, an unrelenting force dragging her toward the antlioch.

She almost wondered if she'd be better off letting Egrin catch them. He'd surely kill Malon . . . of course, he'd probably kill her too, and he'd claim both the circlets. She hated Malon having them, but it would be even worse to leave them to the man who'd pillaged and destroyed Faerune.

They reached the antlioch, and she willingly climbed into the saddle, her senses buzzing from cold and panic. To her surprise, Malon climbed up behind her, then the antlioch leapt forward. His arm around her waist was the only thing that kept her from being tossed back down into the sand.

"What about the others!"

"They'll be right behind us," he explained, his chin near her ear as night wind whipped at both their faces. His free hand clung to the antlioch's shortened wool, but it was mainly his legs digging into the creature's side keeping them both in the saddle.

Realizing she was more hindrance than help, she clenched her thighs and leaned forward. Strands of hair pulled loose from her braid and flew across her face. She must have lost her head wrap somewhere in her bedding, though there was no sun to accost her currently.

There was only the night, far too silent. She could hear huffs of breath from the antlioch, thuds of delicate hooves in the sand. Gentle winds, but nothing else.

Judging by the nearing hoofbeats, the others were not far behind.

"Are you sure we were tracked?" she rasped, fear clutching her throat. "I hear no signs of pursuit."

"Wait for it. He is near. I should have done more to cover our tracks. Reach in the saddlebag for the circlet. You'll need to wear it."

"You're mad!" she argued. "I'm not putting that on."

The desert was slowly turning pink with the first hints of dawn. She kept her eyes ahead, seeing nothing but an open expanse of sand. No, not just sand. What was *that*? Darkness swirled down from the sky. It thickened as it hit the sand, then turned into solid figures. The darkness cleared, and there stood Egrin Dinoba, dressed in black, with four male Dreilore, not just soldiers, but lords.

The antlioch dug its hooves into the sand, skidding to a halt, but they were already too close to Egrin. He'd appeared nearly right in front of him. This close, she could see stolen Faerune moonstone rings on his fingers.

Malon clutched her against him, his breath hot on her cheek. "Put on the circlet, Saida, or we both die here and now."

She heard the other elves' antlioch stopping at their backs, but none ventured past toward Egrin and the Dreilore.

"On the contrary, Saida," Egrin called out, though she wasn't sure how he'd heard Malon's low words, "bring me the circlet, and I will spare you. I will even return you to Faerune, and I will put these traitors to death."

"Saida," Malon pleaded, his arm still around her waist. "He will utterly destroy Faerune, the Empire, and everything else if he has them."

Egrin gestured the Dreilore forward. "Kill them all. Spare the priestess if she cooperates."

The Dreilore all had long white hair with jewels glittering in the dim rays of early morning. They moved with unreal grace, like phantoms with white hair fluttering in the early morning breeze. She knew without a doubt they would have demon magic like those who'd attacked the High Temple. One of them might even be her mother's murderer, Lord Orius. They would be upon them in mere moments.

She shoved her hand into the saddlebag, coming instantly in contact with the cool metal circlet. "I hope you know what you're doing," she hissed to Malon. She withdrew the circlet and placed it upon her brow, tugging her wild hair to lay flat beneath it.

Her fingers went numb as they left the circlet. Stars erupted in her vision, and she swayed in the saddle. She'd never felt anything like it. The magic of the circlet filled her up like a chalice with silver moonlight. It hadn't done that when she touched it before. Suddenly the desert was a distant dream.

Malon had dismounted without her realizing it. He clasped her hand, then helped her down from the saddle before tightly lacing his fingers with hers. "Do not let go.

Together, we can face him. Gods against a single demon."

His words made her hesitate. The Dreilore had stopped their approach, and Egrin's face had turned red, his brow deeply furrowed.

"How?" he growled. "How have you harnessed the moonstones' power in such a way?"

Saida's hand locked with Malon's glowed with white light. She wasn't sure if it was to her eyes alone, or if everyone could see it, but the elves stayed far behind them, and the Dreilore did not advance.

One Dreilore, however, drew a blue-glowing blade. "Will our enchantments cut through their magic?" he asked Egrin, his accent reshaping the words of the common tongue.

"Find out," Egrin ordered. "Claim the circlets, then cut the elves down."

The four Dreilore advanced as one, but Malon just stood there. The only move he made was to lift the back of his free hand, signaling the other elves to stay put. His silver hair floated on torrents of power, and she realized with a start that the loose strands from her braid were doing the same.

"You must trust me," Malon said to her at the last moment. "The circlets are meant to work as a pair. Trust me and I will keep us safe."

He was the last person she wanted to trust, but as the Dreilore reached them, she closed her eyes and surrendered her will to his.

Her hand laced with his began to burn. Her entire body burned. She felt as if she were on fire. She opened her eyes to the sound of shrieking.

Two Dreilore were writhing in the sand. Their blades lay far from their fingers, which now grasped at bubbling, steaming skin. The other two Dreilore backed away, hands raised in surrender.

Malon smiled, his gaze on Egrin, still standing a safe distance away. "You may have pillaged Faerune, but the true heart of my people yet remains. You will not claim the circlets."

Egrin sucked his teeth. He didn't so much as glance at the writhing Dreilore as they fell quiet. Saida presumed they were quite dead.

Egrin gestured the two remaining Dreilore back. "Perhaps I will not claim the circlets today, but I *will* have them." His eyes turned to Saida. "You have until the next full moon to bring them to me, or those remaining in Faerune will all be killed." He turned an icy smile to Malon. "You cannot link the circlets with her if she is unwilling. Let us see how long it takes her to shove a dagger in your back."

Egrin lifted his hand, snapped his fingers, and he and the two remaining Dreilore disappeared in a cloud of darkness.

Saida pulled her hand from Malon's, fell on her knees in the sand, then vomited. She came up with just a trickle of bile, but heaved for a long while. What had she done? Had she given the circlet to Egrin, he wouldn't have turned his sights back to Faerune. He wouldn't be set on going after her father, Elmerah, and everyone else.

She rocked on her knees in the sand. "We have to go back," she wheezed. "We have to protect them."

She felt a hand on her shoulder and quickly shrugged it off, but it returned, this time more forcefully. "Saida," Malon soothed, "he would have gone after them regardless. At least this has bought them time, until the full moon. By then I will have carried out my task, and no demons, nor Dreilore or elves, will be able to stand against us.

Her body shook with silent sobs. She didn't know what to believe. She didn't know what to do to protect her father and her friends.

She especially didn't know what had just happened to her. The magic that had filled her had been pure moonlight, and she could have sworn that deep within it, the goddess Cindra had called her name.

Isara

They'd made it out of the city, and had survived the woods at night. The sunrise caressed Isara's face, this day feeling strange and new to her. Perhaps the gods had not abandoned her after all.

Elmerah and Celen were both talented magic users, and Alluin was fast and deadly with blade and bow. If she were to ever have vengeance for her father's death, these three would be the ones to grant it.

She stroked her horse's mane, tuning out the sounds of Alluin and Celen bickering. She had hardened her heart, knowing her cousin must be stopped. If Egrin truly was a demon, he had to die. But not Daemon. He was as much demon as she, if they were demons at all. She had her own form of magic, but her brother had presented no such gifts. He could still be saved.

Unfortunately, Elmerah would kill him if given the chance. She could not let that happen. It hurt her heart even more than the idea of killing her own cousin, but if Elmerah tried to harm Daemon, she would turn against her. Suppressing even Shadowmarsh magic would be easy.

She sighed, then deeply inhaled the fresh morning air, heavily scented with forest loam and pine. Galterra was a long way off. She still had time to convince Elmerah that Daemon should be spared.

The sound of twigs snapping not far off caught her attention. She tensed, wondering what sort of large creature was passing through the woods. She'd worry about her brother later. He was safe from Elmerah, for now. As for herself and her current companions, the long and perilous journey forward was just beginning.

CHAPTER SIX

Rissine

Rissine flexed her fingers, longing to wring the tiny Akkeri's neck. He blinked up at her with elven eyes surrounded by sallow skin, his hair little more than wisps of decayed fiber barely holding onto his scalp.

She'd always found Akkeri disgusting, and this one was no exception. Except for the strange way he didn't try to kill her. In fact, his eyes held intelligence, and far more calm than she'd ever possessed.

And here she was, threatening him in a private room within the healer's apothecary. He'd remained seated in his small wooden chair, not a threat at all.

She stepped back, *almost* ashamed for looming over him in such a manner.

Seeming to note her calm, he spoke, his words slurred and odd, as if his tongue didn't work quite right. "As I have said, Saida is friend. Elmerah and Alluin are hardly known to me."

Her anger surged. "You're lying. You traveled with them. I saw you off on your journey just south of Galterra."

"I was unconscious much of that. At Valeroot camp, only Saida visits."

She slumped into an empty adjacent chair, stretching her long legs out across the white stone floor. He'd offered her the chair, more than once, but only now did she deign to take it.

The rest of the small whitewashed room was barren, reeking of herbs and ash. She'd been told Merwyn came here daily, receiving different herbs to perhaps regain some of his strength . . . though she imagined he'd never been terribly strong to begin with.

"Did they tell you she was taken?" she asked, hoping to raise some emotion in him, if only to loosen the information she truly desired.

Merwyn's head lowered. "I regret I could not be there to protect her."

It was difficult not to laugh in his face. As if this tiny creature could have protected the priestess better than she and Elmerah.

"Saida must have known Elmerah's plans," she began anew. "Perhaps she would have mentioned to you where she'd go when she left here."

Merwyn shook his head. "Saida not visit much since mother was killed."

Rissine sighed. "You know, if you're to live amongst these pompous elves, you should learn to speak properly."

He didn't seem to have anything to say to that, and only stared at her.

What a waste of time. She would have been better off joining the trackers searching for the *fugitives*.

A knock near the open doorway drew her attention.

Ivran stood just outside, his red-rimmed eyes made painfully obvious by his round spectacles. "A word, Rissine?"

She raised her brows, having initially assumed he was there to see the Akkeri. She stood, then looked down at the small creature. "If you think of anything useful, send word for me at the inn."

Merwyn nodded, seeming relieved that she was leaving him. She began to turn away.

"Rissine," he called out.

She turned back to him.

He had risen from his chair, and was even shorter than she'd imagined. "If you search for Elmerah, you bring me? Elmerah will find Saida."

She looked him up and down.

"He's more formidable than he looks, even with his body and organs damaged by toxins," Ivran said to her back. "He has saved my daughter more than once. If he could help her now, I'd ask you to take him."

She turned back to Ivran. "Who says I'm going anywhere?"

He lifted his brows. "Aren't you?"

Stupid elves and Akkeri. She was sick of them all. "What do you want?" she hissed at him. "Why have you come to find me?"

He stepped back, and she wished she hadn't spoken so harshly. She was used to dealing with pirates and thugs, and had begun to lack talent in the more tactful ways of speech.

She peered both ways down the empty hallway, then lowered her voice. "Alright, yes, I am going after her. Do you know where she has gone?"

Ivran straightened his already straight spectacles, a pause to regain his composure she suspected. "The last time Elmerah and I spoke was when she told me Malon had taken my daughter, to where, she did not know. I believe in Elmerah's mind, the next logical step would be to find the one person who might know Malon's plan. His most powerful ally."

"Egrin Dinoba," Rissine sighed. "You believe she's heading to Galterra? Not back to Skaristead to look for Saida's trail?"

He nodded. "She would not have left Skaristead if there was a trail to be found, and she and Alluin ransacked my cupboards for supplies. Enough supplies to last a long journey."

Her shoulders slumped. "And they stole horses too. All to escape without anyone knowing where they went. If she was openly going after Saida, she could have just said as much. An entourage would have been sent along with her. That she wanted to avoid that means that she must be doing something no one would allow her to do on her own."

Ivran nodded.

Rissine's jaw tightened, realizing she should have seen right to the heart of Elmerah's plan from the start. Her sister was irrational where her emotions were concerned, and she hadn't taken the priestess' abduction well.

"I should have seen this coming," she admitted. "Elmerah can act rashly. Though on the outside she could give up the search for your daughter, she'd never be able to let it go, and all paths lead to Egrin."

"You couldn't have known," Ivran soothed.

But Rissine was beyond soothing. She should have tasked other Arthali to watch her sister through the night.

Merwyn had crept up to her side. Both the Akkeri and Ivran looked up at her, waiting for her response.

Her brow furrowed. Elmerah had already ridden for a full night and morning. There would be no catching up to her. The only thing she could do to stop her, was to reach Galterra first.

She turned to Ivran. "Can you give the orders to ready my ship?"

He nodded. "I believe I can manage that."

She turned to Merwyn, debating her next words. He was small and weak, useless, but he had somehow managed to survive this long. "Meet me at the docks. You're coming with."

"My thanks." With a bob of his head, Merwyn hurried past her down the hall, his scuttling movements restricted by the plain elven tunic and breeches.

Ivran continued watching her. "You will sail to Galterra?"

"I'm not a fool. I will sail to Port Aeluvaria, and catch Elmerah along the way."

"You will stop her from killing the emperor?"

Killing the emperor. Killing a demon. Just how did Elmerah plan to manage such a feat? "I will keep her alive. Elmerah alive is your best chance of rescuing your daughter, and my best chance of keeping the only family I have."

"What about gathering more Arthali?"

She fidgeted, knowing she should keep her next words to herself, but they had weighed upon her so heavily, she could bear them alone no longer. "There are no more Arthali to gather. I have spoken to all the clans. Those I brought with me were the ones willing to fight."

Ivran's jaw dropped. "But—" he seemed to search for the right words. "But why would you tell us more allies were coming? Why promise us an army?"

"Would the High Council have allied themselves with me if they knew?"

"No," he breathed. "No they would not. The Arthali in your company are strong, but not as strong as you or Elmerah. They can offer us little additional protection."

Her anger returned. A familiar warmth. "If you tell anyone, I will prevent Elmerah from finding your daughter."

He furrowed his brow. "There is no need for threats, Rissine. I would not divulge your secret."

"Why?"

He stood a little straighter, though his haggard appearance made him seem old and tired. "Solana believed in my daughter, and my daughter believes in Elmerah. And as much as she'd like us to think differently, Elmerah believes in you." He stepped away. "I'll have your ship prepared. Do not let me down."

He turned away and stepped down the hall. Stunned, she watched his back, feeling an unfamiliar sensation in her heart. Perhaps because he thought Elmerah believed in her. Or perhaps this feeling was the beginnings of madness. She was not sure which, but despite Ivran being a blustering Faerune noble, she would abide by his terms.

She would not let him down.

Elmerah

"We should rest," Celen groaned. "We have ridden down many streambeds, and crossed rocky ground. The trackers will not find us now."

"We cannot risk it. If Rissine finds us—" Elmerah cut

herself off. She had not just run from Rissine, but from the High Council. If this mission were to be successful, no spies could be present to alert Egrin. At least, that's what she kept telling herself. Deep down she knew, that like Alluin, she'd run from the digging, clawing memories of the past. She'd run from Rissine because their relationship could never be resolved.

"She'll what?" Celen pressed, then gripped his reins as his horse stumbled over a loose stone. "What do you really think Rissine would do if she found us?"

"She wouldn't help us kill the emperor, if that's what you're implying."

Alluin and Isara remained silent behind them, thankfully, and she hoped her words did not ring as hollow to them as they did to her. Had she been unwise to leave Rissine behind? Would she have helped them?

She sealed her mouth shut. It didn't matter now. What was done, was done.

"Even if we can go on without rest," Celen continued, "the horses can't. It is only a matter of time before one breaks an ankle. They need a reprieve, preferably by a stream so they can drink their fill."

They'd passed by many streams already. If she were a good leader, they would have stopped at one. But she'd never claimed to be any sort of leader, let alone a good one. "Fine, next stream, we stop. But if Rissine finds us, I will sacrifice you to enable our escape."

At the sound of distant running water, Celen tugged his reins to the right, directing his horse eastward. "I'll sacrifice myself if it means you'll stop acting like a sandcrab."

She didn't reply, and before long they reached the stream and dismounted. Elmerah's rump ached, and her skin itched from the dust. After she'd tied her horse's reins loose enough that the beast could drink and graze, she walked to a rocky area along the stream and knelt.

She removed her black coat, shaking away as much dust as she could, though it would never be as good as new again. Draping her coat across the dry rocks, she knelt and splashed icy water on her face and neck.

"Ilthune curse us," she muttered as her muscles spasmed from the cold, "you'd think this water is melted snow."

"It probably is," Alluin said from behind her. "These streams run all the way down from the Akenyth Province, where they experience heavy snows in winter."

"My thanks for the geography lesson," she said caustically as she stood, flicking cool droplets from her fingers. She looked past him. "Wait, where are Celen and Isara? They were just over there a moment ago."

Alluin whipped around, scanning the seemingly peaceful forest, then turned back to her, his eyes wide. "Fossegrim?"

She shook her head, then leaned down to fetch her coat. "Celen would not fall victim to a Fossegrim's song, at least not so quickly, and we'd see them both asleep on the ground."

Donning her coat, she walked back toward the horses

with fingertips brushing her cutlass. All four horses were still tethered near the stream, but the two riders were missing. She reached the horses and looked further downstream, while Alluin knelt and looked at the ground for tracks.

"Their bootprints circle around the horses," he observed, "but don't lead off anywhere. It's as if they disappeared into thin air."

She ventured a bit further downstream. "Not possible. Celen is far too heavy to flutter away."

Alluin snorted at her sarcasm, but most of his focus remained on the bank. "They didn't cross."

She walked a little farther, then stopped. She was no tracker, but even she could see that no tracks led off in this direction. She turned back to Alluin and the horses.

Alluin was gone.

"Son of a mireling dungbug!" She stormed back toward the horses, unwilling to let them disappear too. "Who or whatever you are, come out and face me!"

She was ready to draw her cutlass in an instant, but no man nor creature revealed itself. The horses stomped their hooves in the thick stream-side grass, but did not seem overly alarmed.

Elmerah looked around the forest, but all was silent. She had no idea what to do. It really was as if they had all disappeared into thin air. She paced around the horses, searching for anything that might seem amiss, wracking her brain for what could have happened. Not Fossegrim, not trolls, nor a wyrm or wyvern. All would have been more obvious in their attack. So would elves, Dreilore, or any other humanoid races. She didn't know these forests well enough to come up with any more possibilities.

She looked up at the sun beating down overhead. She could take the horses and ride on, but if the others returned, they would have no mounts, nor any way of finding her. The other option was to wait, and hope the culprit would return for her too so she could kill it and rescue her friends.

She plopped down in the grass and prepared to wait. She could only hope this cowardly man or creature would not take too long, and that her friends weren't already dead. If Rissine learned she'd only made it this far before failing her mission, she'd never hear the end of it.

CHAPTER SEVEN

Alluin

Alluin walked down the narrow path, his eyes wide as he stared at the creature's back. With him walked Isara and Celen, who'd both been waiting with the . . . he shook his head, unable to believe his eyes. If the myths were real, he was staring at the back of a Fogfaun. Fogfauns' upper halves were human, a bit on the small side, with dark gleaming onyx skin. Their gray furry lower halves had hooves like an antlioch's.

Celen leaned in near Alluin's shoulder. "Where is it taking us? And where is Elmerah?"

Alluin shook his head. He hadn't even felt himself being taken, he was just suddenly on this path with Isara and Celen.

Isara glanced at them both, her eyes huge and wide behind her spectacles. Her curly blonde hair frothed around her face, adding to her befuddled appearance. "The Fogfaun will only come to a realm in great peril. They are harbingers of the end."

"Then what does it want with us?" Celen hissed.

Isara pointed ahead. "Look, there are more of them."

Sure enough, five more Fogfaun waited in the forest ahead, peeking sheepishly around the trunks of aspen and white birch. Shaggy gray hair framed their human-like faces, narrow and delicate, with pure black eyes and skin just a shade lighter. One was female, and it was immediately apparent these creatures felt little sense of modesty.

The Fogfaun leading them stopped and turned around. "You travel with a weather worker," it said, surprising him with words in the common tongue.

"Elmerah?" he blurted, still in shock. "Have you done something to her?" If these creatures were harbingers of the end, as Isara had claimed, then were they all in peril?

"Few weather workers left," the Fogfaun explained, shaking its head. "Very dangerous."

Celen stepped forward. "What do you want? Why have you brought us here?"

Alluin couldn't read the Fogfaun's expression in the slightest. It seemed devoid of emotion.

"Does the weather worker summon the demons?" it asked, ignoring Celen's question.

The demons? Did it mean the Ayperos and giant boars? "No," Alluin answered, "absolutely not. An elf summoned them."

The creature tilted its head. "What is weather work-er's intent? Too many holes torn to the underworld. More demons come through." It pointed off to its right. "Large hole over there."

"It must mean portals," Isara whispered. "There are many myths about portals to the underworld letting demons through. A summoner need only know the words if they possess the power to open them."

"This is madness," Celen interrupted. "What have these creatures done with Elmerah?" Facing the Fogfaun, he raised his voice, "Elmerah is no summoner of demons. She did not create this nearby . . . hole, so you better not have harmed her. Our sole intent in these woods is to travel through them."

The Fogfaun tilted its head to the other side, seeming to think over Celen's words. Finally, it spoke. "Have weather worker close up the hole, and we let you go."

They wanted Elmerah to close up a demon portal? Alluin could admit, he didn't know everything about her magic, but he was quite sure she didn't know how to close up demon portals.

"Fine," Celen said before he could answer. "But you'll have to fetch her and bring her to us first."

The Fogfaun nodded toward Alluin. "You go. Other magic users stay. More valuable allies to the weather worker. She wants them back, she closes up hole."

Alluin looked between Celen and Isara. He already knew Elmerah could not close up the portal. If he left them, it could be forever.

He opened his mouth to argue, but suddenly he was back by the streambed, standing between two horses.

Elmerah looked up at him from her seat in the grass with a scowl. "It's about bloody time, I've been waiting here half the day."

Half the day? It had felt like mere minutes. "You should get up—" he began, then cut himself off. "No, actually, you better stay seated, because you're not going to believe what I have to tell you."

She narrowed an eye and came to her feet. "Well say it fast, I sense strange magics in these woods, and I would like to find Celen and Isara before we investigate."

He glanced around the peaceful woods, then back to her. "That will not be easy. What do you know of demon portals?"

Elmerah

Elmerah wasn't sure which part made her more angry, that these Fogfaun were holding Isara and Celen hostage, or that they had actually thought *she* was the one summoning demons. Although it also raised the question of who had. Was this the place Malon had summoned his demons from, or was there someone else with such magics and their own dark plan? Saida had claimed Hotrath, the High King of the Akkeri, had summoned the Ayperos they'd faced in an Akkeri temple, so perhaps this was his doing too?

She marched through the forest, leading both hers and Celen's horses loosely by their reins. Alluin followed with the other two horses.

She hoped she wasn't leading him into danger, but if she needed to find a demon portal, the strange magic she'd sensed was the place to start. It wasn't far off either, which meant the Fogfaun might be nearby too. She thought her chances of closing the portal slim—she simply didn't know how to do it—but finding it might be the only way to find Celen and Isara. Once she did, she'd teach these stupid Fogfaun a lesson—harbingers of the end though they might be.

Isara

Fogfaun. What could this mean? Was this Egrin's doing, or had the creatures been lured out by Malon's summoning? Isara sat with her back against a tree, Celen sitting beside her. The Fogfaun watched them, but had not spoken further since they sent Alluin away.

She bunched up the edge of her cloak in her fingers, nervously wringing the fabric. If the Fogfaun could transport any of them with a mere thought, what else could they do? The myths said they would appear when a land was doomed to perish, but the myths were overly-poetic and often difficult to interpret. The end of the land could mean a whole myriad of things, and so could the Fogfaun's presence.

Celen bumped her with his elbow, drawing her attention. He was an imposing man with his size and all those scars. She looked up at him sheepishly.

"Don't fret, little sparrow," he consoled. "Ellie is resourceful. She'll get us out of this."

She doubted his words. Elmerah was powerful, but she suspected, not as powerful as the Fogfaun. "That's not what I'm worried about," she whispered. "I want to know why the Fogfaun are here."

"Why don't you ask them?"

She gnawed her lip as she looked at the creatures. They waited, some with eyes or ears turned skyward, as if sensing something.

Anxiety turned her gut. It often did when she was forced to speak, even to normal folk. She looked to the Fogfaun leaning against a gnarled tree trunk, and opened her mouth before her brain could talk her out of it. "Where did you come from? Why are you here?"

The Fogfaun blinked at her for a moment, then straightened. "Demon blood in your veins. Faint."

That wasn't exactly an answer to her question, but she suddenly wished she hadn't asked at all. If these creatures were worried about demon portals, what must they think of her?

Celen watched her, his scarred brow furrowed.

"We come from earth," the Fogfaun continued, his black eyes watching her carefully as if weighing her worth. "Demons upset earth."

Celen sighed. "Do these wretched creatures speak only in riddles?"

The Fogfaun affixed Celen with its unsettling gaze. "Not speaking in riddles, earth worker."

"Are you here to get rid of the demons, then?" Isara asked.

The Fogfaun shrugged. "No getting rid of demons now. Only hope to fill in holes."

So maybe they weren't harbingers of the end, if their intent was to close the portals. If they understood demon magic, perhaps they could even give her the answers she'd searched for all her life. The same answers sought by her father, and perhaps even the reason he was killed.

"What happens to the demons who've already come through?" she pressed, thinking of Egrin. If he really was a demon, he must have come from the underworld at some point.

The Fogfaun looked up to the sky for a moment, as if listening to something only it could hear. Finally, it turned its gaze back to her. "Lesser demons bring death. Greater demons make the earth their own. Reshape it. End it."

Her mouth went dry. She doubted Egrin was a lesser demon like the Ayperos. Did that mean . . . "Is it possible a greater demon has already come through? Perhaps a long time ago?"

The Fogfaun stared at her for a moment, then answered, "Yes, demon king came through. A very long time ago. Only so much magic in land. Limits him. For now."

Her heart skipped a beat, then started racing. Judging by Celen's expression, he'd already figured it out too. Could Egrin be the king of demons, limited only by the land's lack of true magic? But he'd been gathering power for years. He now had more than ever before, yet, he continued his search.

The question left was, what would he do when he had enough?

CHAPTER EIGHT

Alluin

The cavern appeared no different than any other, except for the way it went *straight down*. It was wide enough for a man to descend, if he was willing to risk the fall. Alluin watched Elmerah as she knelt near the rocky lip and peered into the abyss.

"Anyone down there!" she called out, startling him.

He glanced around the quiet forest, then back to their tethered horses, more worried about something in the woods hearing them than something *down there*. It was too mind-boggling to consider a creature might actually be down in that narrow darkness.

Elmerah rocked back on her heels, still observing the hole. "I'm quite sure this is it. It feels . . . dirty, like lamp oil coating my skin." She rubbed her coat-clad arms. "I've no idea how to close it though. It seems Celen would have been better suited to this task."

"The Fogfaun seemed to think you were the only one strong enough to do it," he explained.

She glanced up at the sky, then back down to the hole. "Storms and fire will not close this." She stood. "Those are the only magics known to me."

"If you cannot close it—"

She held up a hand to silence him. "I know. They will not return Celen and Isara, and without Isara, we'll have a difficult time killing the emperor."

"And without Celen?" he asked without thinking, then wondered why he'd even asked it.

She scowled. "He is useful too, and I would regret his loss." She turned away, walked a full circle around the opening, then looked down it again. "Well," she sighed, "I believe the only way I can figure out how to close it is to go down there. There's nothing I can do from here." She raised her eyes to him. "You wait here with the horses."

"Are you mad!" he blurted. "I'm not letting you go down there alone."

"No choice," she said, already leaning her hands on the cavern's edge to dangle her feet down. "There's a slight slope, I might be able to keep my footing, but a rope would help." She looked over her shoulder at him.

"Elmerah, *no*."

"I know you brought a length of rope, Alluin. Be a good boy and go fetch it."

He stared at her, warring with indecision. This might

be the only way to reclaim Isara and Celen, but the thought of Elmerah lowering herself into this unknown cavern made him ill.

She watched him, waiting patiently, because she already knew he had no choice.

"This is insanity," he huffed, then went to fetch the length of rope from his saddlebag. If he ever had another chance at that Fogfaun, he'd send an arrow between its eyes. Elmerah should not be risking herself to close up some demon hole. It had nothing to do with her.

He returned to her with the furled rope, unwound it aways, then handed her one end. "Tie it securely around your waist. If I hear any sounds of struggle, I'm yanking you right back out."

She secured the rope tightly around her waist over her coat.

He took his end and paced around the nearest tree, looping the rope around its trunk for leverage.

"Ready?" Elmerah questioned.

"No," he grumbled, but she was already lowering herself down the hole. He gave her just enough slack as she went, hating every moment of it.

If something happened to her . . . he gritted his teeth and clenched the rope tighter. He could not now consider what that would mean, not to the elves, not to their mission, and especially not what it would mean to *him*.

Elmerah

The cavern was pitch dark, and seemed to go on forever. They'd run out of rope soon, and she would have accomplished nothing. At least the slope had increased as the cavern turned to pure stone. Elmerah inched along on her rear, then as soon as she was able, crawled forward on hands and knees. She was utterly blind, but it would be difficult to draw and light her cutlass in the tight space.

She moved along just a bit further, then the rope grew taut. *Lovely.* She'd run out of length.

She debated her options for a moment. Alluin would be furious, but she wasn't about to return to the surface with nothing accomplished. She'd never see Celen or Isara again.

With knees bent, she leaned back on her heels, her back hunched against the stone above her. She unknotted the rope and removed it from her waist, hoping Alluin would at least leave it dangling so she could climb back out.

Now that she was a bit more upright, she drew her cutlass and encased it in flame, momentarily blinding herself. Her eyes scrunched while she lessened the magic until the flame was just barely sustained, then peered further into the cavern.

It seemed she was almost at the tunnel's end. Her stone surroundings concluded ahead, opening into a dark space.

Gripping her cutlass in one hand, she crawled forward awkwardly, scraping her knuckles on stone. She reached the end, then held her blade into the darkness and peered down. The cavern floor wasn't too far of a drop. She could make the jump, but she'd have an interesting time trying to get back up.

She supposed she'd just have to figure that part out when the time came, though her stomach rebelled against the thought of getting trapped in the cavern. Starving to death in a small, dark, space was not the way she wanted to go.

She said silent prayers to Urus, Cindra, and Arcale. She'd take any god that would listen, if they existed at all. She finally sent a silent apology to Alluin, swung her knees over the ledge, and jumped.

Her feet touched down with a puff of dust, sending a shock through her knees. She straightened and held her burning blade aloft. At her back and on both sides was solid stone, roughly twenty paces across. The rest of the space before her was thick darkness swirling with green light.

"It really is a demon portal," she muttered, then took a tentative step forward. "Now, how to close you?"

The portal rippled like water, then bulged outward, catching flamelight on its newly uneven surface. She scuttled back, holding her cutlass defensively. It bulged further and further, reaching toward her, then a humanoid hand with long black claws broke through.

She realized too late that whatever this creature was,

it had probably been drawn to her fire. A black-scaled arm followed the claws out of the portal. Given the proportions of the arm, this thing was twice her size. She glanced back at the ledge above, too high for her to scale in time.

"Useless gods," she muttered. "First time I decide to pray, and you send me a demon." She held up her cutlass, prepared to fight until her dying breath.

CHAPTER NINE

Alluin

Alluin peered down into the cavern, cursing himself for letting Elmerah go down there alone. Not long after the rope had gone slack, he'd heard distant clanging and unearthly shrieks. Smoke reeking of burnt flesh wafted up from the cavern.

He'd tied the rope around a nearby tree, and now debated whether to climb down, or jump. If Elmerah had removed the rope from her waist, that meant there was solid footing not *too* far below. He might be able to make it down . . . though he'd be no good to her with two broken ankles.

He gripped the rope and began to climb down into the hole, just as the other end went taut. The acrid smoke made him gag.

"Don't come down!" Elmerah called up. "I'm fine!"

Every bone in his body sagged with relief, save his hands on the rope. That cursed witch had scared him witless, and now here she was, calling up as if nothing was amiss.

He hoisted himself out of the hole, then peered over the edge. "Tie the rope back around your waist!" he called down. "I'll help pull you up!"

The rope shifted, scraping along the edge of the cavern, then went still.

He gave a tentative pull, then, feeling the weight at the other end, began hauling it up. If he'd had his wits, he would have taken the time to untie the rope from the tree to use the trunk as leverage, but he wanted her out of the cavern *now*.

He was sweating by the time her head crested the surface, and her hand clamped down on the cavern's edge.

Dark sludge covered her fingers. The same dark, slick, liquid coated her hair and dripped down into her eyes. There was a large tear in the shoulder of her coat, but he couldn't see if there was a wound beneath.

His one hand tightened on the rope while he reached the other out to her. Gripping her hand tightly, he tugged backward, digging his heels into the earth. Her other hand met his, then she was out, and they both toppled to the ground.

He was overwhelmed by the scent of burnt, rotten flesh. She must have used her fire against whatever had attacked her.

"Ouch," Elmerah groaned. "Next time I try to venture off into an abyss, stop me, won't you?"

He sat up, wiping the oily substance now coating his hands onto the grass. "What happened? What is that you're covered in? Is your shoulder injured?"

She rolled over onto her back, her eyes focused on the calm blue sky above. "Well I found the portal. I'm covered in demon blood. And yes, that thing stabbed me with its horrible talons. Hopefully they had no toxic coating."

At her words, he gripped the torn edges of her coat and pulled, tearing her entire sleeve free of her arm.

"Alluin!" she cried out. "I liked this coat!"

He barely heard her words. He wiped her blood away with his sleeve, observing the wound still seeping blood. "It's deep. It will need to be stitched or cauterized." He glanced back toward the horses. He had a needle and sinew in his saddlebag. "How did you manage to climb with such an injury?"

"The possibility of demons nipping at your heels can be quite the motivator."

He wanted to scold her for making quips at a time like this, but he'd spotted shapes moving beyond the horses. The Fogfaun approached, not just the few who'd apprehended them, but dozens. The creatures wove through the trees toward where he knelt, peeking out with wary eyes.

"Alluin, not to rush you, but I'm bleeding out,"

Elmerah said, looking up at him, unaware of the Fogfaun.

"I'll fetch my sinew and silverleaf sap." He knew if he told her what approached, she'd hop to her feet and threaten to kill them unless they returned Celen and Isara. Not that it was a terrible plan, but he'd rather her remain conscious and not lose any more blood.

He rose from her side and approached the creatures, who'd reached their horses, their bodies yet shielded by trees showing fragments of a head here, a furred rump there.

"Weather worker killed greater demon," one rasped as he drew near.

"Few can kill greater demons," another hissed.

"Hole can be filled up now," another said.

"Who is speaking over there!" Elmerah called out.

Alluin narrowed his eyes at the nearest Fogfaun. "You knew there was a greater demon lurking down there, didn't you? That's why you hadn't closed the portal up yourself. You didn't want to face it."

They whispered amongst themselves, until one said, "Yes."

"You could have warned me," he growled, keeping his voice low.

"Alluin?" Elmerah questioned from her position near the hole. "Return to me right this moment."

That she was still lying flat at the sound of voices meant she couldn't rise.

"I must tend her wounds," Alluin said to the Fogfaun. "Can we expect more demons from the portal?"

"Not for long while," one said, its pure black eyes intent on him. "Lesser demons stay far away from greater. Greater wanted out, but too big and heavy to make steep climb out of hole. So it waited." It glanced at the other Fogfaun, then turned back to him. "We heal weather worker."

The creatures scurried past him before he could protest. He followed them toward Elmerah.

"What in the name of Arcale are you!" Elmerah balked as the first reached her.

The creature hovered over her for a minute, then knelt on furred knees.

Alluin neared, intent on questioning how the creatures might heal her, but all he could do was stare. The Fogfaun's small, onyx-toned hands glowed a dark blue over Elmerah's wound. Alluin glanced over his shoulder at the other Fogfaun, who'd formed a semi-circle behind him.

"Alluin," Elmerah said nervously, her eyes finally finding him to her left past the Fogfaun touching her. "What is it doing to me?"

"Healing you, I think."

She turned wide eyes to the creature. "Where are Isara and Celen?"

The creature bowed its shaggy head, seeming deep in concentration. Its hands grew brighter.

Elmerah's eyes slammed shut. Her face scrunched up with pain. "Ilthune's curse that hurts."

The glow dimmed, and the Fogfaun removed its hands from her shoulder. Where once had been a deep, oozing wound, now there was a long blue mark, like a tattooed lightning bolt.

Elmerah sat up abruptly, causing the Fogfaun to scuttle backward. She looked down at her new mark. "You know, I'd been glad to escape the tattoos of my clan, now you've gone and ruined it." She looked to the Fogfaun with narrowed eyes.

"I think perhaps you should be thanking it," Alluin observed.

"For kidnapping our friends and sending me down a hole with a greater demon? I think not."

Ah, so she had heard his conversation with the Fogfaun.

"Where are Celen and Isara?" Elmerah demanded of the creature before her.

It stepped back, keeping its eyes on her.

"Don't you dare disappear," Elmerah warned, reaching for her cutlass with her rump still in the grass.

"Will return them," the Fogfaun who'd healed her said, "but must agree to slay demon king."

More hushed whispers, then, "If you can kill greater demon, you can kill demon king."

Elmerah scoffed. "You want me to kill their *king*? My apologies, but I have quite a few people to kill already. I don't need to add a demon king." She stood, swayed a bit on her feet, then steadied. "Now return my companions or I will be forced to cut you all down."

"Agree to kill demon king," one said. "Give word, then companions returned."

She bared her teeth at them. "Give companions, or me kill *you*." She began to draw her cutlass.

The Fogfaun all chattered frantically, then Isara and Celen appeared out of thin air amongst them.

Elmerah's hand drifted from her cutlass as she crossed her arms. "That's more like it. Kill your own cursed demon king."

Isara was the first to scurry over to Elmerah, with Celen walking more confidently behind. "Demon king?" he asked. "We have some suspicions about that."

"We think it's Egrin," Isara whispered.

The Fogfaun watched Elmerah with wide eyes as she digested the information. Feeling uneasy, Alluin moved closer to his companions.

Elmerah looked to Isara, then Celen, then to the Fogfaun. "Is this true? Is Egrin Dinoba the king of demons?"

One Fogfaun stepped away from the others, boldly straightening to its full, if less than impressive, height. "Many names. Many many names. But yes, Dinoba is one such name."

"Of course it is," Elmerah muttered, her eyes dark with malice. "Of course he is the demon king. He is far more evil than stupid spiders," she gestured to the hole, "or that thing down there." At a conflicting thought, she turned her attention to Isara. "If Egrin is the demon king, a demon who came to this realm on his own, then how are you related to him?"

This seemed a revelation to Isara, who's eyes widened behind her dirty spectacles. "I . . . I don't know? Perhaps he sired children at some point, and I am a grandchild rather than a cousin? From where else would I gain my," she hesitated, seeming to search for the right word, "gifts?"

Elmerah shook her head, turning her sights back to the Fogfaun. "Do you know?"

The creatures simply stared at her.

She glared at the Fogfaun. "Alright you irritating little creatures, I'll kill your demon king for you, whether he's Isara's cousin, grandfather, or anything else, but what will you give me in return?"

Isara opened her mouth to speak.

Alluin gave her a warning look, sure she was about to give away the fact that Elmerah had already planned to kill Egrin and needed no further motivation.

The bravest Fogfaun approached, looking up the long length of Elmerah's body before reaching her eyes. "Weather worker wields lightning and fire, but greater gifts lurk, if you can claim them. This knowledge is gift to you."

Elmerah rolled her eyes. "Your *gift* is useless. I was born with my gifts, and while they have increased in power to a degree, they never change."

The Fogfaun blinked black eyes at her. "Only thing of value we can give."

Elmerah looked to Alluin, who shrugged, then back to the Fogfaun. "Fine," she huffed. "That's alright. I'll kill your demon king, just kindly stay out of my way from this point forward."

The Fogfaun was already backing away. It rejoined the others, and they faded into the forest as if they'd never been.

Alluin stared at the space they'd occupied, almost wondering if this was all just some fanciful dream. Fogfaun, greater demons, and the demon king.

"Let's get going," Elmerah said. "Our journey has been delayed long enough."

Alluin watched her saunter toward the horses. With a shrug, Celen followed, leaving him alone with Isara.

Isara watched the two Arthali with wide eyes, then looked to Alluin. "They don't seem terribly worried to know that Egrin is not only a greater demon, but the demon king."

He sighed and shook his head. "I'm quite sure the only things the Arthali worry about are ale and fine foods."

Elmerah mounted her now untethered horse, then looked back to them. "Hurry it up, will you!"

He started forward, his spirits lower than ever. He'd nearly lost her this day. She'd faced a greater demon, and barely made it out alive. Could she kill the king of demons?

He hung his head slightly as he reached Elmerah and

Celen atop their mounts. He didn't think so. At least not by herself. They'd all been foolish to run off from Faerune alone. Yet without a doubt, now that they had, there was simply no going back.

Saida

S aida had never sweat so much in her life. The day's ride had been torturous after the night of little sleep, and the ever-looming fear that Egrin might return. She hunched in her saddle, pulling her head wrap—which she'd found in her hastily-rolled bedding—a little lower over her eyes. She wasn't sure she and Malon could recreate . . . whatever that was. Whatever that overwhelming magic had been.

Beyond that, she didn't think she wanted to. No one should possess such strength. She could make sure she never felt it again by killing Malon and giving the circlets to Egrin, but then where would that leave Faerune? She hadn't wanted to face the real solution. If Malon was already Egrin's enemy, could she convince him to unite with her to kill the demon emperor? She'd seen the fear in Egrin's eyes. This magic could harm him.

"We'll be there soon," Malon assured, having ridden the entire day at her side.

"You misread my worry," she muttered. She didn't care about reaching Malon's allies. The last full moon had just passed, so the next was still far off. She had time, but they needed to be heading toward Faerune, not away from it.

"It felt right, didn't it?" he said.

She shivered, the sweat dripping down her body suddenly feeling cold. She didn't have to ask what he meant. "It felt wrong."

His silver eyes were on the horizon, the sun creeping ever closer to leaving them in the dark. "Don't lie to yourself, Saida. You are a priestess of the moon. You are one of the only women alive who can channel Cindra's magic."

"The gods' magic cannot be channeled," she hissed. "It is not possible."

"You saw those Dreilore. You cannot deny it."

She shook her head, unwilling to argue further. To her, Malon's words bordered on fanatical. She went silent, listening to their surroundings. The sound of the antlioch's hooves in sand had become a constant rhythm relegated to the periphery of her mind, and beyond that, there was little to focus on.

"What do you plan once we arrive?"

He glanced at the other elves riding silently around them, as if debating whether or not they should hear his answer. Finally, he turned back to her. "The settlement is simply a waypoint. We will show our allies the power we possess," he glanced at the other elves again, "then we will go deeper into the desert."

A few elves muttered amongst themselves, as if

unaware they'd be traveling even deeper into the desert. Saida wondered if the thought made them feel just as ill as she.

"We cannot go deeper," she said, her voice weak. "We must return to Faerune before the full moon."

"We will return when the time is right."

She gripped the front edge of her saddle so tight her fingers ached. She took a breath, forcing her voice to be low, and steady. "Why? Why must we wait?"

"Because I will not return without an army at our backs. The Dreilore are mighty, and you cannot fathom the power Dinoba possesses. Even Galterra's militia should not be taken lightly. Their numbers are great. And now," he shook his head. "I daresay all elves will be against us too. You may think Faerune will welcome you back with open arms, but they will not. To use an artifact like the Crown of Cindra . . . " he trailed off, his tone suggesting she'd been a very bad girl.

"You forced me to use it! I had no choice!" Her antlioch danced beneath her, set off by her emotions.

"An argument that will ring hollow with the remnants of the High Council. You are as much a traitor as I."

"That's not true."

He shrugged. "Believe what you wish, it changes nothing. I will make you one promise. We will return to Faerune before the full moon. In exchange, you must cooperate fully when we meet with the Makali this night, and other tribes in the time that follows."

Tears stung her eyes. It pained her heart to give

Malon what he wanted, but was there any other choice? "Why don't you just summon an army of demons? I know you're capable."

Malon tilted his head as he watched her, his shoulders gently swaying from his antlioch's gait. She'd grown used to only seeing his eyes through the head wrap, and imagined his lips were pursed in consideration. "I'd assumed you and your Arthali witch had figured it out already. Perhaps you're not as clever as I've been led to believe."

She glared at him.

"Very well. While you are correct, the demons make a useful army—against elves and Dreilore—they will not stand against Dinoba. He is their king, more powerful than the greatest of demons. The fact that he abandoned them to the underworld when he came to this land matters little. Most are of low intelligence, and even the more clever demons still respect his power."

She blinked at him. Surely he could not be serious. "His magic is strong, but he cannot be stronger than the greater demons. The myths—"

"The myths are both wrong, and right," he explained. "The demons are extremely powerful whilst in their own realm, but once they're here, they tend to fade. There is not enough magic to sustain them. They are unable to summon power out of thin air like your Arthali, or like Egrin. They are rarities."

"You can summon a wisplight without the aid of moonstones," she accused. "I saw you do it at the Akkeri temple."

"A small feat of earthen magic. The land will let us take small doses here and there, but will not give us magic enough to summon storms, or create destructive flames from nothing."

"Or to suck the air from your lungs," she added, beginning to understand. "That's why Egrin has wanted Elmerah. Her magic is like his, it comes from within, but she can summon it on a massive scale. Perhaps a far greater scale than he."

He laughed. "You are clever after all. Yes, though I do not know for sure, I believe that's why he wants her. He would like to uncover the secret of her gifts."

She pressed her head wrap against her brow to soak up the dripping sweat. At least the sun was going down. She looked forward to a reprieve. "He wants Elmerah, but not Rissine, though he knew Rissine from her time in the Capital."

"Elmerah's sister?" he questioned, then seemed to think about it. "I only met her the one time, but her well of power is small in comparison to Elmerah's."

Her eyes widened as she turned her gaze back to him. "How can you tell? Elmerah thinks her sister far *more* powerful."

"From my limited observations, I would guess Elmerah is limited by her lack of self-belief. Rissine has already reached her full potential. I can tell, because my gifts are similar to yours. I can see beyond what meets the eye." He peered forward, then pointed. "Look, fires. The settlement is near."

She narrowed her eyes against the suddenly sharp rays of dusk, the sun at the final moment before it sunk below the horizon. She could just make out the light of fires, small plumes of smoke, and what looked like sun-faded hide tents.

"Be cautious with your words," he said not just to Saida, but those riding around them. "The Makali are a quick-tempered race. Arguments can quickly turn to bloodshed."

Saida kept her gaze on the distant settlement. Under any other circumstances, she would have been excited at the prospect of such an unusual experience. She'd never met one of the Lukali, nor their less-civilized brethren. Few ventured to Faerune, though she knew occasionally Lukali trade ships traveled up to Galterra during the sun season, when the waves were at their most gentle.

She glanced at Malon—for what, reassurance? She wasn't sure. It was difficult to define one's emotions, when one's greatest enemy was also their sole ally.

CHAPTER TEN

It was full dark when Malon's group reached the settlement, where two Makali sentries stood guard. Saida did her best not to stare, but it was a struggle. The Makalis' skin was a deep, rich brown, much darker than Elmerah's. Their features resembled a human's, save the dainty lower fangs resting over their upper lips. Their gleaming black hair was closely cropped, she presumed to accommodate the blazing heat

Saida had expected primitive dress—they had been depicted to her as little more than savages—but the silver vambraces and greaves were finely crafted. She wondered at the lack of breastplates and other armor to cover their loose linen robes, but thought it best she ask the other elves in private.

The two sentries, both female despite the short hair, stood before massive torches on poles stuck deep into the sand. There were no walls around the settlement, just a circle of torches enclosing the tents, which made sense, considering Makali tribes were nomadic.

Malon dismounted, gesturing for the other elves to stay back. He approached the two female sentries, bowed his head, then began to speak in a language Saida had heard a time or two—practiced in the High Temple by scholars who would accompany trade caravans. The language sounded almost like music, lifting and falling, the words seeming to run into each other like one long word instead of many. She imagined that such a language would be spoken by the nymphs and other magic folk of myth, for it sounded too melodious to be real.

That Malon spoke this language increased the puzzle of his upbringing. Who were his parents to have raised a man who spoke Kaleth, and had a deep understanding of the arcane arts? *And* demons. The conversation seemed to go on forever while Saida studied the hide tents beyond. Other Makali ventured in and out, some pausing to steal a glance at their visitors.

Finally, one sentry nodded, then gestured toward the settlement with her finely honed spear.

Malon turned back to the elves. "You may dismount now. Take from your saddlebags only what you will need for the night. The antlioch will be well-tended."

Saida slid down from her saddle, her body even more stiff than the previous night, and bone-weary. She unfastened a smaller satchel affixed to her saddlebag and slung it over her shoulder, feeling the weight of the circlet within like an anchor pulling her down into the depths of the sea. She glanced at Malon for further instruction, but he had turned to continue his conversation with the female sentry.

Feeling nervous and alone, she took a deep breath, and stepped away from her mount, forcing her mind away from thoughts of Malon, and the circlet resting within the satchel against her hip. She almost felt guilty when her thoughts slipped to the need for a bath, or at least a bucket of water to pour over herself. She should not be considering her own comfort when the lives of all in Faerune might be in peril because of her. She tugged the lower portion of her head wrap loose, sighing at the ecstasy of evening air on her hot, damp skin.

She spotted Phaerille, her head wrap already tugged down, then moved to walk at the woman's side as they strode past the sentries, all the antlioch following obediently in their wake. The hide flap of the first tent was already opening as they neared, revealing three young male Makali dressed in simple robes similar to what Saida and the other elves wore.

One nodded to her as he hurried past. She glanced over her shoulder, watching him as he placed a hand at an antlioch's neck, then guided the creature off the path Saida and the others had taken. The other two young Makali guided two more antlioch, which was enough for the entire herd to follow.

"Saida," Phaerille whispered, startling her. "We're supposed to follow." She pointed ahead.

Saida whipped around, following the aim of Phaerille's finger to a male Makali, this one older and wearing a few pieces of armor like the sentries. He seemed to be waiting for them.

The other elves fidgeted uneasily behind her, and she wondered why they hadn't just moved past while she wasn't paying attention.

Malon reached her other side and leaned in near her shoulder. "Are you well enough to walk? A day in such heat can be dizzying."

She nodded, though she was dizzy, and *tired*. Too tired to trudge through the sand and have a meeting with the Makali clan leaders, but she moved along anyway. Her throat ached, and the still-warm sand tugged at her boots.

Seeming to sense this, Phaerille took Saida's arm and gave an encouraging smile, though she seemed just as worn. They walked on, each woman relying on the other to remain upright. Malon remained silent at her other side, his gaze on the Makali man leading them.

They walked down a path formed by tents on either side, some with open flaps revealing the Makali within either lounging, or enjoying their evening meal. Saida's stomach was so empty it hurt, though she wasn't entirely sure she wanted to know what foods caused the strange, pungent smells emanating from distant cook-fires. The scent reminded her of the yearly visit from the human spice traders to Faerune. The elves purchased few seasonings, mainly just salt, and she had always wished she could procure some of the more exotic spices that would make their way to the Spice District in Galterra.

The Makali guiding them stopped before a tent so massive it could house their entire herd of antlioch, though she supposed its actual intent was to house the clan leaders. Torches like the ones circling the settlement blazed at either side of the closed flap.

"Only two will enter," their guide said in the common tongue. "Others will be shown to the cookfire."

Malon looked over to Saida. "That's our cue. Do you have the circlet?"

She patted the small satchel slung over her shoulder. "I have it, but surely I won't need it?"

"The Makali respect strength," was all he said as their guide opened the tent flap, gesturing for them to venture inside.

Phaerille gave Saida's arm an encouraging squeeze, then turned away to follow the other elves.

Malon pressed his hand into her lower back, urging her toward the candlelight within the tent, which she soon realized actually emanated from glass oil lamps. Her feet were given a reprieve from the sand as they landed upon a massive ornate rug, similar in design to the much smaller rug her mother had imported for their home.

Five Makali sat on plump pillows, the vibrant colors of the fabric echoing those of the rug. The Makali wore fine raw silk in varying shades, and jewels glittered at their fingers. It seemed everything she'd been led to believe was wrong. The Makali were far from primitive. Each of the five, three females and two males, wore silver vambraces just visible at the ends of their sleeves. All had closely cropped hair like the rest of their clan.

Saida jumped as the heavy hide flap *thwapped* shut behind her.

The oldest of the five Makali, a female with gray streaking her black hair, spoke in the common tongue. "Welcome, Moonfolk. We are pleased to entertain you. I trust your journey across the Helshone has been a pleasant one."

The younger male Makali seated to her right grinned, and another female lifted a bejeweled hand to suppress a chuckle.

Malon placed a hand on Saida's shoulder. "We survived, if that is what you mean."

Another Makali laughed, and the air of formality within the tent dissipated.

The older female, who seemed the highest ranking given her position in the middle, smiled warmly at Saida. "A face as lovely as Cindra's. It is no surprise to me that you are a priestess of the moon."

Saida froze, resisting the urge to glance at Malon. As far as she knew, the Makali were without religion. Their myths consisted of wild beasts and wise-folk.

"Do not appear so surprised," the Makali continued. "All know the goddess of the moon, though we may call her by a different name. Come here, child, and let me sense your power."

Malon leaned close to her shoulder. "Urali is the wise woman of this clan. She possesses some earthen magic. Do not be afraid."

Easier said than done, she thought. It wasn't that she felt in immediate peril, but the way this woman, Urali, observed her felt far too intense. The other Makali had fallen silent, watching the exchange.

Saida walked across the rug toward Urali, stopping just out of reach.

Urali looked up at her from her perch on her pillow. "Such a tiny thing," she observed. "Do you have the circlet?"

Saida gulped. This was wrong. She shouldn't be here, discussing this with strangers. She shouldn't be proving to them what shouldn't even be possible.

"Saida," Malon said from behind her, a hint of warning in his tone.

She reached a trembling hand into her bag. If she could prove to these people that she could use the circlet, would it enable them to return to Faerune? Was this the only way to protect her father, Elmerah, and everyone else from the emperor?

Her fingers went icy as she wrapped them around the circlet. She hadn't touched it since unceremoniously snatching it from her brow and shoving it into the saddlebag.

She pulled it free, hearing whispers, not from inside the tent, but inside her head. She almost dropped the circlet to the rug.

Urali's eyes widened, her jaw went slack. "Place the circlet upon your brow, girl."

The whispers grew louder. She couldn't understand what they were saying, but there was a feeling of urgency. Urging her not to do as the Makali asked. Urging her to run from this tent and never look back.

Her boots seemed adhered to the rug, her body wracked with indecision. The whispers were overwhelming. Urali's intent gaze made her feel ill. Saida's eyes fluttered shut, her body swayed. She only realized she'd fallen when she lost her grip on the circlet. Then all went black.

A damp cloth on Saida's brow woke her. The water was warm instead of cool, but it was at least cooler than the stuffy air surrounding her. She opened her eyes to see Phaerille leaning over her, her features conveying worry in the gentle lamplight.

Remembering what had happened, Saida's breathing sped.

"Do not fret," Phaerille soothed. "You are safe. It is just you and I here. Malon waits outside."

Her body relaxed, then tensed again as the nausea hit her. She jolted upright, and Phaerille was just fast enough with the half-full pail of water to keep the carpet from being ruined.

Saida heaved until her throat was raw agony, then

leaned back against her hands, finally able to breathe enough to take in her surroundings. They were in a tent much smaller than the one where they'd met with Urali, though it still boasted an intricately woven rug and a few pillows—more than she'd seen within the other tents when she'd walked past them.

She'd been lying on one such pillow. The pail Phaerille had been dipping the rag in looked like one used to water the antlioch.

She didn't mention it. She'd simply been grateful for the care. And grateful that Malon had waited outside while she was incapacitated.

She wiped the sleeve of her loose robe across her mouth, then glanced over her shoulder at the closed tent flap, noting the lack of light coming from outside. So sunrise was yet to come. At least she hadn't lost too much time.

She turned back to Phaerille. "How long was I out?"

Phaerille pushed her honey blonde hair—a bit matted with sweat—from her face. "Not long, priestess."

"Saida, please, call me Saida." Her thoughts rushed back to Urali, and to the circlet. She held a hand to her suddenly racing heart as her eyes searched the small tent for her satchel.

"Malon has the circlet," Phaerille soothed. "He didn't want to leave it unguarded with only me to protect it."

"I thought you said he's right outside."

Phaerille shrugged. "He is. I simply assumed that was why he took it. Shall I fetch him?"

Saida grabbed her arm before she could rise. "No!" She lowered her voice. "No, that won't be necessary."

Phaerille nodded, sinking back to the ground. "Very well . . . Saida. Do you think yourself able to eat? You should try if you're to have any strength tomorrow. The Makali meat is strange, too filled with spices, but it is edible. I did not have the courage to ask what animal it was before it was hunted."

Saida laughed weakly. "I don't blame you." Those voices. Those urgent whispers. She could not shake them from her mind. They had wanted her to run.

"Please, lie back," Phaerille instructed, misreading her expression.

She shook her head. "No, I'm fine. I will take food, if you don't mind fetching it for me."

"Very well, prie—I mean, Saida."

Saida watched her go, hoping her departure would not mean Malon would come into the tent. She looked down at her legs, draped in the tan robe, wondering if they'd be able to support her. She didn't know if it was the heat, the lack of food, or what had happened in that tent that had utterly drained her, but her body wanted nothing more than to fall back upon the soft pillow.

Unfortunately, her mind disagreed. She needed to retrieve the circlet. Perhaps if she touched it when she was alone, she'd be able to better make out the whispers. But *that*, would require speaking to Malon, and he might not leave her alone once she had it.

She pulled her legs underneath her and stood, swaying, then winced at a sharp pain in her skull. She closed her eyes and leaned her head into her hands for a moment, waiting for the tent to stop spinning.

She must have waited like that for a while, because when she finally lifted her head, Phaerille had returned with a thin wooden tray laden with an enormous hunk of meat and a small pile of cooked grains. Fruits and vegetables would have been easier on her raw stomach, but she supposed such things were rarities in the harsh landscape of the Helshone.

Looking at her disapprovingly, probably because she was standing, Phaerille made her way across the tent and placed the tray at Saida's feet, then set a water skin beside it. "Please rest, Saida, at least until you've had something to eat."

"Can you get the circlet from Malon for me?" she asked. "I promise I'll be good and eat if you'll fetch it for me. I feel uneasy with it out of reach."

Phaerille studied her for a moment. "Very well." She turned and strode back out of the tent.

Saida collapsed, then swung her legs to the side so she could rest on her hip and one hand. She looked down at the hunk of meat, colored a deep red with spice. There were no bones that she could see, and it was a rather large hunk, so it must have come from a sizable animal.

Hopefully not a scorpion.

She heard voices outside the tent, Phaerille speaking with Malon.

The tent flap opened, then shut behind Phaerille, her

face bright red and her eyes downcast. "He says you can have it after you eat, and bathe. He doesn't want you touching it while you are weakened. He fears it will be too much for you."

Her eyes lifted to meet Saida's, clearly anxious for her approval.

This poor woman, Saida thought. It could not be easy to answer to both Malon and herself when they were bound to be perpetually at odds. "It's alright," she soothed. "See?"

She tore off a strip of meat and stuffed it into her mouth. She chewed once, then her eyes went wide. She searched for a place to spit it out.

"You'll get used to it!" Phaerille hurried across the tent, then knelt before her. "Please try to eat it, Saida. We wouldn't want to insult the Makali." She glanced around warily, as if some of the Makali lurked within the tent. She lowered her voice, "I've heard they kill with their bare hands. You saw the armor at their wrists and shins? They punch and kick, and fight with spears. Their limbs are the only areas they need the armor. Nothing breaks through their defenses."

Saida chewed the densely spiced meat. It tasted almost rotten, but also made her tongue burn. She suspected ground fire peppers were part of the flavor.

Phaerille handed her the water skin. "It's easier when you wash it down."

Saida accepted the skin and took a gulp, finding Phaerille's words rang true. Even so, her stomach revolted at the thought of forcing down another bite of meat, so she turned her attention to the grains. There was no utensil, but she found the small, off-white pellets were sticky enough on her fingers to eat a full glob at once.

The bite of grain was mercifully bland compared to the meat. She ate another bite, then drank more water. "How do you know so much about the Makali?"

Phaerille smiled, pleased with herself. "I've known we'd be traveling to the desert for a while. Fallshire has few books, but I found one on a traveling merchant's cart."

Saida nodded encouragingly. "You're from Fallshire?"

She shook her head. "No, but a few of us camped nearby after Faerune fell."

She said it so casually, Saida had to resist the urge to balk. "Were you within the city when it was attacked?"

Another shake of the head. "I've never been to the city. Only my mother was from Faerune. My father was a Valeroot hunter. They fell in love, and my mother left the city to be with him."

Saida lifted her brows. It was not often one heard of Valeroot and Faerune elves falling in love.

Phaerille laughed. "Yes, it is an odd story, but you can imagine how I felt when I first met Malon. He wanted to unite all who had felt wronged by Faerune, and I wanted desperately to fit in somewhere. My pleasure escalated when I learned how many other elves he'd gathered."

"But—" she stared at Phaerille, momentarily lost for

words. Finally, her thoughts solidified. "There could not have been that many of you. Elves are rarely exiled from the city. A few choose to live in the neighboring villages, but they are welcome to come and go from the city."

Phaerille pursed her lips, waiting for Saida to finish, then said, "You truly have no notion of how many have been wronged by the High Council, do you? Malon is right, you have lived a sheltered life."

She shook her head slowly. This could not be true. Yes, the High Council was antiquated in many ways. Perhaps the lower social classes were not treated with as much respect as they should have been. But there couldn't have been so many willing to watch the city fall.

Phaerille's spirits seemed to sink. "Eat your food, priestess," she said softly. "There is a natural spring nearby. I will stand guard while you bathe."

With a deep breath, Saida scooped up more grain. It tasted even more bland than before, or perhaps it was just an effect of her mood. Could she really have been so blind to the plight of the lower classes? Phaerille, she understood. With a Valeroot elf for a father, she'd be looked down upon. But so many others?

She wanted to know all of their stories, beginning with the other elves in their party. What had their lives been like before Faerune fell? How much injustice had they truly endured? She needed to understand.

There were two sides to every coin, and she was finally realizing, she'd only ever seen the side facing the sun.

CHAPTER ELEVEN

Elmerah

The distance Elmerah had put between herself and the demon portal, followed by a full night's rest, had worked wonders to restore her spirits. The spots of sky visible past towering oak boughs hinted at a rainy afternoon, but it was warm enough, and the canopy dense enough, that it should not be too uncomfortable.

Her group kept a leisurely pace, intent on not wearing out their horses now that they were unlikely to be tracked.

Alluin rode at her side, and Celen and Isara rode ahead, seeming to have formed an odd companionship. At least, that's what Elmerah told herself it was. Otherwise, Isara was avoiding her. She had noticed how the little sparrow—for now Celen had put the notion in her head that she was sparrow-like—had avoided her gaze the rest of the previous evening's ride. And how she'd spoken little before they lay to rest for the night, each taking a turn at standing guard.

Now the morning had waned into midday, and Elmerah sensed unease amongst their ranks. Even Alluin seemed to be sulking. It was a rare occasion when *she* was the one in a better mood than everyone else.

She tugged at her uncomfortable coat sleeve, hastily sewn back into place. It wasn't sitting quite right, and the new lightning-shaped mark beneath tingled from time to time. Alluin had tried to wash the blood from his sleeves when they'd reached another stream, but they were stained beyond repair. If she didn't know better, she would think he'd been utterly frantic at the idea of losing her.

A sudden whiff of burnt demon flesh soured her mood. It still clung to her clothing and hair. She had killed a greater demon on her own, but Egrin was far more than a greater demon. While they still had many, *many* days of riding ahead, it might take that much time to come up with a plan. "So," she said, her gaze not on anyone in particular, "not that it changes our mission, but does anyone have any insight on what it means that Egrin is the demon king?"

Isara's spine stiffened so abruptly that her curly blonde hair almost seemed to bristle, but she did not speak.

Noting Isara's reaction, Elmerah looked to Alluin. "Thoughts? Concerns?"

He scowled. "This is not a laughing matter, Elmerah."

"And I'm not laughing. I'm just as worried as the rest of you, but sulking in silence is no way to form a plan. We know that Isara can dampen his magic for a time, this is our only hope of keeping him in place long enough to kill him. But my main worry now is whether or not the demon king *can* be killed."

Celen glanced back at her. He looked utterly gigantic in the saddle, and his poor horse seemed to labor more than the others. "You have slain Ayperos, and whatever it was you faced in that cavern. Why would the emperor be any different?"

She shrugged as Celen turned back around. "Well, he's their king. It has to mean something."

"The Fogfaun seem to believe you capable of slaying him," Alluin suggested. "So it must be possible."

Her thoughts jolted back to the strange creatures, and what they'd told her. The part about her possessing more magic was utter rubbish, *and* they had sent her down a hole after a greater demon. Considering those two matters, she didn't exactly trust anything else they had to say.

Then, there was what had happened when she'd faced that thing in the cavern. She'd fought valiantly, she'd thought, but when the demon pinned her against the cavern wall, its putrid breath hot on her throat, its talons piercing her flesh . . . she thought she was going to die. Then her power had swelled up like a geyser. She had dropped her blade—she had nothing to guide the magic. It didn't matter. She'd become pure flame.

Unnerved by the memory, she absentmindedly fiddled with her reins. She'd come close to such a thing before. She'd wielded fire without a blade, but it had been a small burst. What had happened moments before that demon would have killed her was like a forest fire. It swarmed out of her, eating the demon's flesh from its bones. In mere moments, a greater demon lay dead and charred at her feet.

She wasn't sure why she had withheld details of the event from Alluin—no, that was a lie, she knew why. Wielding such ferocious magic had scared her. Greater demons were fearsome monsters, but what type of creature was she to sear the flesh from their bones with a thought?

It wasn't right. So many folk already feared her, and they had no idea what she could truly do. Until she'd faced that demon, she hadn't even known herself.

Alluin cleared his throat.

She met his gaze, realizing he'd been watching her, and Celen was looking back over his shoulder too.

"What?" she snapped. "If you two have no suggestions on how to defeat Egrin, I must think deep to come up with a plan myself."

"I have a plan," Isara spoke so low, she almost didn't hear.

Elmerah tapped her horse's sides with her heels, trotting up next to Isara while Celen fell back toward Alluin on the narrow path. "Let's hear it then."

Isara peered down at her hands where they twined with her reins, though she should have been looking ahead at the forest for hidden dangers. Her curls bobbed with the movement of her horse. "I think we should lure Egrin out of the city. Once we're close enough, we can start rumors that an Arthali witch and a blonde woman were spotted traveling together. If he knows we are near, unprotected, he will come for us."

Elmerah shook her head. "If it were that easy, he would have come for us while we were in Faerune. Either he doesn't care enough to seek us out, or he fears your magic now that you have turned against him. You are the only person in existence who can stop him from slipping through our fingers. He will not walk willingly into a trap."

Isara finally met her gaze, her eyes tense behind her spectacles.

Elmerah didn't like that tension, it made her suspicious. "What has changed? Why are you so much more worried than before?"

"Helping you escape Egrin was one thing. What we're plotting now is murder."

Elmerah leaned back as far as her saddle would allow. "You did hear the whole part about him being the demon king, correct?"

Isara nodded, then looked back down. "Yes, and it has made me doubt our ability to defeat him. We'll stand a better chance if we face him in a location of our choosing, rather than within the Capital where he'll be surrounded by Dreilore and the militia."

Elmerah sensed that there was something else going on here. That perhaps Isara avoided her gaze because she didn't want to be caught in a lie. The reason was not hard to decipher. Daemon Saredoth would surely be within the city. If they attacked Egrin there, and had a shot at Daemon too, Elmerah would gladly take it.

"If we lure Egrin out," she said evenly, like she was speaking to a spooked mare, "he'll have warning that we are coming. We would lose the small advantage we have. This is the whole reason we departed Faerune the way we did. If we would have stopped to plan, I have no doubt it would have gotten back to Egrin. The Nokken are clever spies."

For a moment, only the gentle *clop clop* of the horse's hooves could be heard. She sensed Celen and Alluin both watching her. Had they already realized Isara's hesitation?

Isara held up her nose, her eyes wide to prevent the moisture resting there from falling. "If you did not want my input on your plan, you shouldn't have asked."

Elmerah chewed her lip, unsure of what to say. If she mentioned Daemon now, and the fact that she could not guarantee his safety, they might lose Isara's aid in the matter entirely. "You must understand why we cannot grant Egrin a warning," she said softly.

Isara wouldn't look at her.

"Leave her be," Celen said to her back. "We have plenty of time to discuss this later. For now, let us worry about surviving the journey."

Elmerah flexed her fingers around her reins. The ability to back away from an argument was not a strength she usually possessed, and it had been difficult enough to keep the annoyance out of her voice.

She took a deep breath, then counted backwards in her mind. "Fine," she said after a moment, her eyes still on Isara. "Perhaps now is not the time."

Isara finally looked at her, a thousand different emotions clear in her eyes. She didn't need to speak any of them. Elmerah understood. Isara wouldn't let her brother die. She'd turn against them all if that's what it took to protect him.

Elmerah realized she was a fool to have thought she could ever convince Isara otherwise. After all, she'd never killed Rissine, and her sister had done far worse than simply catering to a demon emperor.

Rissine

It felt good to be back on the open ocean, the salty wind in her hair. Rissine's new elven-made coat, fashioned from vibrant emerald wool, billowed around her legs as she leaned against the railing. The elves might have been a lot of haughty whelps, but they made the most beautiful clothing. They did not, however, make a worthwhile crew, and that's what she had, a lackluster crew of elves. Her crew consisted of Merwyn, Alluin's sister Vessa, and a handful of Vessa's fellow hunters. Just enough to man the ship.

None of the other Arthali, save Zirin, had been willing to dedicate their time to a secret mission—but she couldn't very well tell them where they were going. Egrin might still have spies within Faerune, and she'd not lead him right to Elmerah.

Heavy boots echoed across the deck behind her, then Zirin stopped at her side. His hair was that extreme shade of black that almost held blue highlights in the sun, with no tones of brown or warmer shades. That dense curly hair fell in a braid down his back, making his large features seem severe.

Eyes almost as black as his hair scanned the calm sea. "The winds won't come easy this day. We won't make as much progress as we'd hoped."

She scowled at the news. She knew she should probably thank him for trying. While the Winter Isles clan could control the winds, the winds had to exist to begin with. There just wasn't enough this day, though she could see rainclouds far off toward the mainland.

Zirin looked to her, waiting for the next command. Beyond his attempt to control the winds, she should have thanked him for coming at all. He'd never even asked what the mission was. The moment she mentioned getting on a ship, he was ready to depart.

Zirin watched as one of the elves hurried past with an oar in her hands—though Rissine could not divine a purpose for the oar up on the deck.

Zirin spat over the railing. "Elves don't know their way around a ship. Useless."

"Hmph." They should both be grateful for the elves too, otherwise, they wouldn't have a crew. She hadn't told Vessa her intent, but Vessa knew. She knew that if Rissine was leaving, she was going in search of her sister, and with her sister, would be Alluin. Zirin probably knew too, but he hadn't mentioned it.

"Storm brewing," he said.

She was about to snap at him for continuing to make conversation, then her eyes widened. The storm that moments ago seemed a gentle thing had darkened. The clouds were so angry they seemed to boil like over-heated stew. She could only guess at how far Elmerah had gotten on her journey, but in all likelihood that storm would cut right across her path.

"You stupid, willful girl," she muttered.

Zirin watched her for a moment, then said, "She's just like you."

He walked away before she could reply, leaving her to turn and stare at his back in shock before turning her sights back to the storm.

Zirin was right. She and Elmerah did not shy from danger, and they did not shy from storms. They sailed with dangerously inept crews, and faced demon emperors all on their own.

Perhaps they were both foolish, but no one would ever call them weak, and to the Arthali, that was all that mattered.

Elmerah

"Leave it to the gods to pick *now* to water the crops!" Celen yelled above the thundering rain.

They had dismounted to lead their tired horses through the muck, searching for anything to provide just a bit of shelter. The heavy boughs overhead poured collected streams of water down atop their heads, like walking through a waterfall.

Elmerah cursed as her boot caught on a slick root. Her wet hair whipped forward into her face as her horse spooked and tugged backward. She slipped and teetered in the mud, but managed to stay upright and not lose her horse. "This is miserable! I don't care if we find shelter. I'd rather just stop moving!"

"Agreed!" Alluin called out from behind her.

It would have been manageable if they were just walking, but trying to lead horses through the muck was dangerous and all together frustrating. "There!" She pointed.

It was as good as they would get. The massive oak might shield just a touch of the rain if they stood right up against its trunk.

Alluin and Isara reached it first, the latter looking ridiculous with her hair plastered to her head, and her spectacles steamy and dripping. Alluin, however, looked as natural as could be with his rich brown hair slicked back, turned darker with moisture, and his sharply cut jaw more prominent without the hair to frame it.

Celen reached her shoulder and leaned in. "You're staring," he whispered, then continued past with his horse.

She smirked, moving forward as Celen found a free lower branch on the oak and tethered his horse, not far from where Isara and Alluin had tethered theirs.

Elmerah's horse snorted and thrashed its head, slowing her progress through the sucking mud. Alluin came back into the heavy deluge to take her mount. She handed over the reins with a nod, then hurried past him to the oak. Relieved by the shelter, she leaned her back against the trunk next to Celen, with Isara on his other side.

This is just my luck, she thought. Caught out in the rain far from her destination, at odds with the only person who could help her save—well, she supposed at this point she was saving all the land, not just her friends and what remained of Faerune.

It was a heavy weight to bear. *Too* heavy. She'd never much cared for responsibilities beyond keeping herself alive and comfortable. Especially when most of the people she was saving would just as soon spit on her, than thank her.

Finished with the horses, Alluin leaned against the oak at her side opposite Celen. Cold droplets still pelted in with gusts of icy wind, but at least here it wasn't like having buckets of water poured on their heads.

Alluin edged closer, his shoulder nearly touching hers. "Let's just hope it lets up before evening."

"At least it washed away the smell of charred demon flesh."

He wiped lingering droplets from his brow. "I noticed the smoke. You must have burned that thing alive."

She swallowed the sudden lump in her throat. "Something like that."

He didn't question her further, and for that she was grateful. Her shoulders began to relax. This wasn't the worst way to wait out a storm.

"Speaking of fire," Celen began from her other side, "you *could* provide us with a bit of warmth about now."

"Water can extinguish even magical flames, you muckfish. I'd waste all my energy trying to keep it lit."

Celen laughed. "It was just a suggestion. If we're going to be here through the night, I might be able to summon us up a bit of shelter."

"I'd rather not have your dirt clods melt into mud atop us while we sleep."

"I meant to make us a temporary shelter with fallen boughs and leaves, you angry whipfish."

Elmerah glared at him as he stepped away from the trunk and turned his attention to Alluin. "Care to join me, elf? We'll let the ladies rest awhile."

Alluin pushed away from the trunk, then followed Celen into the gushing rain to search for materials, leaving her alone with Isara, the one person she'd rather not face right now. She glared at their backs as they faded into the mist. *Traitors.*

Oh well, no time like the present. She grit her teeth and sidled closer to Isara.

Isara peered out into the rain, looking about ready to cry. Maybe she already was. It was difficult to tell with her wet face, and her nose red and sniffly.

Elmerah steeled herself for what she was about to say, as it went against her better judgement, and Alluin would not be pleased. She cleared her throat, but Isara still wouldn't look at her.

She sighed. "I won't kill your brother."

"W-what?" Isara's eyes went wide and filled with child-like hope, facing Elmerah at last.

"I said I won't kill your accursed pompous brother. I promise."

Isara pushed a sopping wet curl behind her ear. Her delicate hands trembled. "Why would you promise this now, when we are finally setting your plan into motion?"

Did she have to make this so bloody difficult? "I detest my sister. She's a venomous viper of a woman. But if you were intent on killing her, I'd strike you down where you stand."

Isara froze halfway through the motion of wiping away another wild curl. "That's not exactly comforting."

"And I'm not one to give comfort. I am, however, a

woman of my word. While I think your brother should die, I can understand why you'd want to protect him. In fact, if you'd agreed straight out to kill him, I don't think you and I would have gotten this far. I would have known from the start that you weren't a person to be trusted."

Isara slid her back down the rough bark, then plopped her rear in the soggy grass and hung her head.

Elmerah didn't think the position looked terribly appealing, but had a feeling Isara expected her to join. She sat gingerly, then waited for her friend to speak.

"I was prepared to turn against you," Isara sighed. "In fact, I had devised a whole wild plot in my mind that after Egrin was gone, I'd suppress your magic and let the militia arrest you. That way, Daemon would be safe."

"Why you little wretch!" Elmerah hissed.

Isara flinched, seeming to shrink in upon herself. "I was wrong," she groaned. "I should have confronted you about it more firmly from the start. I should have had the bravery you just showed me, telling me you'd kill me here and now if I intended to harm Rissine."

Elmerah leaned her back against the trunk with a heavy sigh. "I don't suppose I blame you. No one cares to negotiate with an Arthali. If we're not useful as weapons, we're better dead."

"That's not what I—"

She held up a hand. "I'm used to it. People are afraid of me. If I were an elf or human, I'd be afraid of me too. I'm just as scary as the Dreilore, or a demon." *Perhaps scarier*, she added in her head. *If Alluin had witnessed what I did to that demon, he would have run far, far away from me.*

Isara stared at her, jaw agape. When Elmerah eyed her fully, she snapped it shut. "I'm not afraid of you, Elmerah. With a single thought, I could render you harmless," she glanced at Elmerah's cutlass, running the length of her leg in her seated position. "Well," she amended, "I could render you as harmless as any other skilled swordsperson. I'm not afraid of you any more than I am of Alluin."

"Then why have you been so silent? Why not lay down your terms from the start? Why not just tell me that if Daemon is harmed, you'll turn on me?"

Isara's face, already flushed with cold, grew even redder. "When my father died, I fled. I stayed in Faerune and hid my nose in books. Then I went to Fallshire, hiding myself away even further. This is the first time I've ever truly stood up for what I believe in."

Elmerah laughed softly, shaking her head. This girl was so very young. "You stood up for yourself when you helped me escape Egrin. And you did it before that, when you ran far from Egrin and your brother. Sometimes running *is* standing up for yourself. It may feel cowardly, but it's better than staying in a bad situation."

Finally, Isara smiled. Just a small smile, but it was enough to let Elmerah know they had reached a truce.

Celen came into view in the distance. He slogged toward them with five giant boughs in his muscular arms, and a bushel of wide leaves gripped in his left hand. Alluin was barely visible carrying more boughs and leaves behind him.

"Please tell me you ladies are done talking about us!" Celen called out. "We're entirely soaked!"

Elmerah grinned as he reached them. "My apologies, but I only talk about people who are interesting. You do not qualify." She stood. "Now are you going to build us a shelter, or will you just stand there looking like a troll carrying all those branches?"

Alluin laughed as he reached Celen's back, then tossed his branches onto the ground, maintaining his grip on the neatly stacked leaves, each one as long or longer than his forearm. "At least help us hold up the branches, *Ellie*. Or would you rather sleep in the rain?"

Elmerah narrowed her eyes. "Oh not you too." It was bad enough when Celen called her by the shortened name.

Isara laughed, then moved into the heavier rain to hold up one end of a bough that Celen had leaned against the earth. The weight nearly toppled her. With a grin, Elmerah took the branch's end from Isara and leaned it against the mighty oak.

Together, the four companions built a hasty shelter, then all huddled beneath it, temporarily safe from the rain. Elmerah knew the morning would bring more worries, but for now, she didn't terribly mind being soaking wet, but fairly warm, with Isara's shoulder on one side, and Alluin's on the other.

CHAPTER TWELVE

Saida

Saida paced back and forth across the tent's interior as day waned to night, waiting for Phaerille to return from her search for Malon. She was clean—she'd been baffled in the dark hours of morning to see the crystal clear spring surrounded by strange squat trees with great broad leaves, but she'd been more than grateful to bathe in it—and she was fed. The meat really wasn't *that* bad, once one recovered from the initial shock of it.

Those were about the only two things she had going for her. She'd been stuck inside this tent all day, by Malon's orders, to rest and regain her strength. He'd explained to the Makali that she was simply ill from the heat, and that nothing else was amiss. She was yet to tell him about the whispers, and she wasn't sure she ever would. Now darkness was falling outside the tent, and she was no closer to returning to Faerune.

The tent flap opened without warning, revealing not Phaerille, but Malon, his features tense with a quiet, seething anger. "You have made my life exceedingly difficult," he said, letting the tent flap shut behind him.

She stopped pacing and stilled, unsure how to interpret his mood. She'd never seen him so deeply annoyed, and some folk grew violent in such a state. Still, she could not resist saying, "Any inconveniences I've caused are nothing in comparison to what you've done to me."

His laughter made her jump. He leaned his head forward and rubbed his brow, still laughing. He wasn't wearing the Crown of Arcale, so it must be in the satchel slung across his shoulder, along with the Crown of Cindra. He'd not leave either ornament with anyone else.

He lifted his head and walked toward her. She tensed, but he continued past, then sat on one of the plump pillows.

She turned, tracking his movement.

His shoulders slouched as he settled more comfortably onto the pillow. The tan robe that at first seemed startlingly foreign was beginning to seem natural on him. "Urali is now skeptical of our ability to harness the power of the circlets. She won't say it out loud, but she obviously believes we are trying to trick her. I've spent the day convincing her you simply need your rest, but she has insisted we demonstrate our power before morning."

Saida stepped back toward the pillow furthest from Malon's, then sat. "I do not believe I can agree to that."

His soft smile faded. "We've discussed this. We will not return to Faerune without an army. If we want an army, we must convince Urali. With her approval, we will be able to approach the other clans."

"It's not right. If what happened—if it really is the power of the gods, I will not abuse it in such a way."

He arched a silver brow. "Will you wait idly by while Egrin attacks Faerune then?"

Her fists curled. "No, I will not. But I will also not allow you to use me like a puppet. You have spoken as if a partnership is what you desire. If that is the case, then we must negotiate."

She'd been worried he'd call her a naive little girl, or he'd simply ignore her, but his gaze was considering. After a long observation of her, he spoke, "I see you're beginning to grow up a bit. Good. What do you propose?" He held up a hand before she could speak. "And keep in mind, the Makali will try to kill us if they think we have hidden motives."

She closed her open mouth. Truly, she was so shocked he was actually listening to her, she wasn't sure what to say. All she wanted to do was return to Faerune. She cared not for the Makali, nor this war Malon was attempting to wage.

"Why would they even want to join you?" her thoughts poured out loud. "What do they stand to gain?"

"The Makali have been at war with the Lukali for

centuries," he explained. "You've seen how they live. If a smaller clan wanders too far from an oasis, or if the one they arrive at has dried up, they may die. The Lukali cities are built around the greatest bodies of water within the desert, so they remain strong and safe. Quite safe, in fact, because no potential enemies would dare cross the desert to attack them."

She considered his words, assuming the *oasis* he'd mentioned was the natural spring she'd bathed in, though she'd never heard the term before. "But the Lukali and Makali, they are essentially the same? Other than being born either within a city, or to a nomadic clan?"

Malon nodded.

Such a notion would have made little sense to her before, but after what Malon had done . . . well, it was eerily similar. Elves turned against elves, all for land, power, and status.

"So they want us to help them overthrow the Lukali?"

He laughed. "No. Why claim harsh desert lands, when you can be given lands within the Empire? Even the southern villages with half the resources of Galterra seem like a great boon to the Lukali."

She nodded. "And if you can demonstrate to them the power of the gods, they will believe you capable of granting those lands."

"Precisely."

"There's one issue."

"And that is?" he asked expectantly.

"I don't care about the Makali, or your war, and I won't demonstrate the circlets for them."

"Saida—"

"And," she interrupted, "before you decide to threaten me with Egrin attacking Faerune, know that whatever you try to force me to do, I will fight you every step of the way. I will never give you the power you desire. You will never achieve any of your lofty goals."

His eyes narrowed. "You're mighty full of bluster, Saida. You may hold your leverage, but I too hold mine. Without my help, you'll be stuck here in this desert, and those left in Faerune will be slaughtered. Before you make any more idle threats, you may want to offer a solution to this issue."

Her mind raced for a way to avoid using the circlets for ill. The magic of the gods was not meant for displays of power. Not meant for enlisting an army. Arcale and Cindra gave life. They helped her people make the crops grow. They made the rivers run more fiercely.

"The oasis," she muttered, mostly to herself. "That's it."

Malon watched her steadily. "What about it?"

She stood. "Go to Urali. Tell her come morning, she'll have her proof, but it won't be through an empty display of power."

He watched her a moment longer. "What do you plan?"

"Do you not trust me?"

He shook his head. "No."

She rolled her eyes. "Well you're going to have to."

M alon might have cursed and moaned about the delay to execute their plan, but Saida had managed to make him wait until the small hours of morning, when most of the Makali would be asleep. Urali had been skeptical, but had agreed to wait until dawn for the display of power.

With Malon at her side, Saida approached the bank of the oasis. Soft grass squished underfoot. Squat trees with broad leaves surrounded them. She knelt and dipped her fingers into the water, disrupting the ripples created by the underground spring. The pool wasn't large, just the size of a small pond, but in the desert, it was the giver of life. The water reflected the half-moon overhead, making the surface glow.

Malon crossed his arms and looked down at her. "Will you reveal your plan now, or have you decided to drown me?"

"Shut up and listen." She took a deep breath, watching the water, hoping this would work. She did not have the gifts of a Sun Priestess, but hopefully with the circlet, she could access them.

"I'm *listening*," he said when she didn't speak.

"I've been thinking about the circlets, and where their power comes from. I—" she hesitated. "I don't think the power just comes from the unusually pure moonstones. I really do believe it comes from the gods." She still hadn't told him about the whispers, but hopefully this explanation would be enough for him to understand her resistance to misusing the circlets.

He knelt beside her. "Go on."

She nodded, then looked down at her fingers in the water. "I do not think the gods would will their power to be used for shallow displays to gain an army, but for this," she gestured to the surrounding foliage with her free hand, "for this, I believe Cindra and Arcale would will it. They would like to see the plants grow, and the water expand to help sustain the Makali."

"I thought you did not care about the Makali," he said skeptically.

"I do not care to have them as an army, but no one should have to live not knowing if they'll have enough water to survive."

"It's a clever strategy," he said. "Expanding the oasis is a far greater display of power than what we'd been planning."

She shook her head. "It is not a display of power. It is a gift to these people."

"If it helps you to think of it that way, I will concur."

She glanced at him, then back to the water. Would she hear the whispers again when she donned the circlet? Would what she was about to attempt still anger the gods?

With no answers to her questions, she lifted her hand

from the water and extended it to Malon. "The circlet, please."

Still kneeling, he pulled his satchel forward and removed both circlets. "Correct me if I'm wrong, but Moon Priestesses do not receive training in earthen magic, do they?"

She shook her head.

"Well neither do guardsmen. How will we know what to do?"

She hardly noticed as he placed the circlet in her hand. "Malon, you can summon wisps and demons, you knew how to make the circlets work, but you don't know how to make the plants grow?"

He shrugged.

She would have laughed if she weren't in such a dire situation. Instead, she lifted the circlet and placed it atop her head. Her fingers came away numb, but there were no frantic whispers.

She looked to Malon to see he had already donned the Crown of Arcale. Wordlessly, both stood.

"I think I'll need your hand," she said grudgingly.

He reached out, then laced the fingers of his left hand with her right. Power pulsed between them, more gentle than when they had faced Egrin.

Malon squeezed her hand tightly. "What now?"

She closed her eyes. She had little to go off, but since youth, her mother, assuming her daughter would become a Sun Priestess, had told her how to make the plants grow. Saida had always felt her mother had been disappointed to learn she had no such talent.

Focus, she told herself. She thought first of the pool before her, imagining the small natural spring drawing water up to the surface. In her mind, the water surged with great volume, filling the pool far beyond its banks.

She heard bubbling. Was that the spring? She was too nervous to open her eyes to check. Too nervous too see if her hand linked with Malon glowed with the light of the moon, for she felt that light coursing within her.

Cold water soaked past the laces of her boots, then up the hem of her loose robe. She yipped in surprise, and would have lost her grip on Malon's hand if he weren't holding hers so tightly.

"Keep going," he instructed calmly.

She nodded to herself, letting the water flow around her ankles. She thought of the water seeping into the earth, enriching it with minerals to make healthy plants grow. Then she thought of the plants, of those squat little trees growing tall and mighty. She imagined bushes with plump berries, and medicinal herbs sprouting all over the bank.

She was beginning to sweat with the effort. The circlet felt like a great weight upon her brow.

Open your eyes, Saida. Her eyes fluttered open at the voice's command. Not Malon's voice, but that of a woman . . . inside her head.

She quickly recovered from the sensation of the strange whisper as her eyes beheld what they had done.

They now stood knee-deep in a pool three times the size of what it had been. The once squatty trees towered overhead. A glance back at the bank showed a variety of new plants, peaceful and unmoving in the moonlight.

Malon laughed. "Truly, I did not think this possible."

Tears were in her eyes, though she wasn't sure why. All she knew was that this was a gift, and what they'd done with the circlets before to those Dreilore had been a curse.

"Consider your power proven," a voice said from the banks.

Saida dropped Malon's hand as they both turned to find Urali standing on the bank, a look of zealous awe upon her aged features.

The whispers returned to Saida's mind, frantic once more. Only this time, she could understand a bit more of what they were saying. They were saying that she would never make it back to Faerune, for the woman on the banks would be her demise.

Malon hurried Saida back into her tent as the first rays of dawn stretched over the sand. She wanted nothing more than sleep now, despite her gnawing worry. However, Malon seemed newly energized, practically giddy with excitement.

He let the tent flap fall shut behind them, causing the flames in the oil lamps to flicker. He took both her arms in his hand. "Saida, that was incredible. *You're* incredible."

She pulled away, shaking her head. "Malon, I don't trust Urali. We must leave this place."

His elation wilted, like a delicate flower left out in the Helshone. "What are you talking about? We've proven our power. Soon we'll have the army I desire and we'll go to Faerune, as promised."

Her heart raced. She longed to retrieve the circlet, which had been placed back in Malon's satchel. Had she imagined the voice in her head, warning her against Urali? "No, there's something wrong. Urali will not let me leave this place alive."

Malon watched her for a moment. Even with the lower half of his robe wet, he still seemed well put together, but his eyes were calculating—and his calculations were a force to be reckoned with.

He glanced at the closed tent flap, then stepped closer, lowering his voice. "Tell me why you believe this, and keep your voice down. Urali is not the only Makali who speaks the common tongue."

She fidgeted at his closeness. "I—" she hesitated. He'd probably think her mad, and she didn't really want to share the experience with him, but she knew no other way to make him believe her. "I hear voices when I use the circlet. Sometimes many, but one voice is clear above the rest, a woman whispering in my mind. She told me not to display my power for Urali when we met in her tent. Then just now, the voice told me Urali intends my death." She shook her head, unsure of her own words. "Or she at least intends my downfall."

He leaned closer, his loose silver hair draping around her on either side. "Are you sure of this? I have heard no voices."

She thought about it. Was she sure? Could the voice really be . . . She licked her dry lips. In her heart, she believed the voice to be Cindra, though why a goddess would speak to her was anyone's guess.

She nodded. "Yes, I'm sure. I believe without a doubt Urali intends me harm."

"I wonder why?" he muttered, his gaze going distant. "Does she not truly desire lands further north?"

Saida suspected the question was not actually for her. He was calculating again, searching for Urali's hidden motive. "You believe me?"

He met her eyes. "Saida, what you did out there is something most priestesses train their entire lives to master, and even then, they'd need a group to accomplish such things, and moonstones to focus the power."

"I had the Crown of Cindra. I did nothing special."

He patted her shoulder. "Get some rest. I will speak to some of the Makali in the morning, see if I can't find the root of Urali's intent."

"There's no way I can sleep knowing that woman is out to get me!" she hissed.

He raised his brows at her. "Would you like me to stay with you?"

"Absolutely not. Just give me the circlet."

"If the circlet stays, I stay."

She thought about staying in the tent alone with no way to protect herself. Then she thought about sleeping near her enemy. She found the latter to be the lesser evil, which surprised her. He *was* her enemy, what he had done to Faerune was unforgivable. And yet . . . he was the only person who had ever believed her capable of *more*. It boggled her thoughts. She wanted to hate him, he was the reason her mother was dead.

He did not hold the blade, a small voice said in her mind. Not the voice of Cindra, but her own.

She shook away the voice. He might have thought her mother would be safe during the attack, Cornaith and Immril had survived, but all the other deaths . . .

He knew innocents would die, and he'd gone forward with his plan.

He watched her, waiting for her to make a decision.

"Sleep near the entrance," she grumbled under her breath. "Now give me the circlet."

Without another word, he reached into his satchel and withdrew the circlet, extending it to her.

She took it, then retreated to the far end of the tent. Her thoughts were all a jumble, too many to sort out. The circlet pulsed gently with cool magic in her hand.

It was late enough—or early enough—to be cold, so she curled up on one of the pillows near a warm oil lamp, her back to the small expanse of the tent. Shivering and weary, she curled around herself. A moment later, a blanket was tossed over her, then she heard Malon's gentle steps retreat.

A tear slipped down her cheek. She wanted nothing more in that moment than to speak with her mother, to ask her who she should trust, and what she should do about the traitor turned ally sharing her tent.

Egrin

E grin slumped in the finely-gilded chair, its thick cushions barely dented with his weight. His chamber was strewn with broken furniture, shredded curtains, and shattered earthenware. His bejeweled fingers clenched the chair arms so fiercely the wood cracked. He could tear the entire castle within Galterra to the ground, and his rage would not be sated.

Those cursed elves. He didn't care how they'd learned to use the circlets, he simply wanted the moonstones. He was *so* close, but the magic he'd gathered was not enough. He needed more if he was to reach his full power, and do what he'd originally come to this land to do.

Once he had that power, Galterra, the Dreilore, the Nokken and the elves could all rot. They were merely pawns in this game, playing their roles until he had what he needed.

But those elves . . .

They could end his reign. They could send him back

to the underworld, too weakened and scarred to ever return. He couldn't lose after he'd come so far.

He'd waited centuries to see *her* again. He'd sacrificed everything for her.

He would not fail.

CHAPTER THIRTEEN

Alluin

Alluin had disagreed that it was safe for their group to make way for the main road, but after a long night of rain and close calls with forest beasts, he'd been overruled. While it was true that their horses were weary, and the road would be a faster route of travel, he couldn't shake the feeling that they were being watched. Initially, he'd passed it off as nerves, but the feeling had persisted.

He checked his bow and quiver, fastened to his saddle behind him to assure he could reach them quickly. Celen and Elmerah rode ahead with their hoods tossed back, their heritage clear to any who passed. Even if they weren't being followed, and even if no enemies awaited further down the road, two full-blooded Arthali riding with an elf and a human would stand out, even if they weren't being pursued. Elmerah had been somewhat disguised before with her hood up to shadow her features, and she could perhaps be mistaken for a tall elf or a human with southern heritage, but Celen was unmistakably Arthali, from his height, to his battle scars, to the tattoos crawling up and down his arms, fortunately covered by his fur-trimmed coat at the moment.

Isara rode beside him, for the first time on their journey without a pensive crease to her brow.

"Someone ahead!" Elmerah called back to him and Isara. She and Celen both pulled up their hoods, for what little good it would do now.

Alluin did the same, tugging the green wool of his cloak down to his forehead, just in case.

Elmerah cursed at the sight ahead, but Alluin had already noted that the men in the distance wore the uniforms of Galterra's militia. But what were they doing this far south?

"Should we retreat?" Isara whispered, the militia men yet too far off to hear.

He shook his head. "They've spotted us. Running would make us appear guilty. They may just let us pass."

Elmerah and Celen slowed their horses for him and Isara to catch up, then they rode on more closely together. Alluin noted a handful of men, five visible, perhaps more in the bordering forest. One man knelt by a cookfire on the side of the road. As Alluin's horse crested a rise, signs of a camp became apparent. Copious supplies. These men had been stationed here for a while.

Elmerah glanced back, her eyes landing on Isara. "If they give us any trouble, I'll light their camp on fire. Then you gallop past with Alluin. Celen and I will catch up."

Isara blinked at her with a faint nod, then the group went silent as they neared the men. Three moved to block the road, hands on swords at their belts.

One with an ornate sword hilt and a thick gray beard stepped forward. "Any Faerune elves among you?"

Elmerah reined in her horse and looked down at him. "Not a one, will that be all?"

The militia man gave her a long, hard look, then waved her and Celen past. "Keep an eye out for Akkeri. There've been sightings along the coast near Port Aeluvaria."

Elmerah didn't need to be told twice. She rode on.

Alluin looked each of the men over as he tapped his horse's sides, wondering if they were being lured into a trap. Were they not even going to question what two Arthali were doing riding out on the open road? While the exile had slowly grown less strict, Arthali were still wise to remain in hiding.

He looked to Isara riding next to him and said lowly, "Ride on ahead. I'll catch up."

She did as he asked. He knew it was a risk, but this occurrence was so odd, he stopped his horse near the bearded man. "Any other news from further north?"

The man sneered at him. "None I care to share with you, elf. I'll let you pass, but know this, the Dreilore or

Arthali will kill you before you reach the Capital. Now get out of my sight."

He kicked his horse forward, glad Isara had already gone ahead. He half expected to get an arrow in the back, but nothing came. Elmerah looked to him as he reached her, her eyes wide. *"What in the gods was that about?"* she mouthed.

He shook his head, at a loss, and they rode on. They would discuss it once they were well out of range of the militia's bows. He urged his horse to a trot, and the others followed. They hurried on until they reached a smaller path stemming off from the road. He took it, unable to wait any longer to discuss what the militia man had said. It wasn't the threat, or the disdain for his race, but the Arthali. Why would there be Arthali in the North waiting to kill him?

He looked both ways down the narrow road, then dismounted, bringing his horse to face the others as their boots touched down.

Elmerah's gaze lingered on their narrow view of the main road. "What in Ilthune's name was that about? That man almost seemed to think I was his ally."

Alluin's hands felt numb around his reins as he led his horse closer to the others. "I think he believes you are. Has Rissine mentioned anything about Arthali clans allying themselves with the Empire?"

She tossed her hood back and shook her head. "No, as far as I know, those she found joined her. The clans are broken up and scattered, it was difficult for her to gather many of our kin at once."

Celen stepped a little closer, his gaze wary. "Ellie, do you think Rissine could have been lying? Could she have failed to recruit many of our people because they were already allied with the Empire?"

Isara gazed out at the road, looking tiny next to Celen in her dark blue cloak. "I don't understand how that could happen. How could they go from exiles to allies? *Why* would they do it, when who they believed was Soren Dinoba had destroyed their clans to begin with?"

Alluin watched as Elmerah gently pushed away her horse's muzzle as it tried to nibble at her wild hair. Her eyes locked with his. "And what they said to you? That you would soon be killed, but Faerune elves would not be allowed to pass at all?"

His stomach clenched. When he'd left, there had still been some lingering Valeroot clans in the deep woods. What had been done to them in that time? "We need more information. We'll stop at the next village." He looked to Celen and Elmerah. "You two will venture in. If the people there believe you allies, they will most likely speak to you."

Elmerah shook her head. "Old hatreds are not so easily quelled. Isara will have to go. She'll be more likely to get information than any of us. We need to know what we'll face once we reach Galterra."

"I'll do it," Isara said before Alluin could protest.

He didn't like the idea of her going into a village alone

with no way to protect herself, but something else now held his tongue. That strange feeling had returned. He felt eyes on his back. He glanced over his shoulder, but saw only trees.

"Alluin?" He realized it was the second time Elmerah had said his name. "Is something wrong?"

He shook his head. "Let's move on, if the next village seems friendly enough, we'll send Isara in."

She watched him for a moment more, clearly not believing him. But Isara and Celen were already mounting their horses. Elmerah gave him one last look, then did the same.

He scanned the woods, then climbed into the saddle. He possessed excellent hearing and eyesight. If someone had been following them all this way, staying close enough to spy, he should have spotted them by now. It had to be his nerves playing tricks on him.

They guided their horses to the main path, then continued northward. By his estimations, they'd reach the next village before nightfall. He was both anxious and dreading to learn what had been happening in the Capital. He wasn't sure how much longer he could keep moving forward with his kin dropping like flies all around him.

Elmerah

"Don't look so worried," Elmerah chided. "Celen is watching her."

"I'm not worried," Alluin replied, though the hunch of his shoulders and the deep crease at his eyelids said different. He gripped his bow tightly in one hand, opting not to leave it with the four horses tethered nearby.

Elmerah sat against a tree trunk and stretched her long legs out across soggy fallen leaves, fanning her coat out beneath her. Isara and Celen had gone into the village alone, the latter keeping to the shadows. He would only reveal himself should Isara find trouble.

"They let us pass through the checkpoint," she sighed. "No one is looking for us."

Alluin paced around the small clearing, not far from the road. He was jumpy, though she couldn't divine why now was any different than yesterday. Perhaps he was worried about what the militia man had said.

He stopped to look down at her. "That doesn't mean we're not still in danger.

She scowled at his back as he walked away to peer deeper into the forest. "Would you sit down? You're making my skin itch. Most creatures keep to the deep woods."

"I'm not worried about creatures."

And yet, he continued to watch the trees like they might come alive and attack him.

She sighed. A branch creaked nearby. Alluin shot off like an arrow.

She shook her head as he went out of sight. A perfectly spoiled rest. She got to her feet and went after him, her hand on her cutlass. If he *had* found something, she'd not be caught unawares. And if it was another Fogfaun, well, she had *questions*.

She caught sight of Alluin's back through the trees. He'd stopped walking and was looking around.

"Why are you jumping at shadows?" she asked as she neared, but he held up a hand to silence her.

She glared daggers at his back, but obeyed.

The only warning she had was his hand tightening around his bow, then it was whipped upward, sending an arrow straight into the foliage. A pained shriek assaulted her ears, then a blur of reddish hair and green wool careened down from the canopy, landing with a heavy thud and a groan.

Elmerah unsheathed her cutlass and stepped back, observing the male Nokken now panting and whining on the ground with Alluin's arrow sticking out of his right leg. The Nokken's fox ears were pinned back against his russet hair—probably about shoulder length, but it was difficult to tell with him squirming around on the ground like that.

Alluin nocked another arrow, then aimed it at the Nokken. "Why have you been following us?"

"Been following?" Elmerah asked. "You mean you knew we were being followed?"

Alluin's eyes remained on the groaning Nokken. "Speak now, or I will silence you forever."

"I saw you leave Faerune!" the Nokken cried out. "Don't kill me!"

Elmerah stepped beside Alluin so the Nokken could see them both. "Give us a reason to keep you alive."

The Nokken curled up on his side, his right hand gripping the arrow shaft where it met his flesh. The bloodstain on his green woolen breeches expanded with every small movement. "I didn't mean any harm," he panted. "I was tasked to watch Faerune, and report on anyone coming or going. Then I saw Celen leave with you and grew curious."

Alluin lowered his bow, just enough to ease the tension. "If you know Celen, why follow us in hiding? Why not reveal yourself?"

The Nokken grimaced, revealing sharp teeth. "Celen's clan were admitted within the crystal walls. The Nokken are enemies of Faerune. If that makes me Celen's enemy," he gasped, his hand clenching around the arrow, "then I'd rather not like to face him."

It made sense . . . sort of. "But you'll trail him?" Elmerah asked. "*Why?*"

The Nokken grunted, tossing his head back to remove a lock of hair from his face, then glared up at her. "I thought maybe he was leaving his clan and the elves behind. I thought that if he had a better place to go, somewhere away from the Illuvian forests and this stupid war, that I might be able to go there too. I should have run the other way though when I heard you talking about killing the emperor."

Alluin's bow whipped back up and the Nokken flinched. He was young—Elmerah placed him around eighteen, perhaps a year or two younger.

"Did any of your people follow you?" she asked. "Are any others nearby?"

"No! I was alone when I witnessed Celen leaving Faerune. No one saw me follow him."

She extended her hand toward Alluin, palm outward. "Lower your bow, he's not going anywhere, and he may know of Egrin's next move."

The Nokken blinked amber eyes at her. "You're Elmerah, right? We're supposed to keep a close eye on you."

"Of course you are," she sighed. "Now let's get that arrow out of your leg. I want you alive when Celen returns to verify your identity."

"You would mend my wound?" the Nokken asked, his tone hopeful.

Elmerah knelt beside him. The look in his eyes definitely confirmed his youth. This was no trained spy or assassin. "Yes, I'll mend your wound for now, but be aware, try to flee or harm us in any way, and Alluin will make a new one."

The Nokken nodded frantically. "Yes—I mean no. I mean, I won't run, I promise."

"Very good." She gripped the arrow and yanked.

His scream echoed through the boughs, sending birds scattering across the sky in its wake.

Isara

Isara steeled herself as she prepared to walk into the small tavern, which was also the inn, though she imagined they couldn't have more than one or two beds. There weren't many folk about at this time of day—they were all out tending crops, or fishing in the nearby bay—but she could hear a few voices within. They were too quiet for her to make out the words, especially over the creaking of the bird-shaped rusted sign swaying overhead from an eroded metal post. She could just barely make out the carved letters, the Nightjay Inn.

She straightened her shoulders, realizing she looked silly waiting for so long when she had Celen lurking in the shadows, ready to protect her.

She shook out her curls, squared her shoulders, and straightened her spectacles. "You can protect yourself," she whispered, then pushed the door inward.

Three human faces turned toward her as one, alarmed, then quickly relaxing.

"Just a girl," an older woman said.

"Thank Arcale," said an even older man.

The third was a young woman around Isara's age, with onyx black hair down to her waist, and sparkling blue eyes. "Can we help you? Would you like a room?"

The bar behind where the trio sat was empty. These three must be the proprietors, a girl and her parents.

Isara nodded to each of them. "Just a meal? Or am I mistaken, is this only an inn and not a tavern?" She realized as soon as she said it how stupid the question was. There was clearly a bar right there, stocked with a few small casks of ale.

The young girl stood and walked behind the bar, swishing clean white skirts around her legs. She wiped her hands on her brown apron, then planted them on the bar. "We have cured trout and fresh bread. I'm afraid that's all I can offer you at the moment. Militia men dine like animals when they pass through."

Isara scurried up to the bar and took a stool across from where the girl stood. "Trout sounds lovely, you say the militia passed through? Heading south?"

The girl gave a brief nod, then fetched a fresh loaf of bread from beneath the counter. She set the bread down and pried something open that Isara could not see, filling the space with the scent of cured trout. She piled the loosely held together pieces of fish preserved in gelatine onto a wooden plate, then sliced the loaf of bread with a wicked looking knife that made Isara sweat.

A completed plate was placed before her, along with an unrequested pewter mug of ale.

The girl wiped her hands on her apron again, proudly surveying her handiwork before raising her eyes to Isara. "From where do you hail? Have you traveled far?" She looked her up and down—well what she could see of her from across the bar, then added, "Not on foot, I hope?"

Isara chastised herself for being afraid. These people

were perfectly kind. The girl's parents had resumed their conversation behind her. "No, not far, and from the North," she lied, her mind frantically trying to recall the old maps she'd studied. "From Pence."

The girl's brows lifted. "From Pence? No one's lived there in years. Too many Akkeri attacks."

"I meant near Pence," she quickly amended. "A very small farm. No one knows of the name, so I usually just say I'm from Pence."

The girl watched her a moment, then slowly nodded. "Very well. I hope you enjoy your meal. It'll be two copper gulls."

Isara fished in her coin pouch, knowing full well she should not be spending the gulls, as she had no way to earn more. She hoped any information she might gain would be worth it.

"Any word from the Capital?" she asked, stopping the girl before she could walk away.

Her blue eyes now wary, the girl resumed her original position. "You mean more than the Dreilore and Arthali?"

Isara's eyes darted to her untouched meal, then back up. Would the girl find it odd if she asked about the Arthali?

The girl sighed. "I see you're just as frightened of them as I. I don't know which one is worse. Probably the Dreilore, because there are so many of them, but the Arthali are plenty frightening too."

"I can't believe the emperor lifted the exile," she commiserated, risking the unverified speculation.

"For certain clans, at least. We won't be seeing any Shadowmarsh nor Green Leaf witches." The girl laughed. "A season ago, and I hadn't even heard of the Shadowmarsh clan. Now I'm to report who comes and goes at our inn." She lifted a brow at Isara. "You're not a witch, are you?"

Before she could answer, the girl laughed. "No, too pale, too tiny. The witches are tall, a few passed through with some of the militia heading north."

Isara nearly spit out the sip of ale she'd taken. "You saw them?" she choked.

"Oh yes, heading for Port Aeluvaria. The emperor has them watching all the ports, he says for Akkeri, but I bet it's for the Faerune elves. He won't risk them attacking the Capital."

Isara shoved a bite of trout into her mouth before she could say something she'd regret. As if Faerune, in its current condition, could ever attack the Capital. But that begged the question, why was Egrin watching the ports? None would risk an attack on Galterra.

She turned at the sound of the door opening and gasped, inhaling a fleck of fish. She coughed as Celen strolled up to the bar, natural as can be.

He leaned near her shoulder. "We need to go," he whispered.

The girl behind the bar was staring at Celen as if one

of the gods themselves had strode into her tavern. Her eyes whipped to Isara. "You know him?"

But Celen wasn't looking at the girl, he was still looking at Isara. "*Now*, would be nice."

Isara stumbled from her chair, double checking that she'd placed the two gulls on the counter. "My thanks for the meal!" she blurted as Celen ushered her away from the bar.

She could feel the eyes of the girl and her parents on her back as she hurried out the door. Celen's hand was at her shoulders, guiding her.

Once they were away from the door, he grabbed her hand and tugged her off the main road in between the tavern and a closed-down smithy.

"I thought you were going to wait for me," she gasped.

"My apologies, but I thought you might like to depart before an army of Dreilore arrive."

"Dreilore?" she squeaked.

He tugged her past more buildings, heading east toward the woods. "Heard a farmer talking." He looked both ways down a narrow dirt alley before dragging her past a small sheep pen. "He rushed home from tending his crops, wanted to make sure his wife and child are safely locked away. They'd be more safe hiding in the woods, if you ask me. Can you go a little faster?"

Flustered, she increased her pace. They reached the end of the sheep pen. An open expanse of meadow stood serenely between them and the border of the forest. They broke into a run, the grass swishing around their legs like water.

She dared a glance toward the southern end of the road, stumbling in her panic as she spotted the first of the Dreilore. Were they just passing through, or had they somehow tracked her? She saw no way it could be the latter, but one of the Dreilore pointed to the field, to the exact spot she now stood, her feet rooted in fear.

"Run!" Celen hissed, giving her a tug.

Her mind jolted back to the present, and she ran. She ran until her lungs burned and her legs felt like they might collapse. The Dreilore shouted after them. Did they know who she was, or were they just suspicious of a human and an Arthali fleeing toward the woods?

Reaching the first of the trees felt like slamming into a wave, breaking through, then coming out running on the other side. Her heart thundered in her ears, her footfalls seemed to echo louder on the loamy earth.

Celen kept pace with her, though his legs could easily carry him faster. "Forgive me!" he shouted, then looped an arm around her waist.

Suddenly she was airborne, then her stomach smacked onto Celen's shoulder. She lost her breath. The ground below passed by dizzyingly quick.

"We can't lead them back to Elmerah," he huffed. "We'll run the other way, make sure we escape them before we find her."

"Why are they chasing us?" she forced out against the shoulder pushing into her stomach.

"Those militia men at the checkpoint took note of us, and the Dreilore are coming from their direction. They might have realized either who you are, or Ellie."

The trees whipped by them, but Celen never seemed to tire. Isara felt helpless and useless atop his shoulder, and she could only hope she'd not been the one they recognized. She'd hate to once again be the trap which led Egrin to Elmerah.

CHAPTER FOURTEEN

Elmerah

Elmerah stretched her neck from side to side, irritated. Alluin was back to his pacing, but now for a different reason. "They should be back by now," he said, more to himself than to Elmerah or Killian, their Nokken prisoner.

At least, he was acting like a prisoner. Elmerah rolled her eyes to Killian, sitting across from her, both leaning their backs against tree trunks. Alluin had been the one to tend his arrow wound. It wasn't a bad one, deep, but far from hitting anything vital. The young man had been lucky Alluin didn't pierce his heart.

Elmerah crossed her arms, peering at Killian suspiciously now that he was bandaged and ready for questioning. "Are you sure none of your people followed you?"

His fox ears flicked forward at her words, a bit unnerving since she wasn't used to spending time around Nokken. "I told you, I was on my own when I saw you leave Faerune. No one would have been around to follow me, and I would have noticed if they had," his accent grew thicker with his rushed words. "I'm a good tracker. *I would have noticed.*"

She lifted her hands in a soothing gesture. "Calm down, I was just asking. Now why were you watching Faerune on your own? Isn't that the sort of task entrusted to a full scouting party?"

Killian shrugged, averting his amber gaze.

"*Kil...li....an,*" she warned, drawing out the syllables of his name.

He looked to her, then to Alluin—still watching the woods—then back to her.

She tilted her head. "Might I remind you, we can still reinsert that arrow into your flesh."

Killian winced, placing a hand to his bandaged leg. "Alright, alright. The truth is, watching Faerune is a bit of a punishment. Nothing ever happens. We watch for days, but hardly anyone comes and goes. If they do, we wait until our replacement shows up, then we go back to camp and report what we saw."

She considered his words, thinking them truthful. She knew well enough that the High Council had been resting on its laurels, keeping everyone inside, though they should have been moving forward. "Do your people only watch Faerune, or do you watch the neighboring villages as well?"

"Skaristead, Fallshire, a few others. The villages are less of a punishment. At least in Skaristead I could make myself look like an elf and go into the tavern."

Alluin walked up to her side. "Skaristead?"

He need not say more. She knew his exact worry. Had the Nokken been watching Skaristead the night Saida was taken? If Malon had given Saida to Egrin, it was irrelevant, but if he had other plans . . . She let out a long breath. If Malon was keeping the Crown of Arcale for himself, Egrin would be after him. And if the Nokken saw what had transpired and where Malon had taken Saida, he'd know where to search.

Killian looked worried. "Did I say something wrong?"

Alluin shook his head. "It doesn't matter. There's nothing we can do now except move forward. We should look for Isara and Celen, they may need our help."

She stood, stretching out her stiff legs. "If we do that, they may return here and find us gone. We can't both go."

"I'll go," Killian offered.

Elmerah snorted, rolled her eyes, then looked back to Alluin. "You go, you're stealthier than I, but if they're in trouble you bloody well better come back and find me. Don't go rushing into danger on your own."

"Wouldn't dream of it. You'll be fine with . . . " his gaze drifted to Killian.

Elmerah grinned wickedly. "Don't worry, we'll spend this time getting to know one another." She turned her grin to Killian, who hunched his shoulders and inched his back further down the trunk.

Alluin surprised her by placing a hand on her shoulder, not a casual gentle pat, but a meaningful squeeze. She watched him for an explanation.

"Please, be careful."

She blinked. "I'm not the one possibly walking into a trap."

He smiled, though it didn't reach his worried green eyes. "Humor me, will you? If a troll happens upon you, don't antagonize it."

She lifted a hand to her chest. "Me? I'm hardly antagonistic."

He gave her shoulder a final squeeze, then turned away. "I'll head straight northwest to the village, and I'll come back the same route. If I don't return by nightfall, come find me along the way."

"I'll be finding you well before that," she said, but he was already gone, and she was left with only Killian for company.

She walked across dead twigs and leaves, then plopped down in the soggy grass right beside him.

He squirmed, but didn't try to move away.

She didn't like Alluin leaving, but at least she had entertainment while he was gone. "Now Killian, I think it's time you told me everything you know about the emperor's plan." She patted his leg right above the bandaged wound. "And remember, Arthali can smell lies. I'll know if you leave anything out."

Killian took a trembling breath. "Where do you want me to start?"

Isara

Panting and sweaty, Celen let Isara down to her feet. The Dreilore weren't just following them because they ran, they were searching for her specifically. That fact had been proven by the way the Dreilore dogged their steps deeper and deeper into the woods.

Her body trembled from the panic of it all, though signs of pursuit had not been heard for quite some time. "Do you think they'll track us?"

Celen wiped sweat from his brow, then shucked his coat, baring the tattoos on his well-muscled arms. "No. My magic may not be quite as impressive as Elmerah's, but it's useful when covering one's tracks."

She wrapped her cloak tightly around her arms, feeling cold though the weather was moderate. "I think your magic quite impressive, actually. The way you shifted the earth outside the crystal walls to save Alluin was incredible."

Draping his coat over one arm, he looked around. Occasionally a bird flitted from branch to branch, but there was no other sound or movement. The forest seemed almost cheerful.

"You'll have to save your flattery for later," he said as

he watched a bird swoop down near them, then back up. "Now that we've evaded the Dreilore, we need to find Elmerah, and not run amok of any deep woods creatures while we're at it. I don't imagine there will be Fossegrim this far north, but there may be trolls, and I don't know these forests well enough to evade them."

"Trolls?" she gasped. She'd never seen an actual troll in the flesh, though she'd studied them extensively.

Celen nodded. "Now," he spun a slow circle, "by my estimations, Ellie is that way." He pointed.

She grimaced. "Forgive me, but you're pointing north. Elmerah and Alluin should be to the south of us, and closer to the road, so slightly west, if I'm correct on how far we traveled. It was a bit difficult to tell since I was watching the ground go by behind your feet."

He winked. "My apologies for that. It's the easiest way to carry someone, and we needed to move quickly."

She thought other means of carrying her might have been just as easy for such a large man, but bit her tongue. "You saved my life, or at least my imprisonment, no apologies necessary."

"So you think they were after you? I thought so too. One of the militia men must have realized who you were."

She nodded. "I look a lot like Daemon, unfortunately. I'd not be surprised if the militia men were ordered to keep an eye out for me."

"It's a good thing. It lets us know that Egrin is scared of you."

She lifted her brows, too shocked to reply.

He rolled his eyes. "The emperor wants you, and he wants Ellie, but never came and snatched either of you from Faerune. He knows that together, you may be able to defeat him, and he wasn't willing to risk it." He looked around again. "So if that way is north," he pointed, "we should go that way." He swung his arm in the opposite direction.

She placed a hand at his wrist and pushed so his finger was pointing a little more westward. "Yes, southwest, correct."

He grinned and lowered his hand. "Well then, let's go. I hope you're alright to walk on your own the rest of the way."

"I'm fine," she said, though she wasn't. Her legs felt like thistle jelly and her brain felt filled with fog. She'd hidden from Egrin and Daemon for so long. Now that they knew she was still alive, and had allied herself with the opposition, there would be no returning to that quiet life. She wasn't sure she would return even if she could.

Celen walked casually at her side, seeming unworried. "So the Dreilore, you can eliminate the enchantments on their blades?"

"Yes?"

He nodded. "Good. If they catch us, be sure to do that. I don't need them neutralizing my magic."

"Do you think they'll find us?"

He shrugged. "They're Dreilore, the monsters from the North who mine magic metals and have held their lands against any opposition for centuries. What do you think?"

A lump formed in her throat. If she had to choose what she was the most afraid of, it would be the Dreilore. Yet, if she ever wanted to learn what had happened to her father, they would hold the answers, because as far as she knew, they'd killed him.

They might kill her too, before all was said and done, but she'd do her best to avoid it.

Daemon

Daemon Saredoth did *not* enjoy life on the road, nor did he enjoy traveling with a pack of Dreilore. He brushed dirt from his red velvet pantaloons, thinking *pack* was a fitting term. They were more like wolves than men and women, always hunting, or else sunning themselves and looking at you like they might eat you.

Or like they might just kill you and leave you for the real wolves.

He glanced at each of the five Dreilore who'd remained with him while the others searched the woods. When Egrin had tasked him with obtaining his sister, he hadn't thought it would be difficult. Isara was impressionable, and didn't like to argue. She shouldn't be hard to convince . . . only he couldn't find the blasted girl. If it weren't for the militia men recognizing her, he'd still have no idea where she was. Fortunately, the men had been instructed to report her position and not try to apprehend her. According to them, she traveled with two Arthali and an elf. The elf was of little consequence, but the Arthali complicated things. A few militia men would have been no match if said Arthali had even a fraction of the power the Shadowmarsh witches possessed. Or if one actually was a Shadowmarsh witch. The Volund sisters had made their stance against Egrin clear, it could easily be one of them traveling with Isara.

He sighed, tired of waiting near the pathetic little village. He should have gone to Isara and taken her by force from Faerune, but it would have been such a long way to travel, and he knew she'd wander northward eventually. It had been much easier to place militia at every port, and blocking every road. Messengers checked in with each group periodically.

He drummed his jeweled fingers on his thighs. "What's taking them so long?"

The one Dreilore of their regiment with long hair, denoting his status, looked to him with malice in his ember-filled eyes. "They are skilled trackers. She will not evade them for long."

Daemon sneered, then quickly regretted it at the look the Dreilore gave him. *Wolves*, they were all wolves. "They'd better not harm her," he muttered.

"Capture the girl, capture the female Arthali, kill all others. Those are our orders."

He drummed his fingers again. *Kill all others.* Egrin had grown rash, it seemed he no longer even cared for this war. It was as if land and status were of no consequence to him.

Daemon might have considered fleeing, but he was in far too deep, and he knew Egrin would eventually locate him if he ran. He wasn't as valuable—nor as dangerous—as his sister, he needed to remember that. He'd find her, and use her to guarantee his own safety. There was no other choice.

CHAPTER FIFTEEN

Saida

Saida wrapped her arms around her belly, cradling herself against sharp pains, undoubtedly an effect of that spiced meat. Her stomach simply did not agree with it, though her temporary incapacitation could not have come at a worse time. Malon had been gone all day —hopefully questioning the Makali as promised, and she'd been left in her tent with Phaerille. The tent flap was tied open with the idea of letting in a nice breeze, but there was no breeze to be had.

Phaerille came down on her knees beside her, seeming healthy and content, perfectly fine from eating the meat. "Perhaps cooling down at the oasis would ease your pain."

Saida shook her head. The Makali would surely all be

at the oasis, observing how it had grown and flourished overnight. She pressed her hands over her stomach, terrified to face them. Would they view her as savior, or witch? Neither option was comforting, or true.

Phaerille frowned. "I wish there was something I could do for you."

She winced against another sharp pain. "Do you wish that as one friend to another, or because you believe I am what Malon portrays me to be?" She didn't mean the words to sound harsh, but she was sweating and annoyed. She wanted out of this cursed tent, but there was nowhere else to go.

Phaerille silenced, looking down at her hands in her lap.

"I apologize," Saida groaned. "I did not mean to snap at you. I've never experienced pain like this in my life."

Phaerille lifted her worried gaze. "Perhaps it is not the meat. Something more serious might be wrong. I have no training as a healer, but you seem quite ill."

The pain cut through her, intensifying. She slumped over on the rug and curled herself in a little ball.

Phaerille hurried to her side, then knelt, placing her palm upon Saida's brow. "You're burning up, it's more than just the desert heat. I'll see if the Makali have a healer."

She gripped Phaerille's wrist before she could rise. "No! Do not tell the Makali I am ill. Find Malon. *Please.*" Her eyes snapped shut, anything else she might have said drowned out by the pain.

The light seeping through her closed eyelids shifted as Phaerille left the tent, then went dark as she closed the flap behind her.

She groaned, left alone in the dark, unable to defend herself if Urali came to kill her. Or maybe she'd done her work more subtly through poison, and this pain was her body slowly dying, for it surely felt that way.

She wasn't sure how much time passed before she sensed a new presence at her side.

"Saida?" Malon's voice. "How long have you been like this?"

The pain had spread from her stomach to her head. She opened her eyes to mere slits. "It started this morning, but has only grown worse." She inhaled sharply, reeling against sudden nausea.

His cool hand rested on her brow, then pulled away. "I do not believe this to be from the food."

She heard him shuffling through a bag, then cool metal slid across her brow. Whispers exploded through her mind, frantic, like when she'd first met Urali.

"Take it off!" she rasped. "They're too loud!"

He removed the circlet, but the whispers continued. Her trembling hand shot to one ear, the other buried against her pillow.

"This is definitely not from the food," he muttered, rolling her onto her back though her body protested the movement.

Sweat seeped from her pores, coating her clammy skin and eliciting chills despite the oppressive heat.

"What's happening to her?" Phaerille's voice cut through the whispers.

Saida hadn't realized she was in the tent.

"I think it's a curse," he explained. "There is a dark residue on her spirit."

What in the gods was he talking about? Her thoughts were unable to compete with the whispers. She could not make out what they were saying, only that they were frantic and frightened.

"Saida," Malon said evenly. "I'm going to place the circlet in your hand. You must grip onto it no matter how loud it gets. I'll need your help to cure you."

"You know how to cure her?" Phaerille asked, her voice seeming to call out from the other side of a great abyss.

"No," Malon said, his voice closer, but somehow just as distant. "I know little of curses. I think she's going to have to force it out herself."

The pain had dulled, or else it was just her mind shutting it away. She couldn't move, think, nor breathe. The cool weight of the circlet landed in her outstretched palm and moonlight shot through her. Her fingers flexed, gripping the metal, the only remaining thing that felt real.

She hadn't heard Malon move to her other side, but he now gripped her free hand. She knew it was him the moment moonlight was met with sun. A fist closed around her heart, dark pain shutting out the light.

Her body shot upright as she struggled for breath, but

her eyes wouldn't open. She was sure her heart no longer beat.

"Fight it, Saida. Draw on my magic."

She focused on his words, and on the feeling of sunlight stemming from his hand joined with hers, but the light ebbed. The world went pitch black. She was no longer in the tent with Phaerille and Malon, no longer in the tent at all. She was on her feet, walking through a land of unending darkness, with no way in or out.

S he seemed to walk through the darkness for hours, frightened and entirely alone, but also grateful the pain was gone. She'd been cut off from Malon's magic, and with it, the only chance of her survival.

The darkness wasn't all bad though. At least here, nothing hurt. She no longer felt her physical pain, nor the deep aching brought on by her mother's death. She hadn't realized just how much it hurt until it was gone.

Perhaps she'd be able to join her mother soon, maybe at the end of this dark place . . . if it ever ended.

"*Saida,*" a voice slithered through her mind, dark and sticky like sap. "*Rest now, Saida.*"

Her feet grew heavy, her bones weary. Rest. Yes, rest sounded just right. She sat on the ground, though it wasn't earth nor anything else corporeal, just pure darkness.

Now that she wasn't moving, she actually began to

think. Where was she, and where was Malon? Her mother may wait at the end of this, but what of her father?

"Rest, Saida. It is time for sleep."

A haze set in around her. The air grew thick with smoky vapor. She had no choice but to inhale it, and she was so very tired. Distantly, she recognized that something was in her hand—the circlet!—but when she tried to focus on it, it seemed like it wasn't really there. Nothing was really here in this place of darkness.

She blinked rapidly, pulling out of her daze at the thought of the circlet, and beyond that, her father. He was still alive, and in danger. If she did not face Egrin before the full moon, he would die.

Her breath caught, then stuck. Thick sludge blocked her airway. She lifted a hand and clawed at the agony in her throat. Something massive grew out of her, like a slimy tree root sprouting from her insides. She tried to cough, gagged, then a viscous snake of darkness climbed upward, filling her mouth.

She fell forward onto all fours, heaving with what little air she could draw through her nose. *Her father. Elmerah. Alluin.* They would all be left unprotected. They could not defeat Egrin on their own, but with the circlets, with the power she and Malon possessed, they stood a chance.

She gagged as the thick sludge surged out of her mouth in a violent current, splattering onto the darkness beneath her palms. It speckled her skin with moist globules. Every part of her body wanted to give in and die, but she continued to choke and heave. *Her father. Elmerah. Alluin.* The rest of the Faerune and Valeroot elves. Merwyn. Even Rissine.

She gave one last mighty heave with the remainder of her strength, and the rest of the sludge left her, solid enough to form a shape like a giant slug. It landed with a heavy, moist thunk onto the ground, just as the darkness faded away.

She was no longer trapped in that dark space, she was in the tent on all fours, the circlet gripped in her fingers, and Malon's hand upon her back. Beneath her, the carpet was covered with a black viscous puddle.

She trembled, taking shallow breaths, not yet able to move. She could feel the liquid around her mouth and on her face. "What was that?" she rasped.

She spotted Phaerille out of the corner of her eye, her back pressed against the tent wall.

Malon gripped her shoulders, helping her to sit away from the puddle. "You were cursed, Saida."

"By whom?" she panted.

"I cannot be sure, but I intend to find out."

She could find no more words. All she could do was sit and relearn how to breathe. The circlet was still in her hand, silent now, though faintly pulsing with power.

She wasn't sure if she'd fought off the curse alone, or if the gods had aided her, but she would not let this gift go to waste. Her family and friends were in danger. If she could beat a curse, she could beat a demon. Any other ends were simply not an option.

CHAPTER SIXTEEN

Isara

Isara and Celen hadn't made it far in Elmerah's direction before spotting several Dreilore searching the woods. Luckily Celen had seen them first, and their retreat was drowned out by a rushing stream. They now hid under a small crag, their bootprints obscured with Celen's magic.

Isara pressed her back against the rough stone. Celen, in the same position at her side, didn't seem worried, but she was beginning to realize Celen never seemed worried. He strolled through life like nothing could touch him, even when Dreilore swarmed the forest around him.

She stifled a scream as someone darted out from behind a tree, realizing just in time that it was Alluin. Clutching his bow in one hand, he leaned his back against the crag, scanning what they could see of the forest ahead while Isara balked at him.

"What are you doing here?" Celen whispered over Isara's head. She would have almost enjoyed the shock in his voice if they weren't in immediate peril.

Alluin's gaze remained outward. "Elmerah was worried about you, rightly so, it seems. We cannot lead these Dreilore back to her."

"My thoughts exactly," Celen whispered. "We were hoping to wait them out."

Alluin shook his head, tossing rich brown strands over his shoulder. "Not likely, I saw Daemon Saredoth waiting near the village. This is no simple hunt for the Dreilore. They will not return without their quarry."

Isara made herself small as Celen leaned closer to speak to Alluin, not seeming to notice he was squishing her, overwhelming her senses with smells of sweat and forest. "Speaking of hunting, how did you find us? I covered our tracks."

"Yes," Alluin said somewhat caustically. "Too well. One need only look for twigs broken from passing, and grass trampled, but with no tracks in the earth to match."

Isara turned to see Celen wince. "Fair point. I'm not used to being tracked on land."

Hushed voices thick with the accent of the Akenyth Province grew near, then faded. It seemed the Dreilore weren't quite as perceptive as Alluin. Even so, she did not doubt their ability to eventually find them. Then Alluin and Celen would be killed.

She couldn't let that happen. "I should surrender. If they locate me, they'll end the search, and you can safely return to Elmerah."

"Absolutely not," Celen and Alluin whispered in unison.

Voices grew near again, then faded.

"They're circling us." Alluin's words were barely audible. "Starting wide then working their way in. A few more passes and they'll be upon us."

Her mind raced. She was running out of time. If Daemon was at the village, the Dreilore most likely had been ordered to take her prisoner. If she was going to be taken prisoner either way, she'd rather be the only one involved in the conflict.

Celen and Alluin were both looking out at the woods. Just a few more passes, Alluin had said. She couldn't let time run out. Not wanting to give away her intentions, she didn't so much as inhale. She wrapped her magic around Celen so he could not raise the earth at her feet, kicked Alluin in the shin, then ran.

Twigs snagged at her curls and scratched her face, but she pressed forward almost blindly, focusing her will on disabling Celen. If Daemon was waiting at the village, the Dreilore would bring her right to him. He might be the closest ally of a demon, but he would never harm her.

She heard Dreilore voices and veered toward them, hoping they wouldn't react on instinct and cut her down. She hated to do this to Celen and Alluin, knowing they'd feel guilty, but Elmerah would understand the practicality of her choice and her intention therein. Once Elmerah faced Egrin, she'd have an ally waiting to assist her in taking him down.

Alluin

Alluin tugged against Celen's grasp on his arm, wanting to go after Isara, but the man was built like a boulder and had a grip like a blacksmith's vice. "We have to go after her!" he hissed.

Celen gave Alluin's arm a yank, slamming his shoulder against the crag. "She disabled my magic as she ran. She does not want us to follow."

In that moment, Alluin didn't have a care for what Isara wanted. "They'll take her to Egrin," he growled.

"And there she will wait to assist us when the time comes. We won't let him keep her."

Alluin stopped struggling. Celen was right, and Isara was already gone. He could no longer hear her footsteps, and the Dreilore would not have been hard for her to find.

"We will not squander her bravery," Celen lowered his voice. "We will wait here while the Dreilore leave the woods, then we'll go back to Elmerah. We will continue on as planned. Isara will be fine."

Alluin exhaled, then willfully pressed his back against

the crag. "Elmerah awaits us with a young Nokken named Killian. He claims to know you."

Too tall for the space, Celen hunched his back where the crag jutted forward. The position didn't seem comfortable, but was at least concealing. "You cannot be serious. Killian?"

Alluin sucked his teeth, annoyed with all of it, and worried for Isara. "Is he a threat?"

"Killian wouldn't hurt a fly, unless it was with his own stupidity. Why did he follow?"

"He seemed to think you were fleeing the war. He hoped you had a safe place in mind, and he could come with you."

Celen buried his face in his hands and shook his head. "That sounds about right, and you left him with Elmerah?" He lowered his hands to look at Alluin.

He nodded.

"Oh good gods, she'll eat him alive."

Celen's distress almost made him smile. *Almost.* Any mirth he might have found was lost in thoughts of Isara being marched out of the woods by Dreilore to a brother she trusted far more than she should. He hoped she'd be kept alive, but there was absolutely no guarantee.

Isara

The first Dreilore Isara found were a male and female pair, and they were *not* happy to see her. Or at least that's how it seemed. Maybe the Dreilore were never happy. They were too busy being terrifying.

The pair had taken one look at her as she rushed toward them, then each drew glowing blades, one green, one blue. Isara couldn't have guessed what the blades were enchanted to do, though she knew she could easily disable their magic if need be.

. . . Which would do her little good now, as they marched her out of the forest with blades occasionally poking into her back.

They'd come across six other Dreilore as they walked, all male, who upon seeing them, moved on ahead. It seemed only two of them were needed to nudge along a weakling like her. She was right to assume the Dreilore would have found her no matter what. They worked in methodical circles, it seemed, a well-planned maneuver which enabled them to comb the woods with a small party, and to check in with each other periodically.

At least, that was the conclusion Isara had reached, and she'd had a long, nerve-wracking walk to reach it.

The sight of intense sunlight at the edge of the forest was almost a relief. At least once they reached Daemon, she'd no longer have blades poking into her back.

They exited the trees into the meadow she and Celen had run across earlier. Eleven more Dreilore were waiting on the southern end of the road with

Daemon, his blond hair the only way she was able to distinguish him at the distance. That meant eight Dreilore had gone into the woods, while five waited near the village.

She shook her head as she walked. *Stupid,* she thought. *I'm so stupid.* Observing the Dreilore's tactics would do her no good now.

Spotting her, the party moved their way, Daemon in the lead. He looked just as pompous as ever, perhaps more so than she remembered. The red velvet pantaloons were almost as garish as the brocade tunic.

He tossed his pin-straight hair behind his back as he reached her. She was probably one of the only people left alive who knew that he straightened it with a hot iron every night. Naturally, it was as curly as hers. He'd flee like a damsel anytime the sky looked like it might rain and wet his perfect locks.

He looked her up and down, taking in her simple, though finely made tunic and dirty blue cloak. "Sister, poverty does not become you."

She gave him a similar assessing look. "Some things are more important than jewels upon your fingers."

His eyes widened at her tone. "You've grown a sharp tongue, Isara. If I were you, I'd whittle it down before we reach our cousin."

She was surprised he was still referring to Egrin as their cousin. Didn't he realize Egrin had been alive for centuries, not born to their father's long-dead brother as they'd thought?

Daemon lifted a hand over his shoulder and snapped his fingers. "Bind her hands, then fetch the horses."

She glanced past him to the waiting Dreilore, who seemed void of intention to obey Daemon's order. She hadn't seen any horses before, and they did not seem like they were going to fetch them regardless.

Daemon glanced over his shoulder, then sighed. "Cursed Dreilore." He grabbed her arm. "The horses are back with the rest of the contingent. We didn't want to startle the villagers, only for you to escape in the chaos."

He dragged her across the meadow toward the road, the Dreilore silently falling into line behind them.

"Daemon," she rasped, stumbling as he dragged her along, "you don't know what you're doing! Egrin—"

He stopped for a moment to look at her. "I realize exactly what Egrin is. Do you think me so dense? I've remained by his side for years." He tugged her arm.

Teeth gritted, she tugged back. "If you know, then how can you aid him!"

"Better than standing against him, sister, you will learn that in time."

She had hoped to talk sense into him once he knew the full truth, but he already knew. He knew Egrin was a demon, and he didn't care. "That answer isn't good enough."

He shook her by his grip on her arm, then yanked her forward.

This time she went with him, wanting to keep her shoulder in its socket.

He walked ahead, tugging her behind him with his too long stride. "Isara, quit being foolish. Our choices are to live long lives with riches and protection, or to fall into ruin like the elves. Can you honestly tell me you prefer the latter?"

She pushed up her spectacles with her free hand. More Dreilore had come into view. Twenty, thirty? She could not tell. Their ranks went on and on, taking up most of the southern road. Even if she could make Daemon see reason, they'd never escape so many.

She glared at his hand on her arm as he continued to drag her behind him. "I will enjoy the look on your face when Egrin is defeated."

Daemon laughed, not looking back at her. "Don't antagonize me, sister. I'm the reason you're still alive."

She fought the tears welling up in her eyes, but it was no use. Her only hope now was to wait for Elmerah to save her, and hope she'd keep her promise. Because even now with Daemon at his worst, she knew she could not let him die. Even now, part of her was overjoyed to see him again, her only family, and all she would ever have.

CHAPTER SEVENTEEN

Saida

S aida sat on the intricately woven rug with legs crossed, knees open beneath her tan robe. She ran her fingers across the circlet, turning it over and over again in her hands. She was surprised Malon had left it with her. Maybe he thought it would protect her from another curse.

He'd also left her with every elf in their party, all crammed inside her tent. The male elves had been spared the horrific details. The black sludge had been scrubbed up, the stain covered with a pillow, and she'd been given a clean robe. The elves were told only that there may be danger, and to not let Saida out of sight.

Which was vexing, considering she wanted to get to Urali before she cursed her again. She hid that desire, avoiding eye contact with the other elves, some seated, and a few stationed just inside and outside the entrance. Malon would not condemn Urali without proof, but she knew it was her. The malevolent look in her eye that night at the oasis was unmistakable. She didn't know if Urali wanted to kill her, or trap and use her, but she was not inclined to wait around and find out.

Phaerille stood near the door with two male elves. It was hard to tell them apart in the long tan robes with their backs to her, but Phaerille was a bit smaller, and her shoulders were hunched. Since seeing Saida vomit up the black mass, she'd avoided her as if she were diseased.

Saida turned the circlet over again in her hand. It had remained silent, perhaps because she was temporarily out of danger? But that begged an even more confusing question. Was the circlet actually protecting her?

Voices outside the tent drew her gaze, just as the flap opened to reveal two male elves and a rather daunting young female Makali peering inward.

"She claims it's time for the settlement to move," one of the elves explained as he stepped inside. "A herd of," he glanced at the Makali, "gukokam, was it?"

She nodded, leaning on the pole of a wicked looking spear. The sleeves of her loose robes revealed silver vambraces. A warrior. Every elf in the tent eyed both her and her weapon warily.

"A herd of gukokam will come to the oasis soon," the elf next to her continued. "Apparently we do not want to be here when they arrive."

Saida stood, fastening the circlet at the belt of her robe. *What in Cindra's light was a gukokam?*

The female Makali looked past the other elves, her dark eyes landing on Saida. "Time to take down tents. You come with me."

A protest was on the tip of her tongue, but Phaerille had already stepped in front of the Makali. "Where Lady Saida goes, so go we. She is not to be left alone."

"Urali says to bring her," the Makali argued, stepping around Phaerille, but three more elves had already blocked her path. She glared at them all, then turned her dark eyes toward Saida. "You must come with me now," she urged, her tone pleading. "Unless you want to walk the dark place again."

Saida's jaw fell open. Did she mean the curse? She hadn't told Phaerille or Malon exactly what she had experienced. "Are you threatening me? Where is Malon?"

"He awaits us, please come."

That gave her pause. She almost believed it, but real-ized Malon would never expect her to trust one of the Makali after what had happened to her. "Tell him to come here for me, and we will go wherever you want together."

The Makali chewed her lip, glancing at the other elves before landing her eyes back on Saida. "Time is short. Please, I would keep you in the light, priestess."

Saida glanced at Phaerille and the other elves. There was something this Makali wanted to say, but not in front of them? A whisper shivered through her mind. *"Go with her."*

She swallowed the lump in her throat. Something was wrong. There was a reason Malon had not returned. She stepped toward the Makali. "Take me to him."

Phaerille gripped her arm as she tried to walk past. "You cannot! This woman cannot be trusted." She gestured to the Makali.

Saida patted Phaerille's hand, then pulled away. "All will be well. Prepare for departure with the others." She met the Makali's hopeful gaze and nodded.

"No, Saida." Phaerille gripped her arm again.

Saida pulled away, surprised at Phaerille's fervor. "I can take care of myself, do not worry." She glanced at the male elves still blocking the exit. "Step aside."

"But Malon said—" one began to argue.

She held up her hand. "I am going to Malon now. Do not worry." She walked toward them. They would either get out of her way, or she'd push past them. She hoped, after what they'd seen her do to the Dreilore with the circlet, they would choose the former.

They did. Soon she was out in the sun with the Makali woman at her side. The elves whispered frantically inside the tent, clearly unsure of whose orders they should be obeying at this point.

The Makali gestured to the wide path between the tents. The camp had come alive with others, some already taking down tents in the midday heat.

Saida realized as she began to walk how much the

shade of the tent had helped. Without her head wrap, she felt like her skin might blister. The female Makali wrapped her own dark hair as she walked at her side, a well-practiced movement with which the other elves had fumbled.

"Thank you for trusting me," the Makali muttered, leaning in close once her mouth was hidden by tan fabric. "Malon is in trouble. You are in great danger, and not just from gukokam."

"I figured as much. Why are you helping us, and why could you not speak in front of my people?"

The Makali's eyes darted nervously around the camp. A few had turned to watch Saida's passing. "I help because you would bring life to the desert," she whispered. "That is what's important. I am called Brosod." She glanced around again. "And I believe you have a traitor in your party. Someone to feed you Urali's curse."

So it had been the food! It wasn't just the spices, someone had . . . put a curse in her food? But the one who brought her meals was Phaerille, so that couldn't be right.

Shouts erupted behind them. They were speaking Kaleth, but Saida interpreted the meaning well enough. Spear in one hand, Brosod gripped her arm with the other. "Run!"

"Saida!" Phaerille's voice called after her.

She ran. Phaerille could not help her now, she needed to find Malon. Her heart thundered as her boots slipped in the sand. Her loose robe seemed to have a mind of its own, tangling around her knees and threatening to trip her. Brosod gripped her arm, keeping her aloft.

"He is at the oasis," Brosod panted at her side. "Trapped there. You will free him." She glanced back, then tugged Saida's arm so hard it nearly popped out of its socket.

The force of it launched Saida forward. Losing her balance, she skinned her palms in the hot sand, then collapsed. Panicked, she rolled over, thinking she'd been betrayed by Brosod, but the woman had turned to face a bevy of Makali warriors, gleaming spears pointed her way. They barked orders in Kaleth.

Brosod shook her head, pointing her spear toward the other warriors. "She has given us water, *life*. You will not have her."

Phaerille and the other elves had caught up to stand behind the Makali warriors. The male elves seemed confused, unsure of where to stand, but Phaerille looked almost . . . excited? It was an expression Saida never would have expected given the circumstances.

She got to her feet, reaching for the circlet at her belt. The Makali warriors closed in around her and Brosod.

Still holding her spear defensively, Brosod glanced back, then quickly returned her gaze to the approaching warriors. "I am sorry, priestess, I have failed you."

With trembling hands, Saida placed the circlet upon her brow. She didn't know if she could make it work without Malon and the other circlet—remembering the Dreilore, she was not sure if she wanted to make it work at all. But while the Makali might not kill her, they would surely kill Brosod for betraying them.

For a moment, the circlet was silent, then a clear voice rang through her mind. *"Be still, the moment will soon come."*

Low voices cut across the crowd gathering amidst partially disassembled tents. Saida watched as the Makali standing furthest back moved, then those ahead stepped aside, parting the crowd like water to form a path. Urali walked down that path, confidently gripping an ornate wooden staff with opaque blue stones embedded into the carved designs. She wore vibrant red silks today, standing out like a cardinal amongst a sea of tan.

Saida took an instinctive step back, then froze at a sharp tip pressed between her shoulder blades. A glance showed a handful of Makali warriors behind her, one pressing a spear to her back. She lifted her hands in surrender. The circlet remained silent upon her brow.

"Bring her to me!" Urali ordered. "Kill the traitor!"

"No!" Saida gasped, stepping away from the spears and closer to Brosod. There was no way to protect her from all sides. They were surrounded.

"Challenge her," the voice whispered in her mind.

"I challenge you!" Saida echoed, stepping forward. The crowd went utterly silent. "I challenge you, Urali," she repeated, making things up as she went. "If I win, you spare Brosod's life."

Outraged shouts erupted through the crowd. She

wasn't even sure what she was doing, but it had certainly gotten their attention.

Standing not ten paces away, Urali lowered her chin, peering at Saida from beneath her dark, wrinkled brow. "You know not the customs of my people, little girl. We do not use weapons when challenged. That circlet on your brow must be cast aside."

Saida licked her cracked lips, hoping the circlet would give her further instruction, but nothing came. The other elves in her party were now surrounded by Makali with spears near their throats. But Phaerille—Phaerille had moved to stand at the front of the crowd, behind Urali.

The loose ends of the plot twined into place. Brosod believed they had a traitor in their midst, because someone had fed her a curse. She didn't want to believe it, but that traitor was Phaerille.

Urali watched her cooly. "Remove the circlet, Saida, or your challenge means nothing. Brosod will be killed."

"Do not do it," Brosod whispered.

Saida removed the circlet, then extended it toward Brosod. "Please, keep this safe for me."

Brosod extended her palms. "I cannot!"

Saida shook the circlet at her, knowing she'd soon regret this, but she couldn't let Brosod be killed. "You just proved you would die for me. Please, you are the only one here I can trust."

Brosod's eyes widened from within the folds of her head wrap as her trembling hand lifted to take the circlet, gripping it tightly as if it might flutter away on a breeze.

Saida struggled to take in a full breath. The moment the circlet left her grip, panic consumed her. *Where in Arcale was Malon? Was it as Brosod had said, that he was trapped at the oasis?* She could see trees in the distance, but too much of the camp stood between.

She whipped her gaze around as Urali walked forward, a twisted smile on her lips. The other Makali had stepped back, forming a large circle around them. No one moved toward Brosod. It seemed a challenge was binding to these people. If she defeated Urali, would Brosod be allowed to live?

It was a foolish question if she'd ever thought one. She'd never defeat Urali in hand to hand combat. Aged as she was, the woman had probably been trained to fight since she could first walk. Urali would pummel her into pulp.

Glancing to the captured elves, the surrounding Makali, then to Urali, Saida moved toward the center of the circle.

Phaerille shoved her way between two male Makali nearest Saida. "You'll never be able to beat her," she taunted as Saida passed. "You should just give in now."

Saida wanted to glare at her, but could not risk removing her eyes from Urali. "Why would you betray us?" she asked Phaerille. "I thought you viewed Malon as your savior."

"Malon, yes. You, no. He is too good a man for a worthless thing like you."

The final thread twined into place, making her feel

sick. Phaerille was in love with Malon, and she wanted Saida out of the way. She'd played her from the start.

Urali lifted her bejeweled hands, revealing the silver vambraces beneath her sleeves. "I will make this quick. Once I have your circlet, Malon will have no choice but to make *me* his Cindra."

Saida's back went rigid. She didn't for a moment assume Urali was in love with Malon too, but now the curse made sense. Urali wanted her out of the way, because she believed she could fulfill her role. A role which Malon needed filled one way or another.

She lifted her hands defensively. She'd been trained to fight, but her skill was with a staff, and Urali had cast hers aside. Hand to hand combat was not foreign to her, but she hadn't sparred in years.

"You cursed me," Saida accused, hoping to grant herself a moment before Urali attacked.

Urali grinned. "Yes."

"You have magic then, enough to use the circlet?"

"Yes."

"And Phaerille?"

"She cares not for power. I sensed her desires the moment she entered my camp. I knew she would agree to feed you my curse."

"So you used her?" Saida spat. "And now you would claim Malon, and the circlet?"

Urali laughed. "She can have your man, I desire the magic of the circlets."

More nimble than she seemed, Urali hopped back on one foot and swiped at Saida with the other.

Saida dove to the sand, missing the blow, but the sand slowed her movements. Urali's sandal-clad foot crashed down, kicking her in the gut.

Saida rolled across the sand, gasping for air, then struggled to her feet. She lifted her hands again. Malon would not be coming to save her, and it was obvious no one else here would. She was on her own.

She stepped to the side, remembering the movements she'd been taught by practicing with guardsmen as a girl. She might have lost many learned skills, but she would not go down without a fight.

She eyed Urali defiantly, and as one, they began to dance.

Malon

Malon's blood boiled. If Saida were with him and they had the circlets, he'd sear the skin from the Makali warriors' bones. He'd come to the oasis in search of Urali, and he'd been met with an ambush. He should have seen it coming, but he'd truly believed Urali would not risk losing his goodwill. Not when there was so much to be gained.

He struggled to roll his stiff shoulders, pushing his back against one of the newly grown trees, his wrists bound at a painful angle on the other side of the trunk. One of the younger women of high status, Oga, spun the Crown of Arcale on her long finger, leering at him. She was young and beautiful, but Malon would gladly kill her too.

He strained against his bindings. "What is Urali doing to Saida? Where is she?"

Oga grinned. Five male warriors flanked her. The others had gone with Urali.

"*Where* is she?" he demanded once again.

"You can say farewell to your woman, *elf*. Urali has more magic than she. With the Crown of Cindra, she will turn the entire desert into an oasis."

He gritted his teeth, squinting his eyes against the near-blinding sun. Saida needed him. He had brought her here and promised to keep her safe, and now she would die while he was tied to this cursed tree.

He took a steadying breath, trying to calm his temper. "Tell Urali that if any harm befalls Saida, I will not help her. I will leave this entire desert to desiccate."

Oga bared her prominent lower canines. "You will have no choice in the matter, elf, you are our prisoner now." Her eyes darted southward at a distant rumble.

"Gokugam," one of the men muttered, clenching his spear. "We must move soon."

Malon tensed. He'd never encountered the gokugam directly, but had seen evidence of passing herds. They were massive creatures, even their young weighed thrice as much as a full grown male troll. Thick gray skin, impenetrable to even the most finely-honed blade, protected them from the sun. Their tusks could impale a man in seconds. The eight antlioch tethered to the nearby trees now made sense. They would need to ride swiftly to escape the gokugam, but ... only eight? What of the rest of Urali's clan?

The male warriors spoke in Kaleth, perhaps not realizing he could understand them. They intended to move him, tie him to an antlioch and transport him away from the oasis before the gokugam reached it. The rest of the clan would travel away on foot, unaware of Urali's plan to regrow the desert.

Three male warriors approached. This would be his only chance to rescue Saida, if she was even still alive. He needed to retrieve the Crown of Arcale from Oga, preferably from her cold, dead fingers.

The distant rumbles intensified. Still speaking in Kaleth, Oga ordered the male warriors to release him.

Malon forced his body to relax as the warriors reached him. One lifted his spear, pressing it against his throat.

He swallowed, feeling a sharp prick as the spear punctured his skin.

Another warrior walked around the tree and worked at the ropes binding his hands. The ground trembled beneath their feet, reverberating through Malon's bones. The warrior fumbling at his ropes muttered a particularly foul curse in Kaleth.

"Hurry up," Oga hissed, clasping the circlet with both

hands against her chest over her tan robe. "Urali will be back soon, and we must be ready."

"Cursed ropes," the warrior on the other side of the trunk said in the common tongue. "Straighten your hands, elf."

He realized his hands were balled into fists, pulling the rope too taut. He relaxed them, willing the warrior to hurry. He needed his hands free if he was going to wring Oga's neck.

The warrior tugged the rope suddenly, slamming Malon's back against the trunk, then cursed. "You tied it too tight," he muttered, presumably speaking to the other warrior who'd moved to try the knots. "Cut it."

Malon hissed as the sharp point of the warrior's spear sliced across his hand on its way to cutting the ropes. Free at last, he began to move his hands forward, but the Makali guarding him applied more pressure to the spear at his throat.

"Do not move, elf. Keep your hands where they are."

"Hurry!" Oga urged, her dark eyes on the horizon past Malon's back.

The rumbles had grown so intense, he knew the massive, slow-moving gokugam would be visible in the distance, but he couldn't turn to look with the spear forcing his neck against the tree.

A warrior came around the tree with the cut ropes, gesturing for him to put his wrists together in front of him.

He could not let them bind him again. If he remained trapped, everything would be over.

He relaxed his body, acting as if he fully intended to extend his wrists. He would have to rely on the hope that they'd been ordered to keep him alive. He balled his hands into fists, pushed his throat slightly against the spear, and lashed out.

Saida

Saida rolled in the sand, her body a hot, pulsing heartbeat of agony. Urali had won the fight long ago, but the beating continued. She wasn't sure if the rumbling of the ground was from her own blood pumping in her ears, or something else.

Another kick landed to her stomach, sending crimson-tinged saliva spewing from her mouth. Murmurs throughout the crowd grew louder as Urali stepped over her, casting her in shadow.

Saida rolled onto her back, sure the end was near, but too weak to defend herself.

Urali grinned down at her, but spoke to the surrounding crowd. "Kill the traitor, bring me the circlet."

The rumbling wasn't in her ears after all. The ground shook, tossing flecks of sand across her bare palms. Her mind muddled by pain and exhaustion, she almost thought Cindra had come to save her, but then she remembered the gokugam Brosod had mentioned.

"Curse the gods," Urali hissed, glancing southward before looking back down to Saida. "Time to end this." She lifted her foot, aiming it at Saida's neck.

The ground shook so violently, Saida cried out, the fresh cuts and bruises all singing at once. She whipped her head to the side, seeing Urali on her rump in the sand, thrown from her feet by the trembling earth. Makali shouted all around them, running in different directions.

Urali let loose a string of foul curses, scurrying to her feet as Saida struggled to sit up. Her wounded body seized up, and she fell back to the sand.

Urali stood over her. "Now you die!"

"Lady Saida!" A blur of tan robes cut across her vision. Urali disappeared in a tumbling mass of robes and elven fists.

The remaining male elves surrounded Saida. "Get to your feet," one urged. She recognized the voice, Luc. Arms gripped her, sending bolts of agony through her battered body. She could no longer see Urali struggling against the other male elves.

Luc wrapped his arm beneath her shoulders, holding her upright. "My apologies. They would have killed us had we tried before."

She would have said she didn't expect anyone to die for her, but it was all she could do to grit her teeth and move in the direction Luc guided her. Makali hurried around them, shouting orders, rolling up hides, and fleeing.

"Brosod," she groaned, her eyes rolling upward, the sun above but a dizzying display of light. Sweat and blood dripped down her face, making her skin wet and sticky.

"I am here," Brosod's voice answered from Luc's other side. "I have the circlet. We must hurry. If we travel away from the oasis, the gokugam will not bother us."

"We must find Malon," Luc argued. "The last we saw of him, he was heading toward the oasis. I fear the Makali have taken him prisoner."

The sand dragged at Saida's boots, and salty blood dripped from her nose into her mouth, somehow cooler than the hot sun on her skin.

"The gokugam will trample any near the water they hope to drink," Brosod said.

The shouts died down behind them as they hurried across the sand. Saida sensed the other elves following close, but could hardly make sense of things. She'd taken a few blows to the head, or perhaps this was the heat and exhaustion.

"They have him!" Luc gasped.

She opened her eyes, only then realizing they'd closed. The desert swam like she was viewing a scene through water atop glass. Three Makali warriors surrounded Malon, spears all pointed toward his throat and chest. Two bodies on the ground. A female Makali standing back, a moonstone circlet glinting in her hands.

The other elves ran past to aid Malon, leaving her alone with Luc and Brosod.

Luc let her down to her knees on the trembling sand. "Stay here, priestess."

"The gokugam!" Brosod shouted.

The rumbles were so loud, they drowned out the shouts of elves attacking the Makali, and Brosod's words as she knelt by Saida's side. Seeming to realize this, Brosod produced the circlet from within the folds of her cloak, and placed it atop Saida's brow.

She gripped Saida's shoulder, leaning close to her ear. "You must save us."

The circlet's cool magic soothed Saida's hot brow. The desert faded from view. Everything was moonlight, but she didn't know what to do with it. Malon did not possess the Crown of Arcale, and she could not reach him now even if he did. She distantly registered that the elves fought the Makali to protect Malon, but they were running out of time. The destruction of the gokugam grew near.

She could do nothing kneeling in the sand . . . except feel the sand. She reached down, desperately searching for more life in the desert. The earth answered. Water swam upward, soaking her robe. Trees, she needed more trees and water to block the gokugam. Instead of them coming to the oasis, the oasis would go to them. They were animals, not monsters, they deserved the water as much as any Makali.

Water surged up from the earth, a new trembling

taking hold as trees sprouted from nothing out of the sand. They grew so rapidly, shade abruptly cut across Saida's face.

More shouts not far off. She opened her eyes, but could not see against the blaring sun in that direction, its rays cutting solid lines through trees against glistening water.

But she didn't need to see. She felt it the moment Malon reclaimed the Crown of Arcale. Even without touching, his magic called to her. She knelt in cool running water with Brosod at her side, and waited for him to come.

"You foul witch!" Urali's voice hissed behind her. Something hit Brosod, ripping her away from Saida's side.

Saida fell forward into cool running water, slipping and bobbing as she tried to turn around. Water surged into her mouth, choking her. She turned onto her rump in the sand beneath the water in time to see Urali hefting a hatchet over her head.

The hatchet swung down. With the water weighting her movements, she was too slow to avoid it. Things seemed to be happening in half-time, slow, like a dream.

A hand clutched her shoulder, Malon's magic swam through her, and Saida focused all her hatred and pain on her enemy. Sunlight flared out of her, hitting Urali.

Flames crawled across Urali's skin, fed by magic. Urali shrieked and dropped the hatchet, then fell into the water, but the flames licking up her clothing would not quench. Unearthly wails bubbled up from the surface of the water.

Saida dug her boots into the sand beneath the pool and pushed back, trying to rise, wanting to escape the horrifying sight. "Make it stop!" It was too horrible. No one should die in such a way, not even Urali.

The shrieking continued. Malon wrapped his arms around Saida's waist and lifted her to her feet. "There is no stopping it," he muttered close to her cheek. "And she would have done far worse to you."

Tears fell down her cheeks, mingling with fresh water and blood. Urali's shrieks ended in a sound like a long exhale. Her charred corpse bobbed in the water, a grotesque reminder of what happened when you tried to steal the magic of the gods.

Saida clutched her stomach just above where Malon's arms still held her. She was glad for the cooling water now up to her waist, carrying the husk of Urali in the other direction.

Malon's voice sounded in her ear. "The ground has ceased its shaking. You managed to divert the gukogam with another pool of water. We are safe."

Her breath came too fast, panic and tears consuming her. "I tried to fight, but in the end, I needed you to save me."

His cheek pressed against hers, an oddly intimate gesture. "You are not the one who needs saving, Saida, you never were."

She didn't know what he meant. They stood together

in the cool water surrounded by shade trees as her strength left her, and everything went black. It was a good blackness, absent of scalding sunlight and charred corpses. She was safe, and for now, Malon would watch over her.

For better or for worse, she was in this thing with him. There was no going back now.

CHAPTER EIGHTEEN

Elmerah

"Can we stop yet?" Killian whined.

Elmerah sucked her teeth, gripping her reins so tightly her knuckles went white. "Just be glad you are still alive," she growled. *And why was he still alive?* she thought. He was not useful in the slightest. All he knew of the emperor's plans was that he wanted the elves and Arthali watched. He'd had nothing interesting to tell her at all.

So why was he riding with her, Celen, and Alluin?

Her lips twisted sideways while glaring at the rump of the horse Killian rode just ahead of her. With Isara gone, they'd had a spare horse, and they couldn't very well let him go with all he knew of their plan. And no one quite had the heart to kill him.

"We *should* actually stop soon," Alluin sighed, horse

and rider bringing up the rear. "The sun is almost gone, and we must find a safe place to sleep . . . if such a place even exists."

Elmerah glanced back at him. "You know as well as I there is no safe place in the deep woods, but at least here, we won't run into a contingent of Dreilore. I hope."

"Don't act so worried," Celen said from ahead of them. "These woods cannot be any more dangerous than the Illuvian forests, and Killian and I have survived those woods for years."

"They're worse," she and Alluin said in unison.

"I'm hungry," Killian chimed in.

"Shut up!" Elmerah hissed, her ire quickly returning. She knew where it was coming from, and perhaps Killian did not deserve her harsh words, but the Dreilore who'd taken Isara were not here, and neither was that slime-bellied Daemon Saredoth. A man who'd have his own sister apprehended by Dreilore had sunk to the lowest depths.

She almost had to laugh, recalling how Rissine had once had her apprehended by pirates.

"Alright," she sighed, loosening her grip on her reins to twine her fingers into her horse's matted mane. "Let's make camp. We should reach Port Aeluvaria tomorrow, and I want us all rested and ready. Perhaps there we will find word of the Dreilore who apprehended Isara, though we can already be quite sure where they're going."

Alluin hurried his horse forward, weaving through

the trees to ride at her side. He gave her a knowing look that could have meant ten different things, but she didn't need any help deciphering it. They had lost Saida, now Isara, and the lives of countless elves. Their mission was more important now than ever. Yet, their chance of success had been shrinking from the moment they'd first started out, just an elf and an Arthali, with the fate of everything and everyone resting in their battleworn hands.

Alluin

An uneasy air floated through their small camp that night. No suitable shelter could be found, so Alluin, Elmerah, and Killian rested with their backs to the rotted insides of a massive, halfway hollowed out oak. Across from their campfire, Celen stood far enough from the light to keep a sharp view into the darkness.

It was Alluin's turn to rest, but sleep evaded him. Perhaps it was Killian snoring loudly to his left, or Elmerah restless to his right.

She turned toward him as he shifted his weight, pulling his bedroll up to his chest, his legs extended toward the fire. Flamelight danced in her dark, weary eyes. "What do you think we'll find at the port?" she asked softly.

He shook his head. He'd been worried over the same

thing. News of more slaughtered elves? A blockade preventing any of his kind from traveling further north toward the Capital?

"I'm preparing myself for the worst."

She shook her head. "Perhaps we shouldn't stop. We risked acquiring information once, and look where it got us. We may be better off keeping to the woods."

"We would be going in blind to the Capital."

Her shoulder moved against his as she shrugged. "Better than going in with any less of us."

A loud snore from Killian made him tense. At this rate, the Nokken would draw every troll and wyvern in the forest. He nudged Killian gently with his elbow.

Killian groaned, sliding down the rotten inner trunk to lay on his side in the dirt. After a moment, he tugged at the bedroll wrapping his legs, wiggling about until it was up to his shoulders.

Alluin felt Elmerah leaning near the back of his shoulder to peer at Killian. "Is he still dead asleep?"

"I think so. I'm not sure how he's survived this long in the woods sleeping so deeply . . . and loudly."

Celen stepped closer to the fire. "The Nokken who live in the forest often sleep in trees, and those within their larger settlements are well-protected."

Elmerah sat up straight, facing Celen. "And how do you know so much about them?"

Celen shrugged, gripping a wicked-looking knife in his hand, though his magic would offer better protection than any blade. "My clan lived in the forests for years. We encountered their kind often enough, but they rarely gave us any trouble."

Alluin glanced down at Killian, not for the first time wondering why the Nokken had chosen to side with the emperor. He turned his gaze up to Celen. "They were spying for Egrin some time before Faerune fell. Long enough to infiltrate the city and successfully pose as healers to poison the High Council. You never noticed any strange activity?"

Celen's brow furrowed. "Why would I invest resources into watching the Nokken? Save a few scouts keeping an eye on the road from time to time, we stayed far from Faerune."

Alluin sighed, realizing he'd unintentionally accused Celen of something. "It was a simple question. I'm wondering why the Nokken would spy for Dinoba, and how long it's been going on."

Elmerah laughed quietly. "You know, I probably should have asked Killian that while he was still afraid of me. I was so set on gaining information about Egrin, I ignored the Nokken's role in matters."

"You could just ask me now," Killian's drowsy voice interrupted.

Alluin glared down at him, finding his eyes open to narrow slits. "How long have you been awake?"

Killian sat up, pulling half out of his bedroll. "Not such a light sleeper after all, eh?" Despite his words, his amber eyes drooped, and his russet hair stuck out in all directions against his sagging fox ears.

Alluin gestured for him to go on. "Well then, answer the question."

Killian glanced up at Celen, then over to Alluin. "It's a bit humiliating."

Celen loomed closer, the fire casting his face into grim lines. "We've all been forced into humiliating roles at one time or another."

This seemed to give Killian courage. He sat up a little straighter, his hands clutching the bedroll's hem, now piled in his lap. "The truth is, he threatened us. My people are happy in the forests, it's where we belong. Promises of land and riches did not entice us," he hesitated. "Well, they did not entice most of us. Some traveled all the way to the Capital in hopes that Dinoba would grant them a different life."

"He threatened to kill you?" Elmerah asked.

Killian rapidly shook his head. "No, no. We are skilled fighters. We would not back down to such a threat. His threat was far greater than the loss of lives. He threatened to destroy the forests. He said he would burn everything to the ground, and would summon demons to keep us from fighting the blaze. We would be left alive, but with no home." His words tumbled out so quickly he had to pause to take a deep breath. "The forest is part of who we are. We could not lose it, and so, we agreed to be his spies. It seemed our only option, and truly, he was not asking much of us."

Alluin wondered if he should warn him that Rissine had killed several Nokken who'd gone to the Capital, but it would undoubtedly do little good. The lad was already filled with turmoil.

"So why did you run?" Elmerah asked. "If you love the Illuvian forests so deeply, why would you leave them?"

Killian looked down at his lap. "I could see what was coming. The emperor's threat was slowly tearing my people apart. Even my sister, Cheta, went to the Capital, and she was to become the next clan leader. Those who remained behind argued over what was right. Were we cowards to aid the emperor? Did we even deserve the forests if we could not protect them against such threats?"

To Alluin, it sounded all too familiar. He'd spent his time in the Capital arguing with his uncle, and with the rest of his clan. Should they risk everything for a better life, or should they cower and do what was needed to keep the life they had?

Killian was watching Celen, seemingly waiting for a reaction. When Celen said nothing, he asked, "Do you think me a coward?"

Celen's brows lifted. "Why does it matter what I think of you?"

Killian shrugged, looking back down at his lap. He didn't need to say out loud why it mattered, it was obvious to all that he looked up to Celen. Well, obvious to everyone but Celen himself, it seemed.

Elmerah reached around Alluin's back to pat Killian's shoulder. "People are stupid. Clan leaders, Nokken, elves and Arthali, all horribly stupid. We cannot account for the actions of others, especially those in charge. We can only account for ourselves."

Killian's head hung lower. "Yes, and I ran away."

"To find a better life for yourself."

Killian shrugged again, his head still hanging low. "I miss my sister. She was the only one who was ever kind to me. I thought once she led the clan, things would be better, but she left."

Elmerah didn't seem to know what to do with that one. She retracted her hand from Killian's shoulder, then nudged Alluin's arm. "I did my best," she whispered, "now you go."

Alluin sighed, thinking of his own sister. She might have allied herself with Rissine in the Capital, but when it came to life or death for her clan, she'd done the right thing.

He couldn't say that though. Killian's sister was likely still working for the emperor if she'd gone to the Capital, or she might be dead.

Celen spoke, saving him. "If you want to do the right thing, help us kill the emperor. *He's* the whole reason you're in this mess. Once he's gone, you can go back to the forest, and maybe your sister will go with you."

Alluin eyed him sharply, but it was Elmerah who said, "He's just a lad. He's more a liability than anything."

Celen crossed his arms. "He's Nokken. He can shapechange. Don't you think that might come in handy? You're so worried about going to the port, but Killian can simply make himself look human and march into any establishment he chooses. He can do the same at the Capital."

"He might be killed," Elmerah hissed.

Alluin didn't dare point out that they'd already almost killed him.

"I'll do it," Killian blurted. "Let me come with you, and I'll do whatever you ask. I can change into *anyone*."

"Absolutely not," Elmerah growled.

Alluin wanted to agree with her, but . . . the outlook for them all was too dire. And why should Elmerah risk herself to reach the emperor, when having a shapechanger could facilitate a safer passage into the Capital? Killian could even infiltrate the Dreilore to find out Egrin's exact location.

Elmerah was looking at him, clearly waiting for him to agree.

"I think we should let him come," he decided. "We already turned away the help of your sister. We cannot continue making such choices." He bit his tongue. He couldn't say any more, couldn't tell her how desperate he was. Saida might be gone, if he lost Elmerah too, he'd be well and truly alone, and utterly incapable of avenging the growing list of lives lost.

Elmerah glared at him. "He is little more than a child."

"That's not true," Killian argued. "I'm of age. If I want to help kill the emperor, I'll help kill the emperor."

Elmerah threw her hands up, tossing the bedroll away from her legs. "Fine! Let's lose another innocent then. What does it matter now?"

"We're all part of this war, Ellie," Celen lectured. "Whether we like it or not."

Realizing Celen's face was lit more brightly than before, Alluin cast his eyes toward his boot-clad feet, growing warmer by the second. The campfire had blazed upward, though the wood beneath had diminished to embers.

Elmerah seemed to notice it next, and the fire quickly died down.

"Was that—" he began to ask.

"It was simply the wind," Elmerah hissed. "Now let's get some rest while we still can." She leaned back against the rotted out tree, crossed her arms, and closed her eyes.

Alluin looked up to Celen, who stared worriedly at Elmerah. Had she stoked the fire with her magic by accident? He didn't realize that was a possibility until now, but the panic in her voice while she chastised him supported the theory.

"It's been a long day and even longer night," he said to Celen and Killian. He climbed out of his bedroll and came to his feet. "Take your turn at rest, Celen. I'll stand watch."

Celen took Alluin's previous spot next to Elmerah, then leaned over and whispered something in her ear.

Her eyes still closed, she shook her head.

Killian watched them both for a moment, then snuggled back down into his bedroll.

Alluin stepped out into the darkness to keep watch, his thoughts all tangled like seaweed. He hadn't forgotten what the Fogfaun had said about Elmerah's magic. He didn't even really know what it meant, but now was the absolute worst time for her to lose control. He hated that they needed to depend on her to defeat Egrin, but that didn't make it any less true.

Saida

Saida huddled near a roaring campfire, a coarse blanket wrapped around her shoulders. The fleeing Makali had left behind enough supplies for their party to survive, though she could summon no gratitude for the boon. Her group now camped at the far end of the oasis. Though there was now a small forest on the far side of the pool, the occasional sounds of the gokugam unnerved her. They'd gone fairly still since reaching the water, and according to Brosod, they'd rest there for several days, mostly draining the oasis before moving on to another.

Saida glanced at Brosod, huddled at her side, seated in the rapidly cooling sand. Across the fire stood a few other elves talking with Malon, his silver hair naked to the moonlight, and the circlet upon his brow. She had a feeling he'd not be removing it again anytime soon, not after what had happened. He spoke in hushed tones to the other elves, and she wondered what he was saying. Phaerille had not been seen since the Makali fled.

Saida shivered, disgusted with how easily Phaerille had tricked her.

"You're cold," Brosod said, beginning to remove the blanket from her shoulders, though they were both near a blazing fire.

Saida lifted a hand to stop her. "No, I am well, keep your blanket."

With a nod, Brosod's pensive eyes stared into the flames.

Saida watched her in her peripheral vision, wondering what she was feeling. Brosod had forsaken her entire clan when she helped Saida. Even though most Makali had not realized Urali's intent, going against her was a death sentence. She still could not fully comprehend why Brosod had done so.

"How did you know about the curse?" she asked softly. "You knew what Urali had done to me."

Brosod shrugged, her eyes on the blanket edges clasped tightly in her hands.

"Brosod?"

Her shoulders rose and fell with a deep inhale. "Because I hunted the animal for the curse." Her eyes darted to Saida's face. "I did not know what it was for, I swear it. Then I heard others whispering that you had fallen ill. The animal Urali wanted was a nightstinger. The coincidence was too great."

Saida considered her next words, unsure of how she felt about Brosod's role in matters. "A nightstinger?" she asked finally.

Brosod nodded. "A small scorpion, very deadly. The venom can be used to numb the skin if one is injured, but it can also be used for a specific curse which fills one's mind and soul with darkness. The animal's death is used to place power behind the curse."

Saida inhaled deeply. The curse was not Brosod's fault. She'd simply done what Urali had asked of her. "Are there any longterm effects?"

"No, if the subject of the curse manages to expel it from their body, which I assume you did as you are speaking to me now, the curse is ended."

Feeling eyes on her, Saida glanced past the fire to find Malon watching. Their eyes met. "Well that's something at least," she muttered distantly.

"Once I realized what had been done, I knew it was upon me to make it right. You granted the desert life, and the Makali repaid you with a curse."

Malon looked away, and Saida turned her attention back to Brosod. "Consider us even, though I worry what you'll do now. Can you return to your clan?"

Brosod lifted her brows in surprise, then shook her head, raking long fingers through her short, onyx black hair. "I cannot return. An elder will be elevated to fill Urali's place, and I would be put to death. No wise man or woman would allow a traitor to live for fear I'd act against the clan again."

"But you cannot survive on your own in the desert . . . "

Brosod's lips pulled back into a tight, bitter smile,

pressing her protruding lower canines against her upper lip. "I would rather be claimed by the desert, than to die for a crime that was not a crime at all. I'm more worried about you. You came here to form an army, but no Makali will follow you after what happened."

Saida pulled her blanket more tightly around her shoulders, looking across the fire toward Malon and the others, speaking too lowly for her to hear. "I never wanted an army, Brosod. I want to return to Faerune. If I do not reach my home before the full moon, Egrin Dinoba will kill my father."

"You should have enough supplies to make it, and with Malon, you are strong. I'm sure you can save them."

She nodded. After what she'd done to Urali, she almost believed Brosod's words. "You could come with us. I know it would be a difficult life being away from your kin, but it would still be a life."

Brosod leaned forward, plucking up another brick of condensed fibers—a special craft of the Makali—to throw into the fire. "I would sooner approach one of the great cities. On my own, I may stand a small chance of being admitted."

Saida watched Brosod's expression for any hints of a lie. "Do you truly believe that? They would take you in?"

Brosod's downward glance and shrug said that was likely not the case.

She placed her hand on Brosod's shoulder. "We'll figure it out. You saved my life, now I will return the favor."

Both women looked up as Malon and Luc approached, leaving the other elves to rest for what remained of the night.

"We will go to Hekala," Malon announced. "We may have lost our Makali army, but the Lukali could still be convinced. We will grow them a great oasis in return for an army."

Brosod gasped.

Saida merely sucked her teeth, she'd been prepared for this. "No, we will not. We've tried things your way, now we'll do them mine. We will return to Faerune."

Malon crossed his arms. "I've told you my terms, Saida. I will not go without an army. If I returned to Faerune, the elves would put me to death, and if I defended myself with the circlet against any you care about, *you* would put me to death."

Saida stood, still clutching the blanket around her. She *had* to reach her father. "Then don't go with me."

"If we part, Egrin will kill each of us and take the circlets."

"Then come to Faerune, and I will protect you."

Brosod rose and took a step back, her attention darting between Saida and Malon. With a considering look, Luc stepped back near her, separating himself from the impending argument.

"Saida," Malon said patiently, "we've been over this. We cannot return to Faerune without an army."

Words spilled from her mouth, revealing the thoughts which had plagued her since the start. It might be foolish, but deep down, she knew the only option. "Then we won't return to Faerune. Let us go to the Capital and kill Egrin Dinoba. Once he is gone, we will no longer be bound to one another."

If she didn't know any better, she'd think she'd hurt his feelings. He watched her for several heartbeats. "You want rid of me so badly, you would attempt to assassinate a demon?"

She hesitated, unsure if she had the fortitude for such a task, then nodded sharply. If Malon would not return to Faerune, and she would not venture deeper into the desert, attacking Egrin at the Capital was the only choice.

He considered her words for a moment, his reflective eyes glinting in the moonlight with his back to the fire. "And if we meet armies of Dreilore in our path?"

"We cut them down."

"And human militia?"

"The same."

Malon stepped toward her, reaching out for a brief moment, then let his hands fall. "I thought you unwilling to abuse the power of the gods."

His words made her heart sputter. She waited for the circlet at her belt to whisper in her mind, or for her conscience to object, but no hidden voices came. "I will defeat the emperor not for land, nor power, but to protect those who cannot protect themselves. Will you join me?"

Malon lifted his brows. Brosod and Luc huddled near

the fire, watching the conversation with seemingly bated breath.

"Yes, Saida. That is a plan I could stand behind. Though I would prefer to do so with my army. Countless opponents stand between us and Egrin Dinoba. They will not be so easily overcome."

"We'll find Elmerah first," she suggested. "She will help."

Malon snorted. "You would place so much faith in a single witch?"

A chill breeze gusted her back, as if it were pushing her forward, urging her down this new path. "I would place all the faith in the world in a single witch."

Malon looked to Luc, who shrugged, then looked back to her. "Is this just a trick to lure me into Faerune?"

Another trickle of wind pulled a lock of hair free from the collar of her robe. This whole time she'd wanted to protect Faerune not only to save her father, but because Alluin and Elmerah might still be there. But would they be? Really, she shouldn't have been worried about quite so many lives. Alluin and Elmerah would never rest idly on their laurels for so long.

"Well?" Malon pressed. "Is it?"

"I do not believe Elmerah is in Faerune," she explained. "She wouldn't have stayed behind after I was taken, and since she's not here rescuing me, I know where she went."

Malon waited for her to continue.

She hesitated. She hoped she was wrong, but if she

knew her friend at all . . . "I think she's going after Egrin herself. That was always the plan. And after you took me," she shook her head, "she would not be aware that you were no longer working with Egrin. She'd assume you were taking me to him."

He tilted his head. "Then how do you propose we find her?"

Now that, she did not know. Her mind had not yet raced that far ahead. Would Elmerah have sailed, or would she have gone on horseback? If Malon would not return to Faerune with her, she had no way of finding out. No way of tracking her at all.

Brosod stepped forward from the shadows. "If this is a friend you know well, I may be able to help you locate her."

"How?" Malon demanded before Saida could speak.

Brosod hunched her shoulders at his tone. "I may not be the most skilled curseworker in my clan, but if you can supply the magic, I could guide you. If you know her energy well enough, you could track her."

Malon watched Brosod suspiciously, but Saida would not pass up an opportunity to find Elmerah, not even if it required a curse.

She stepped away from Malon and toward Brosod. "You would travel with us, even out of the desert?"

Brosod hung her head. "It is not a fate I would choose for myself, but if I can help you, I will do it."

Saida knew she was asking much. Brosod had lived her entire life in the desert, it might be harsh, but it was her home. Yet, what other choice did she have? "How soon can we start?"

Brosod lifted her head, glancing warily at Malon and Luc, then turned back to Saida. "We can gather the materials tomorrow. It's a simple curse, it should not even require a sacrifice. Once we have all we need, we can cast it the next night by moonlight."

"And how can we trust this curse will not harm us if we cast it?" Malon asked.

"It would not harm you," Brosod said patiently, "because you will not be the caster. It must be Saida, as this woman you hope to find is her friend."

"So it could possibly harm me?" Saida asked.

Brosod nodded. "All curses come with risks. To wield unnatural powers is to risk those powers turning on you." She glanced at the circlet at Saida's belt. "But you seem able to manage such things."

"I'll do it."

"Saida," Malon cautioned. "You've known this woman a day. Do not give your trust so easily."

She met Brosod's waiting gaze, then said to Malon, "I trust her. Tomorrow we will head north, and gather the needed ingredients along the way. We will not proceed with an army, but we will have the only person who has ever come close to defeating Egrin Dinoba."

Malon crossed his arms.

She could tell he was on the brink of arguing for his cursed army again. She braced her hands on her hips. "I will not go further into the desert, Malon. You had your chance at an army, now it is my turn."

He sighed loudly and lowered his arms. "Fine, we will try it your way, though I'm not sure how you plan to catch the witch if she's already on her way to the Capital."

She wasn't sure either, but there was nothing she could do about that now. She could only look toward the next step, and that was divining Elmerah's location. Isara and Alluin would likely be with her.

After everything, they would return to their original plan: assassinate the emperor, and perhaps Daemon, then move forward from there. Except now, now they had the power of the circlets, which Egrin truly feared.

He feared what she and Malon could do together, and he was right to fear them. She was utterly terrified herself.

CHAPTER NINETEEN

Elmerah

Elmerah breathed in the salty coastal air near Port Aeluvaria. Normally the scent would have inspired a longing for home, now it just filled her with a sense of dread. She and Alluin waited near the road leading to the port. Celen and Killian had gone ahead, the latter disguised as human instead of Dreilore, for imitating the accent of the Akenyth Province proved too difficult for him.

Elmerah smiled softly despite her nerves. It hadn't been for lack of trying on Killian's part. He'd been quite keen on sauntering into port as a Dreilore, inspiring the common folk to quake in their boots at the sight of him.

She shifted her weight to her other leg, glancing at Alluin seated in the grass. Her smile wilted. "This doesn't feel right."

He looked up at her, his green eyes filled with distant thoughts. "What do you mean?"

She shrugged, gazing in the direction of the port, though the ships were too far off to see through the trees. "A sliver of doubt nags at me. Call it instinct. We didn't listen to yours with Isara, and look what happened."

He stood, glancing at the nearby horses, then back to her. "Do you want to go to the port? We may risk their safety—and ours. This close to the Capital, Egrin could have spread word of your description, and I'd likely be the only Valeroot elf stupid enough to show my heritage in these parts."

She frowned. He was right, Celen and Killian should be fine. No one would recognize Celen, and they were simply gathering information about the goings on in the Capital. Yet that could not soothe the churning in her gut.

"Let's just get a little closer," she suggested. "I'd like to be nearby should something go amiss."

Alluin nodded. "I'll fetch the horses."

"No telling me I'm being silly?"

He smiled. "No, and I won't even rub it in that you brushed off my valid worries about Isara."

She scowled. "Shut up and get the horses."

Rissine

I t felt good to place her boots upon the dock after several days at sea, but something strange was afoot at Port Aeluvaria. The man waiting to register her arrival was Arthali. Only a halfblood, she could tell just from looking at him, but one of her people would never be tasked as portmaster within the Empire. It was unheard of.

Yet, here he was, looking down at his wood-mounted parchment, quill poised. "From where do you hail?"

She had the hood of her emerald coat pulled up, but this man obviously wasn't paying attention, else he'd have paid her more heed. "From the North," she lied. "On my way to the Helshone to retrieve a shipment of spices."

He scribbled on his parchment. "Name?"

She blinked at him, glad she'd left Zirin aboard the ship, lest he pummel the halfblood for his impertinence. "Melia Korinth."

"How long will you stay at port?" He finally looked at her, really looked at her, and his eyes widened slightly.

Just long enough to find word of my sister, she thought. "Two days. Perhaps three." More lies. She'd abandon the ship at port if she must. There was no way she'd try to sail further north and dock at Galterra.

The halfblood scrawled a few more words on his parchment, glanced around them warily, then back to her. "Were you sent by the emperor?" he whispered. "I was told to expect a contingent of Arthali."

She started to raise her brows, but quickly schooled

245

her expression. "Yes, that's correct. I wasn't aware anyone at port would know. Do you have any information for me?"

Another wary glance. "No word of the Shadowmarsh witches you're to hunt. Dreilore should arrive here by midday, bringing word from further south."

She nearly choked. Egrin had enlisted other Arthali, and he was sending them to *hunt* her? Her magic flared inside her with sudden intensity. That little demonic worm. Those traitorous Arthali. They'd not join her cause, but they'd hunt their own kind?

She supposed it was no surprise. They'd been willing to kill her entire clan to save their own hides. She and Elmerah had only been spared because they were hardly out of childhood at the time.

She cleared her throat. "Does anyone else at port know of my task?"

He shook his head. "Only the few other Arthali stationed here. We all must know our task to secure our place within the Capital."

A shiver snaked up her spine. This was just like before. Egrin was finishing the job he started, enlisting Arthali to kill or capture the last two remaining witches of her clan. Was he afraid to face her himself, or was the task simply not critical to him?

The halfblood watched her, his features turning suspicious.

She squared her shoulders. "Have I been provided

lodgings, or am I to stand out on the docks for all of eternity?"

"But what of the rest of your contingent? Surely you don't intend to hunt *Shadowmarsh* witches on your own."

She glared. "I'd not have been entrusted with this task if I weren't capable, and my crew must see to the ship before they disembark. Now are we done here? I've things to do."

He hastily bowed, scribbled something else on his parchment, then scurried away.

Rissine clenched and unclenched her fists, debating whether or not to board her ship and flee. If a contingent of Arthali were being sent to hunt her, they'd surely be powerful fullbloods. They would not accept the task if they did not think themselves capable of defeating her. She should run and save her own hide, but . . . Elmerah was somewhere out there, perhaps even nearby, and she might have no idea what awaited her.

Yet, if she left her crew for long, they'd risk running afoul of the Arthali as they reached port.

A throat cleared above her. She looked up. Zirin peered down at her from the deck.

Using old Arthali signals taught to her as a girl, she gestured for him to wait on board. She'd quickly search for information, then return to her ship, either to flee with her crew, or order them to disembark. She held little love for any on board, but she'd not leave them to die by Arthali hands.

Zirin watched her for a moment, nodded, then his head disappeared.

She turned her attention to the nearby settlement, unnervingly serene given the time today. Aeluvaria was one of the largest port towns along the coast outside of the Capital and Faerune. Relatively close to Galterra, it was usually well-guarded by militia.

She spotted a grey uniform here and there among the folk bustling about beyond the dock, but not as many as there should have been. Which begged the question, what was more important to Egrin than protecting the dock? Where had the rest of the militia been sent?

Noticing the halfblood portmaster eyeing her from further down the dock, she started walking. She'd not need to hide her heritage here if Egrin had enlisted other Arthali, she just needed to hide from anyone she knew. She'd made many enemies during her time in Galterra. If there was a price on her head, they'd turn her in.

She reached the end of the dock, stepping across a few more planks leading to solid ground. Her legs seemed to sway awkwardly, but she knew it was just a mental effect from her time at sea. A militia man eyed her as she walked by, but made no move to question her.

She straightened her shoulders and continued walking, debating tossing back her hood. While many in Galterra respected her since she had connections to the emperor, she was not used to walking through a settlement entirely unhindered. In the Capital there was always the odd militia man, or drunkard who thought they could push her around because she was the only Arthali they'd seen in their miserable, sheltered lives.

They'd been wrong, but it didn't change how wary she'd always felt walking the streets in daylight.

She walked past the storage houses, where goods from nearby farms awaited transport to Galterra, then into the center of town. There were more taverns and inns here than anything else, vying to pry coins away from tired sailors needing a reprieve.

Any one of them would do. She needed to learn what was going on here before the Arthali arrived to *hunt* her. And before the Dreilore arrived, the ones the portmaster had mentioned. She wasn't sure which was worse.

The thought struck her as she walked through the wide-open doors of the busiest tavern, that the Arthali might have already captured Elmerah. The portmaster hadn't seemed to think so, but word could travel slowly at times. If Egrin already had her sister, he knew he'd have Rissine too. Elmerah was her only weakness, one she'd sacrifice her life for.

Though she doubted Elmerah would do the same for her.

She caught a few odd glances of tavern patrons as her boots echoed across the wooden floor. The open doors and long windows along the sun-facing wall left no doubt what type of woman lurked beneath the emerald hood.

As she approached the bar, she noted the distinct lack of elves in the tavern. She'd expected no blonde or silver locks from Faerune, but outside of the capital, Valeroot elves often worked farms, and some even joined trade crews. Yet not a single elf glanced her way.

Arthali welcome, and elves exiled. How strange life could be.

She reached the bar, quickly catching the attention of the elderly man pouring ale. The seated young couple she'd stepped between wordlessly climbed from their stools, moving slow like she might strike them, then scurried away.

Arthali welcome, yes, but still feared, it seemed. So the land had not been *completely* turned on its head.

The barkeep reached her, brushing a meaty palm over thinning gray hair. "What'll it be?"

She reached into her coin pouch, withdrawing a rare rhodium gull, one of many earned during her time in the Capital. The man's eyes widened. The gull could feed his entire family for a year.

She slid it across the bar, leaning toward him in its tracks. She lowered her voice, "Every scrap of information in your skull. I want to know who has passed through this port, and why. Whispers of the Dreilore, plots of the Arthali, all of it."

The barkeep licked chapped lips, reaching trembling fingers toward the gull. "Not here, too many eyes and ears," he whispered. "Meet me out back."

She swiped up the gull before he could snatch it. "I'll see you there."

She turned and sauntered out of the tavern, hoping

she'd chosen right in her source of information. Barkeeps knew more than most in any settlement, and the aged ones knew most of all, because no one expected they cared enough to listen.

Celen

"Stop fidgeting," Celen muttered under his breath. Killian might look like a normal, sandy-haired young human man, still dressed in his woolen tunic and breeches, but his shifty eyes and hand-wringing were sure to give him away. If one of the militia men stopped them, Celen had little doubt Killian would panic and blurt out every scrap of information unfortunate enough to pass through his little mind.

"Crowds make me wary," Killian whispered, eyeing those milling about at the center of the port.

"It's not even crowded." Celen surveyed each of the taverns for the busiest one. They'd get their information, learn what they faced within the Capital, then get out.

"No elves," Killian muttered, his brown eyes darting about. "No elves, no Dreilore, but some Arthali."

Celen stiffened. He hadn't noticed the lack of elves. Not a pointy ear in sight. "The Arthali you see are just halfbloods." Their skin was a bit too light, their features telling the tale of roots within the Empire. "Let's go in there," he pointed to the open doors of a large tavern.

"We'll have a drink and a good listen to the other patrons."

Killian nodded a little too quickly, the illusion of his sandy hair flopping forward.

With a heavy sigh, Celen led the way across the square and into the tavern. He quickly surveyed the patrons, wary of any lingering Militia, then strode across the room with Killian at his side. Whispers followed him as he approached the bar. *"Another one." "Has to be a full-blood, he's so tall." "She was almost just as tall as him."*

Celen's shoulder blades itched. Too many eyes on his back. And where was the barkeep? The dull, scuffed wood held a few empty mugs and plates, with no one around to clear them.

Killian subtly tugged at Celen's sleeve, drawing his attention behind him. Every pair of eyes in the place whipped downward. He suddenly regretted entering the tavern. He'd thought with all the halfbloods around, he wouldn't be much of a spectacle, but he was tall even for an Arthali, and his scars were an unusual characteristic. He could only be grateful his tattoos were covered by his coat.

He turned around and leaned his back against the bar, making sure the eyes remained downward. With no barkeep here to question, he'd need to make a casual escape. Couldn't seem too conspicuous lest someone report him. "Let's get out of here," he grumbled to Killian. "Might be better to ask a few questions down at the docks."

Killian nodded. "The barkeep is out back. Heard some whispers." He reached a hand toward the nearest stool as if to lean on it, a casual gesture, but his hand slipped across the wood and he nearly fell.

Celen cringed as Killian quickly righted himself. "How did you pick up on that?" he whispered. "You still have fox ears hidden under there?"

"My appearance is illusion. I can still smell the foul stale sweat in this place, and I can hear them all whispering about your scars."

Celen nodded subtly. "Let's go out back then." He raised his voice, just enough to seem casual. "No barkeep, let's move on."

Killian nodded a little too quickly, then hurried toward the door with Celen at his heels.

Celen felt the eyes on his back as soon as it was turned, and wondered if Elmerah had dealt with this in the Capital too. He'd known enough about the continent to hide in the woods when his ship wrecked on the shores, but he hadn't realized just how bad it could be.

The open sunny sky above the square was a welcome relief. Not paying attention, Killian turned left while he turned right. He had to reach back one arm to grab Killian's sleeve and turn him around, then they both proceeded to walk around the tavern toward the back.

Celen neared the building's back corner, then hearing voices, he slowed and leaned against the wall.

An old, raspy voice spoke, "I swear, that's all any of us

know. You'll find no other information within this port. Now, my gull?"

"This was hardly worth my trouble," a female voice growled, and Celen had to stifle a gasp. He knew Rissine would search for her sister, but he'd never thought she would have already made it this far. She must have set sail within a day of learning Elmerah was gone.

His palms sweated as he leaned against the outer tavern wall, with Killian pressed against his shoulder. He had to decide quickly. If he didn't confront her now, he might lose her, but maybe he *wanted* to lose her. Would she be a help, or hindrance? Would she protect Elmerah, or just drag her by the ear all the way back to Faerune?

His decision was quickly made for him. Killian inhaled sharply through his nose, sputtered for a moment, then let out a stifled sneeze.

"What was that?" Rissine hissed. "Did someone follow you out here?"

"No, and I want nothing to do with it. Give me my payment so I can return to my tavern."

"Here," Rissine grumbled, followed by the sound of footsteps and a door opening and shutting.

He had to decide now. Flee, or try and reason with the most difficult woman he'd ever met.

"Get behind me," he sighed to Killian. "And keep quiet. She could strike you down in a heartbeat."

Killian obeyed without question, just as Rissine came into sight around the corner of a stack of crates. She didn't see him immediately, but when she turned her eyes filled with a moment of recognition, then pure, untainted hatred.

"You!" She stormed toward him down the narrow dirt alley, wild black hair whipping behind her. "Where is my sister?"

He held up his hands. "She's safe, let's not act rashly, you'll need me to lead you to her."

She stopped in front of him, angrily tugging her emerald coat straight. "You utter fool. How could you put her into danger like this? Do you realize purebloods have been sent to hunt her?"

He lifted his brows. "What in Arcale's light are you talking about, woman?"

"The information I was given the moment I arrived at port, from an Arthali halfblood portmaster," she fumed. "Now where is she? Our hunters could arrive any moment."

"Outside of town," he answered honestly, realizing now was no time for pretense. "If those Arthali have any Brambletooth witches with them—"

"They'll easily track her magic, mine, and yours," Rissine finished for him. She looked past his shoulder. "Who is this trembling little man hiding behind you?"

"An ally," he explained. "Now let's go."

"I have a crew. Valeroot elves, the little Akkeri, and Zirin."

Celen fidgeted, ready to make like a silverfish darting away from a whale. "Will they wait on your ship until otherwise instructed?"

She nodded.

"And the hunters, should they have a Brambletooth amongst them, will sense Zirin's magic. We need to get them out of there."

Rissine shocked him by seeming torn. "Elmerah—"

He nodded, understanding her dilemma. To fetch her crew, and possibly leave Elmerah vulnerable so nearby, or to leave the crew, and let them deal with Arthali hunters. "Elmerah can take care of herself for now, and Alluin is with her. He won't let anyone sneak up on them. Now let's get your crew and get out of here." He turned to head toward the docks.

A hand on his shoulder stopped him, and he turned back around, shocked Rissine would even touch him. "I cannot lose her, Celen."

"I know, neither can I, but if we're to flee the port, we can't just leave your crew to die. Now let's go."

This time, Rissine followed, then quickly took the lead, heading west toward the docks.

Celen could only hope this wouldn't prove to be the biggest mistake of his life.

CHAPTER TWENTY

Rissine

E very step toward the docks felt like a stride in the
wrong direction, but Celen was right, she couldn't
desert her crew just because Elmerah was near. If she'd
foreseen finding her sister this quickly, she'd have abandoned her ship and taken her crew with her from the
start. She only wanted them ready to sail should she find
news of Elmerah somewhere far off.

Celen grasped her shoulder before she reached the
first planks of the dock. Holding back his alleged ally
with his other arm, he removed his hand from her
shoulder and pointed ahead. "Look."

Rissine followed the aim of his finger. A ship far out
at sea cut across the blinding afternoon sun. She could
not make out the color of its sails, but only so many ships

came into port each day. Some days there would be no ships at all. Chances were, this one carried the Arthali.

An old primal fear, instilled in her when she was but a girl, flared to life. Her mother's corpse. Elmerah's tear-filled eyes. "We must hurry," she rasped.

Her heart beat steadily in her throat as she made her way down the docks, keeping an even pace, exuding exterior calm. Inwardly, her mind raced over and over that fateful day so long ago, when she was given the choice to save her mother, or her sister. She knew the gathering Arthali could kill her in an instant, could kill her mother, her sister, and anyone else they chose. She'd had no choice then, but she did have one now. She wouldn't let them take anyone else from her.

Moving toward the ship, Celen and his little *ally* followed her lead. She had time, she told herself. She had time before that ship would reach the docks. She could get her crew off the ship, flee to the woods, and warn Elmerah. Together, they could come up with a plan.

Spotting her, the portmaster approached as if to bar her way. Did he realize she'd lied about her identity? Had the incoming ship given away her ruse? The look on his face said yes, and he'd soon rat her out, if he hadn't already.

With malice in her dark eyes, her gait remained steady as she unsheathed her blade.

The portmaster, but a few paces away, took one long look at her, Celen, and the squirrelly little man behind them, then turned and scurried the other way.

As she reached the ship, Rissine heard chatter and sensed movement back at the edge of port. The militia lingering there would have seen her draw her blade. Time was short.

"Zirin!" she shouted, hoping he waited on deck and not below in the cabins. "Now!"

Zirin and Vessa both leaned over the ship's railing as she neared. Zirin cast one look toward port, then darted away.

Confident Zirin would gather her Valeroot crew, Rissine turned around, tightening her grip on her blade, prepared to protect her allies from any militia who dared stand in their way.

Elmerah

Elmerah reined in her horse, needing silence. "Do you hear that?"

Alluin's mount had already halted just ahead of hers. They'd left the other two horses hidden at the edge of the woods. He lifted a pointed ear toward the sky. "Shouting, lots of shouting. Something's happening at the port."

She clenched her reins. "Those cotton-brained fools."

"It could have nothing to do with them."

"Or *everything* to do with them." She kicked her horse's sides, leaning forward in the saddle as the beast took off like a cannonball.

She heard hoofbeats over the sound of whipping wind as Alluin's mount followed hers.

Idiot, she thought, narrowing her eyes. *I'm such an idiot.* She should have never let them go, not after what happened with Isara.

Their mounts carried them swiftly down the road, kicking up a cloud of dust in their wake. She focused on her magic, wanting it fully built and ready to strike, though she'd no idea what she'd find at port.

The first squat wooden buildings came into sight. She knew little of the port, but surmised the fastest way to the docks would be right through the middle of town.

Alluin's horse charged up beside hers as they reached the first buildings bisected by the road. "I know the port! Sharp left up here. The docks are at the northwestern end."

"How do you know they're at the docks!" she shouted over thundering hooves. The few people milling about in the streets took one look at the charging horses and ran through the nearest doorways.

"Taverns are near the docks! That's where they would have gone!"

The sky darkening overhead had her questioning whether she'd summoned her magic too early, but no. She felt it like a deep still well in the pit of her gut. These sudden dark clouds were not her doing. Either a storm had brewed unnaturally fast, or . . .

"I think Rissine is here!"

Alluin didn't answer. Instead, he leaned forward,

focused on weaving his horse through the streets and evading any people too slow to get out of the way.

Elmerah's horse huffed and grunted with every gallop, giving off heat where she grasped the reins near its shoulders. She let Alluin take the lead, her horse just a step behind, following as he led them through the town and toward the coast. Thunder rumbled, setting her teeth on edge. What in Ilthune's cursed name was Rissine doing at the port?

"Just ahead!" Alluin shouted back to her.

They'd reached the northern end of town, and took a sharp left toward the coast. The docks ahead swarmed with militia. There was one ship already anchored, and another nearing port.

Beyond the charging militia was Rissine, lit up with circling lightning, keeping the militia back from those who waited beyond.

Elmerah and Alluin slowed their horses. Behind Rissine were Celen, Killian, and a host of Valeroot elves. Should the militia's arrows break through Rissine's lightning, they would be overtaken in a moment.

She drew her horse to a halt, dismounted, and let go of the reins, freeing the horse to run out of danger. Her magic swarmed upward. "We have to help them," she panted. The second she loosed her magic, the militia would turn on her too.

Alluin dismounted, unstrapped his bow from the back of his horse's saddle, then freed his mount. He reached for the quiver slung over his shoulder. "I'll follow your lead."

"Now that's what I like to hear." Magic poured out of her, a more mighty torrent than she'd ever experienced. Fire erupted on the road ahead, blazing forward though there was no fuel save her magic. It cut toward the docks and the militia beyond, just as Rissine's lightning rained down from overhead.

In the time of a single inhale, the entire port erupted into chaos.

Isara

Isara could hardly believe her eyes as lightning seemed to engulf the port. Daemon's contingent had just crested the rise of the southern road when the horses began to panic.

The horse she'd been given reared up, struggling against its reins fastened tight to the front of Daemon's saddle.

Daemon's attention was mostly occupied by his own panicked mount, but he found time to shout, "Control your horse!"

All Isara could manage was to grip tightly to her saddle and brace her legs around her horse's trunk. Some Dreilore approached on foot, and others dismounted all around them, their black leather armor giving them an air of *otherness*. If she was thrown and knocked unconscious, she wouldn't be able to help Elmerah, for surely that was who waited at the port ahead.

The Dreilore lord with their contingent calmly sidled up toward Isara's horse, grabbed the reins where they met the bit, then tugged her mount into submission. The beast stomped its hooves erratically, but lowered its head in the Dreilore's grasp.

In the moment of relative stillness, Isara took a shaky breath, then looked up as the first drops of cold rain speckled her cheeks.

Now in control of his own mount, Daemon looked to the Dreilore lord. "Take Isara and a few soldiers into the woods and make a wide path around the port. I'll go with the rest of the contingent to the docks, see if we can't capture us a Shadowmarsh witch."

"No!" Isara cried, kicking her horse's sides.

The Dreilore lord reined in her horse, gesturing to some of the soldiers on the road behind them. She swung her leg over the saddle and slid down, but the Dreilore lord was there, looping an arm around her waist.

"Struggle," he whispered in his thick accent, "and I will break your legs. You are wanted alive, but not necessarily whole."

She winced, cowering at his closeness. She could sense the strength in his arms. She might be able to disable the enchantments on his blade, but she could not fight him.

Dreilore soldiers closed in around her, most on foot but a few still on mounts. One took her horse.

The Dreilore holding her tightly barked orders she couldn't understand, then began dragging her away from the road.

She pulled away, casting her eyes back toward Daemon, but he'd already started riding toward the port, most of the contingent surging past her in his wake.

The Dreilore holding her gave a harsh yank, bringing her tight against him, his long white hair brushing her cheek. He dragged her further from the road. She whipped her gaze upward at a deafening peal of thunder. A black line cut across the rolling dark clouds, opening up a wound which gushed rain down upon them.

Her wet spectacles half-blinding her, and her sodden cloak tangling around her stumbling feet, Isara was dragged into the woods. Dragged away from any chance of warning Elmerah that an entire contingent of Dreilore —with blades and shackles that could nullify her magic— were on their way.

CHAPTER TWENTY-ONE

"F aster," the Dreilore lord hissed in Isara's ear as he shoved her from behind. She regretted ever sliding down from her mount, but with the rutted earth and thick brambles of the forest, she'd have been forced to dismount regardless. They'd reached the edge of the storm, finally out of the rain, but thoroughly soaked to the skin. Despite the wall of trees standing between her and the port, she could still hear the sounds of chaos in the distance. She estimated they had in fact come closer to the port, but further east away from the road.

"You've no idea—oof!" He shoved her back so hard she pitched forward, toppling right into prickly brambles. Little thorns snagged her cloak and drew blood on her skin.

The Dreilore lord and the three others accompanying him all stared down at her, their unusual eyes flickering with burning embers.

"Move," the lord ordered, tossing a lock of bejeweled white hair behind his shoulder.

Stuck halfway sitting in the brambles, she raised a bloody hand to straighten her spectacles. The cut on her palm wasn't deep, but burned like a bee sting thanks to the mild irritants in the thorns.

"I'm stuck," she lied, grasping at the small chance to delay being taken too far away from the port to find her way again. She felt torn in so many ways, and could not deny that now, half of her worry was for Daemon. If he ordered his Dreilore to attack Elmerah, what might she do in retaliation?

The Dreilore lord reached down, grabbed her wrist, and tugged. She pushed off with her feet, using the momentum to drive her forward, hoping to topple the Dreilore . . . but his grip stopped her dead in her tracks. He squeezed her wrist so hard she cried out, her knees buckling beneath her.

"Unhand the girl!"

Isara thought for a moment she imagined the voice, but the Dreilore all turned in that direction. A handful of Valeroot elves and an Akkeri blocked the way west toward the port. Sweat shone on their brows. Four elves aimed unwavering arrows at the Dreilore.

The Dreilore lord raised Isara's wrist in his grasp, pulling her up on her toe tips, but his words were for the female elf who'd spoken. "Would you like to die this day, elf?"

Isara watched the elves, wide eyed. She recognized

one of them from Faerune, Alluin's sister, Vessa. Another female seemed vaguely familiar.

Vessa's raised bow did not falter. "Do not make me laugh, Dreilore. You are outnumbered, and no one is faster than a Valeroot hunter with a bow."

At a nod from their lord, the three other Dreilore drew glowing blades and approached the elves.

All Isara could do was watch as bowstrings tightened, and the first arrows flew in her direction.

One of the Dreilore went down quickly, but the other two launched themselves at their opponents.

Isara's eyes widened. The Dreilore were so graceful and fast, as if they had muscles that humans and elves did not. One slashed at Vessa with a green glowing blade, nearly disemboweling her.

With a gasp, Isara summoned her magic, quenching the Dreilore's glowing blades. It would make their finely honed edges no less dangerous, but there was nothing else she could do.

One Dreilore hesitated at the sight of his quenched weapon, just a heartbeat, but it was enough for an elf standing further back to send an arrow straight through his heart. The third Dreilore stepped back, now facing the elves on his own.

"My apologies," the Dreilore lord holding her painfully aloft muttered, "but you are not worth dying for."

Isara fell to the ground, looking up just in time to see

a wave of black smoke dissipating. The Dreilore lord was gone.

She scrambled to her feet, realizing the lord had not been speaking to her, but to the remaining Dreilore now backing away from the elves, almost reaching her. It seemed Egrin had only granted magic to the higher standing lords, and this lord had left his soldier to die.

He froze as three bows raised his way.

"Don't!" Isara cried, already horrified by the two dead Dreilore at her feet. "There has been enough killing these days, and we need to help my friend at the docks." *And find my brother*, she added silently.

Vessa lowered her bow, just slightly, her green gaze on the Dreilore. "Now would be the time for you to flee. Consider yourself lucky."

With a confused glance at Isara, the Dreilore turned tail and ran deeper into the woods.

The elves lowered their bows as they approached. Isara couldn't fathom how they'd happened upon her, but she was most shocked to see Merwyn, who she'd met a time or two in Faerune.

Though he leaned on a fine elven cane for support, he reached her before the elves. His sickly skin seemed out of place in the soft sunlight filtering through the trees. "Lucky we found you. Elmerah bade us flee—" he hesitated, glancing at Vessa. "But we should not have left her. She could use our help." He looked to Isara. "Your help especially."

His slurred words were a bit difficult to understand.

She looked up to Vessa. "What does he mean? I saw the lightning. What's happening at port?"

Vessa raked her free hand through her short hair, revealing pointed ears beneath the tousled locks. "We sailed here with Rissine, searching for Elmerah and my brother, but we had the misfortune of arriving at the same time as an Arthali ship. The militia attacked us, and we might have been overwhelmed had Elmerah not arrived. She and my brother are still at the port, we just left them. I imagine the Arthali ship has docked by now."

"An Arthali ship?" she gasped. Vessa made it sound like a bad thing, so they could not be allies of Rissine. That meant . . . "Egrin sent them? Who are they after?"

"Rissine and Elmerah."

Her thoughts raced. The militia had attacked, Rissine and Elmerah now faced an entire ship of Arthali, and Daemon had ridden into port with a contingent of Dreilore. That entire port was about to be obliterated, and those she cared about would be caught in the middle.

She clutched a hand to her chest, willing her heart to stop racing. "We must return to the port. Have you any mounts?"

Vessa shook her head. "We ran all the way here, and we're not going back. I swore to my brother I would not. Their extra mounts should be somewhere near."

Isara stepped toward her. How could she even consider abandoning Alluin? "Your brother is going to die if we don't go back!"

Vessa flinched like she'd been struck. She wiped the

sweat from her brow and shook her head. "I tried to get him to leave, but he wouldn't leave Elmerah." Her voice hitched. "He's chosen to protect that witch 'till the end. If I return he'll be watching two backs instead of one, and it could get him killed."

Frantic, Isara looked to Merwyn next.

He lowered his nearly bald head. "I will follow, but you must run ahead. I will slow you down."

She glared at the elves, but it appeared none would change their minds. She could hear the distant sea. She'd find the way to port on her own. If she made it in time, she could disable Arthali magic and Dreilore enchantments alike. She was the only one who could curtail the bloodshed yet to come . . . if she could make it there fast enough.

Her breath huffed out. "Fine, Merwyn and I will save them." She glanced at the small Akkeri, doubting he'd do much good, though she was still glad she didn't have to go alone.

She turned, listening again for the sound of the distant coast. The Dreilore had not taken her far, she should be able to find her way. Hearing shouts and clangs of steel over the distant crashing tide, she started walking, feeling the eyes of the elves heavy upon her back.

She'd only taken a few steps when Vessa caught up to her side. "Wait," she gasped, her brow creased with worry. She stared off through the trees for a heartbeat, then a look of grim determination set in. "We're going to have to run if we hope to make it in time. If we're lucky, we'll find my brother's spare mounts along the way."

"I thought you weren't coming."

"The others can hide on their own. I've made a bad habit of choosing the coward's way out in the past, and I am riddled with regrets."

Isara nodded. She knew just how Vessa felt. "Let's go."

She turned to run, realizing Merwyn had scurried ahead, darting through the brush like a rabbit.

Slow me down? Isara thought, then jogged after him with Vessa at her side.

Vessa clutched her bow tight to her side, avoiding the curling brambles. "That little creature is braver than us all," she panted.

Isara didn't answer, her tongue tied in half-regret for guilting Vessa into coming after Alluin had convinced her to flee. She hoped she wouldn't get her killed.

She hated seeing death, and couldn't understand how others could kill at all. Unfortunately, that seemed like all everyone wanted to do.

Alluin

Alluin held his bow at the ready, though he had but a single arrow left, and no time to retrieve those he'd loosed. Storm clouds surged overhead, seeming almost sentient in their fervor. The accompanying winds carried the scent of ocean salt, blowing his hair back from his face. Before him Elmerah, Rissine, Celen, and another Arthali that Rissine had brought with her formed a living wall at the start of the docks. Bodies, dead or unconscious, were sprawled all around, some unlucky ones bobbing in the rocky tide below.

Elmerah cast a worried glance back toward him, her cutlass ablaze and her hair soaking wet. "Go after your sister, you fool! You stand no chance of surviving this!"

At the end of the docks a ship had cast anchor, and nine Arthali had disembarked. They were tall, dark, and terrifying, all dressed in the different fashions of their clans, some in furs, some in leather, some in more subtle linens and silks. Those with arms bare to the gusting coastal wind bore tattoos, the designs as varied as their clothing.

A female with white fur at her collar and tattoos that swirled like angry winds approached ahead of the others and called out, "Shadowmarsh witches! You make our task too easy!" She didn't spare a glance for the bodies she stepped over and around, followed by the rest of her crew. Her curly hair swirled with gusts of coastal wind.

Alluin watched as Elmerah looked to Rissine, and he didn't miss the worry in their eyes. They were afraid, more afraid than he'd ever seen either of them.

Elmerah wanted him to run. He'd convinced his sister, Killian, Merwyn, and the others to run, but he would not leave her. If this was where it ended, they would go down together.

Rissine's storm clouds echoed with thunder overhead, or maybe they were Elmerah's, though her cutlass burned brightly with flame.

Rissine raised her rapier toward the sky, and a thin line of lightning stuck, meeting the tip of her blade. "Tunisa, you coward!" she called out. "You claimed you did not want to leave the North when I found you."

The woman in white furs, presumably Tunisa, laughed. Her eyes were lighter than Elmerah's, almost gold. "We were already in talks with the emperor, you fool. If I'd have known my task then, you'd be in a cage." She neared the end of the dock, stopping roughly ten paces back. Her golden eyes flicked up at the sound of hoofbeats on the road beyond. "Oh, how perfect," she laughed.

Alluin glanced behind them, spotting horses in the distance, Dreilore riders atop their backs. Countless more Dreilore marched on foot, and at the head of the group rode Daemon Saredoth.

Elmerah was the first to react, breaking the line with her sister, Celen, and the other male Arthali to move to Alluin's side. "You should have run when you had the chance."

His fingers flexed around his bow. "I'll always watch your back, Elmerah."

"For what good it will do now." Her cutlass blazed brighter, bathing them both in warm yellow light. The flames flickered in the storm winds like a campfire on the coast.

"You handle the Dreilore!" Rissine called back to her. "The Arthali scum are mine!"

Elmerah's flames reflected in the depths of her dark eyes as she bared her teeth. "You always get to have all the fun!"

Rissine didn't answer. Alluin glanced back to see Tunisa lifting her arms, violent winds swirling around her. With a whip of lightning, Rissine charged, and Alluin turned just in time to watch Elmerah charging in the other direction. Forgetting Rissine and the Arthali, Alluin ran after Elmerah, watching her back, as promised.

Elmerah

Elmerah was already exhausted, and she knew without a doubt she'd not win against so many Dreilore, their drawn blades glowing with enchantments. But what else could she do? There was no escape, and she'd not go down without a fight. She wouldn't go back to Egrin's cage willingly, they'd have to kill her first.

She pushed more fire into her blade as her boots pounded the hard-packed muddy earth. Those on horses fell back, leaving the lower ranking foot-soldiers in Elmerah's path. Her fire blazed brighter with every step, jumping from her blade to form hot orange rivulets around her.

"Take her alive!" one Dreilore shouted.

The order would be their undoing. They couldn't kill her, but she'd rain death down upon them like a fiery goddess. Or a *demon*.

She stopped walking as the soldiers neared, swiping at her fire with their blades, making it sputter out in places with their enchantments.

She pushed her magic further, hoping Alluin was well out of reach. The fire seemed to pulse in rhythm with her heartbeat. The beat of a drum leading her to war. Arms extended, her body heaved until all she could see, hear, and feel was fire. It boiled the blood in her veins, and singed the ends of her hair, filling her senses with an acrid stench.

The odor gave her pause, and her magic faltered, then flared back to life. Her own fire should not be able to burn her. Beyond the flames she could barely see the waiting Dreilore, enchanted blades raised to protect them from her magic. She couldn't sense Alluin behind her, nor could she hear Rissine and the others.

But she couldn't let her fire go out. If it went out, the Dreilore would take her, and they would kill Alluin.

She inhaled, scalding her lungs. Her skin *burned.* She inhaled as deeply as she could manage, then like a fiery hurricane, her magic thundered outward toward all who stood before her, leaving her gasping in its wake.

Screams. All she could hear were screams, but there was no pulling back now. She continually forced more magic outward until her fire exploded in a final current.

She smelled burnt hair and burnt flesh. The screams intensified, and she collapsed to the ground on all fours, her eyes seared with afterimages of fiery orange. Her right hand pinned her cutlass to the earth, but she was too weak to lift it. Someone was grunting in pain, and she realized distantly, it was her. The smell of burnt hair was overwhelming, and her skin felt as if it might melt from her bones. Her lungs cried out for cool air, but none seemed to come.

Tears stung her eyes like molten metal as she opened them and beheld the sight before her. Charred bodies were strewn all around her, too much smoke to see beyond them.

The smoke swirled with movement, then someone stepped forward. Daemon Saredoth held a cloth over his mouth and nose, his eyes crinkled in disgust. He stopped before her, rapier drawn. "Quite the feat, witch, but I doubt you could do it again without rest. Unfortunately, I simply do not think it wise to leave you alive when you possess such power. Egrin will have your sister, and that will be enough."

He lifted his rapier.

Still on her hands and knees, she tried to summon her magic, but it was like grasping frayed ends of string. Her cutlass was useless pinned beneath her right hand. She'd given everything she had to defeat the Dreilore.

Daemon poised his rapier's tip downward, ready to plunge through her back and into her heart.

She forced her gaze upward, prepared to look death right in the eye.

Daemon smiled, then his body reeled backward like an invisible force had hit him, but it wasn't an invisible force. An arrow protruded from his chest.

Gripping the arrow shaft, he blinked down at it in shock, then toppled over and did not move.

Elmerah knew she should try to rise, but the smoke had cleared beyond Daemon, and she could behold what she had done. *So many.* She'd killed so many of them. Far off, the rest of the contingent fled. Their enchantments had not held up to her fire. The nearest buildings burned. Any innocents in the port were either hiding or dead, because other than the fleeing Dreilore, nothing moved.

Nothing moved?

"Rissine!" she gasped, coming up to her knees. There was no lightning, no thunder, only smoke and slowly clearing clouds. How much time had passed since she started summoning her fire? She couldn't seem to make sense of things.

She stumbled to her feet, grabbing her cutlass with her less-burned left hand. Alluin was there, helping her. She realized dizzily that he'd saved her from Daemon. It had been Alluin's arrow protruding from his chest.

He held her gingerly. "You're badly burned, you shouldn't move."

She looked down at her wrists. Her coat sleeves had burned away, leaving angry red skin, charred and weeping. "Rissine!" she rasped. "My sister!"

She turned her head toward the docks, but there was too much smoke in her vision, she could see nothing in the distance. She hadn't even realized how far she'd charged into the Dreilore ranks until that moment, leaving her sister behind to face the other Arthali.

She wrapped her right arm around Alluin's shoulder, flaking pieces of charred fabric from what remained of her sleeve. He braced her with his arm around her waist, which was the least damaged part of her body, still covered by her clothing and coat.

She staggered toward the sound of the ocean with Alluin's strong arm keeping her upright. "Could you see what happened to them?" she rasped.

"No, I was watching you, but the sky went still not long ago."

The sky went still. The words pierced her heart. If the sky was still, then Rissine was—

They came out on the other side of the smoke, where the enemy Arthali waited, roughly twenty paces away at the edge of the docks.

Elmerah's breath caught in her throat. Celen was on his knees, head hung, each wrist cuffed with what had to be magic-nullifying shackles. Zirin lay on his side, unmoving, but since he too wore shackles, he must be alive.

Then there was Rissine, shackled but still standing, with Tunisa's bone-hilted dagger at her throat. The rest of Tunisa's men and women stood behind her, waiting patiently.

Tunisa's eyes met Elmerah's as she forced Rissine a few steps forward toward the final planks of the dock where they met land. "Be a good girl and come here. Let us shackle you and perhaps I'll let your sister live."

Elmerah tried to stand on her own, but found her legs unable to hold her, and was left leaning heavily on Alluin. She couldn't let them shackle her. She'd not go back to Egrin, but Rissine . . .

Tunisa smiled. "We only need one of you, Elmerah. Either you come to me willingly, or I'll slit Rissine's throat and take you by force. You are clearly too weak to fight."

"Don't—" Rissine's words were cut off by the blade at her throat. She bared her teeth.

Her words weren't needed. Elmerah knew Rissine would never want her little sister to trade her life away.

She lowered her chin, glaring at Tunisa through burnt locks of hair. "Release my sister, or I will kill all of you where you stand." She gestured with her free arm to the charred corpses littering the ground behind her.

Tunisa laughed, her long curls whipping about in the coastal wind. "I think you're quite burned out right now. You can hardly stand."

Elmerah searched for her magic, finding a weak, flickering flame inside her. She reached for it, but suddenly, it went out.

Her brow furrowed. That wasn't right. Though she was out of energy, and unable to summon her magic outwardly, inwardly she should be able to feel it. Had she completely burnt herself out? Was such a thing even possible?

Tunisa watched her with a smug smile. Elmerah was out of options.

She didn't want to go to Egrin, she *couldn't*. She couldn't be caged and subjected to his torture again. But Rissine . . . "Alluin," she breathed. "Leave me here. Let them take me."

"No."

"I will not let her harm Rissine. If I go to Egrin now, you can still save me, but if I don't go, we're all dead. Leave me here and flee. Find Vessa and the others."

His arm tightened around her waist. "I will not leave you, Elmerah. If we go down here and now, we go together."

"We haven't got all day!" Tunisa taunted, raising her voice over gusting winds. "Wait too long and more Dreilore will come to claim you!" She nodded to an older male Arthali beside her. "Go and fetch her, would you?"

He stepped forward from the group, flexing bare arms tattooed with designs almost identical to Celen's. He stepped off the docks and onto solid land.

Elmerah tensed. "Brace yourself," she muttered to Alluin. "He can move the earth."

The Arthali male splayed his meaty hands before him and smiled.

Elmerah waited for the earth to tremble, but nothing happened. The only movement was the gently gusting wind.

"What is the issue?" Tunisa hissed.

The Arthali male's smile wilted around the edges. He glanced back at Tunisa. "I can't summon my magic. Something is wrong."

Elmerah was so relieved she could have cried if her eyes weren't burning and bone dry. She hadn't used up her magic, someone was nullifying them all, and the only person who could do that was Isara. From a distance, she likely could not be accurate, and so had suppressed *all* magic.

"Do you think Isara is near?" Alluin whispered.

She gave the slightest of nods. "It makes sense. She was with Daemon. Perhaps he had her under guard somewhere nearby while he came here with his Dreilore." She licked her cracked lips. "But Daemon—"

She'd promised Isara she wouldn't harm Daemon, and now he was dead.

Tunisa and the other Arthali muttered amongst themselves, glancing around for the source of what hindered them. It was clear none of them could summon magic . . . though that didn't remove the blade from Rissine's throat. Celen had lifted his head to watch them all, but seemed unable to stand.

Her face red and pinched with frustration, Tunisa gestured to those standing behind her. Two male Arthali with blades unsheathed, and one female aiming a bow approached. The arrow's tip was aimed at Alluin, not Elmerah. He unsheathed a dagger with his free hand, but it would do him little good against a bow.

Elmerah clung to him, too weak to flee or do anything else. Her cutlass hung loosely from her left hand. Isara might have nullified everyone's magic, but they were still outnumbered.

The female with the bow grinned as she and the others neared. "Prepare to lose your elven lover."

Her words left Elmerah a heartbeat to act. The Arthali drew back her bowstring.

Elmerah screamed at the sound of an arrow flying free. Alluin tried to spin her behind him, but she threw herself against his body, taking them both to the ground. Her charred arms and face were pure pain, both icy and burning at once. She'd landed on top of Alluin, spreading her body over his to shield him from incoming attack.

"Are you hurt?" she rasped. "Are you hurt!"

She glanced toward the woman with the bow, sure the next arrow would soon come, but the woman lay dead on her side, blood pooling onto the hard-packed earth beneath her. The bow and the arrow she'd drawn lay useless near her fingertips.

"Elmerah," Alluin groaned. "Elmerah I need you to move so I can rise."

She rolled off him, and looked up to find Vessa aiming an arrow at the other two Arthali. Beside her stood Merwyn and Isara. More elves approached, panting and sweaty, from where they'd hidden behind smoldering buildings.

"My thanks for the horses, brother," Vessa said, her

gaze and bow unwavering from the Arthali. "Though we could have used more than two."

Elmerah struggled to sit up, then let Alluin help her to stand.

Alluin replied to his sister with an uneasy nod as Elmerah looked to the docks, her eyes searching for Rissine.

Tunisa, her face puckered with ugly rage, still held her near the edge of the docks.

"Stupid elves!" Tunisa growled. Elmerah barely heard her words over the wind. "We'll take Rissine and the others on board. Leave Elmerah for the Dreilore."

"No!" she cried, lunging forward, but stopping short as Alluin held her back.

"You're too weak to fight!" he grunted, his arms locked around her waist. "The rest of you, go!"

The elves hurried past them, toward the docks with bows and weapons raised.

Elmerah tugged against Alluin, too weak to struggle as Tunisa forced Rissine toward the ship at knifepoint. Rissine's throat trickled blood around the blade's tip, seeping down onto her emerald coat.

Tunisa eyed the approaching elves wildly, shielding her body behind Rissine. "One more step, one arrow fired, and I will slit her throat!"

The elves hesitated.

As Elmerah watched on helplessly, one of the Arthali at Tunisa's back hefted a gleaming axe, dull side turned downward, then clobbered Tunisa on the back of the head. She fell like a sack of manure, freeing Rissine to spin around and kick the nearest Arthali in the face.

Vessa, Merwyn, and the other elves rushed onto the docks.

Elmerah pulled away from Alluin. "Help them!"

But he was already releasing her. He ran toward the docks while the other Arthali were still trying to figure out what had just happened. The elves darted forward with weapons raised. Celen's face scrunched with pain as he grabbed the smallest Arthali by the legs, yanking his feet out from under him before throwing him off the dock into the sea well below.

The Arthali who'd attacked Tunisa stood back from the chaos as his hair flowed from black to red, then fox ears appeared.

It was bloody Killian! Elmerah slumped into the dirt, unable to do anything but watch. How long had Killian been waiting in disguise amongst the Arthali?

Isara moved to her side, then knelt. "Don't worry, I'll keep their magic at bay."

Elmerah kept her eyes glued to the docks. Rissine evaded another Arthali grabbing for her, then kicked him in the back as he barreled past. Another charged her, his sword held high, but received an elven arrow in his chest. Down he went into the sea.

"Leave her!" an Arthali shouted. "Without magic, we'll be shot down!" One of the men picked up Tunisa and tossed her over his shoulder, and together the Arthali fled back toward their ship, leaving their prisoners behind.

Vessa knelt to check on Celen, who'd slumped over after throwing that Arthali off the docks. Others attended Zirin.

The nearest elven archers glanced back to Elmerah. "Do we go after them?" one asked. "Stop them from sailing away?"

Elmerah hunched her back, pressing her knees into the dirt as relief flooded through her. The Arthali were leaving. With their magic suppressed, they'd not face armed elves.

She shook her head, feeling numb. "No, let them flee. Let us be done with killing this day." She could still smell burnt flesh on the wind. It was only a matter of time before Isara surveyed the bodies, and realized her brother was amongst them.

She wasn't sure if she should laugh, cry, or curl up in the dirt and just die right there. Somehow, Alluin and Rissine were both safe—no thanks to her.

Elmerah looked up to Isara, but she had already turned, her gaze on something in the distance.

Elmerah turned too. The smoke had cleared, and in the center of charred bodies, a blond-haired figure dressed in velvet was staggering to its feet.

CHAPTER TWENTY-TWO

Daemon stood amongst the bodies of his Dreilore soldiers. The arrow still protruded from his chest, staining his garish brocade tunic with blood.

"Cut him down!" one elf shouted.

"No!" Isara screamed, rushing toward him. She stumbled across bodies, her tattered cloak whipping wildly behind her.

"You foolish girl!" Daemon gasped at his sister as she reached him, his hushed but sharp words echoing across the crashing tide.

Alluin returned to Elmerah's side and helped her back to her feet.

She wrapped her arm around his shoulders, her gaze on Daemon and Isara. "You missed his heart."

"You promised Isara you would not kill him."

She wasn't sure whether to laugh or cry. "He's still wounded, he may yet die."

He held her waist tightly, steadying her as she swayed. "He was about to kill you. I did what I could."

She smiled, but it soon wilted. He'd done better than her. She'd obliterated everyone in her path. It wasn't like she hadn't killed before, and she held no love for Dreilore, but . . . they hadn't stood a chance. Killing in such a way wasn't natural. Magic like hers shouldn't exist.

"Zirin and Celen?" she asked breathily. "Are they well?"

Alluin nodded. "The Arthali will think twice before attacking again after having their magic nullified. On equal footing, my people are better fighters than yours." His gaze drifted to Isara as she helped Daemon to lie back on the ground. "What do we do?"

She ignored the subtle insult. He was right regardless. Staring at Daemon, she shook her head. "Well, at least he's still alive. I'm still trying to decide if that's a good or bad thing."

"The Dreilore may return to fetch him."

She licked her cracked, burnt lips, glancing back at her sister kneeling and hitting her shackles on a rock. Killian and two elves had Celen on his feet, and Zirin had been moved off the docks onto the ground.

"We need to get out of here," she decided. "We should board Rissine's ship for now. Get out to sea before the rest of the Dreilore return." She glanced back. The Arthali ship was making great progress, probably Tunisa's doing, since she was of the Winter Isle's clans.

She worried for a moment that they might return with their magic no longer nullified, but the ship grew smaller and smaller, heading northwest. Of course, with Isara around, they'd probably made the right choice. She turned her attention back to Alluin.

"What about them?" He nodded toward Isara and Daemon.

One of the elves approached before she could answer.

Elmerah glanced at her, then had to glance again. It was Vail, the healer they'd left behind in Faerune.

Vail looked Elmerah over with calm assessment, her green tunic and darker green breeches neat and unstained.

"I didn't see you with the others," Elmerah observed, suddenly feeling awkward with how she was clinging to Alluin.

Vail pushed a lock of rich brown hair behind her pointed ear. "I am not a fighter, Elmerah. I waited out of sight. I joined Rissine's crew because they needed a healer." She glanced down at Elmerah's limply hanging hand, then up to the other near Alluin's shoulder. "Hold out your hands please, I must assess the extent of your injuries."

Elmerah shook her head. "Tend Daemon's arrow wound first."

Vail's eyes widened.

"He wants us all dead!" Vail argued.

"Yes, he does, but we don't have time for big decisions

right now. We'll take him out to sea. Isara claims he has no magic, so he won't be able to harm anyone."

Vail hesitated, then nodded. "We have two of your mounts. We can use one to transport him to the ship. We can make a stretcher to hoist him on board." She glanced at Alluin, then turned and walked away.

Elmerah sighed. Everything hurt, but what she wanted now most of all was rest, and to wipe away the images of all the burnt corpses she'd created. She looked to Alluin. "Take me to my sister, please."

Not commenting on her choice to kidnap Daemon, he helped her turn and walk toward Rissine, still struggling with her shackles.

Rissine stopped clanging her shackles as they reached her. Her dark eyes raised and landed on Elmerah.

"Is your ship ready to sail? I'd like to leave land before the Dreilore return."

Rissine watched her for a long moment, unsaid words passing through her calculating gaze. "Your fire—"

"Later," Elmerah cut her off. "Plenty of time to talk about that later."

Rissine's gaze flicked to Alluin, then she nodded. She climbed to her feet, extending her shackled hands. "I can't get these off without my magic."

Elmerah glanced back toward Isara, now kneeling beside Vail, who had removed Daemon's arrow. Her instinct warred with compassion. Daemon needed to die, but Isara needed him to live. "Isara can nullify the enchantment long enough to damage the shackles, but it will have to wait awhile." She looked back to Rissine. "Your ship?"

Rissine scowled, but nodded. "The elves can sail . . . well enough."

Aided by Killian and an elf, Celen hobbled toward them. Killian's face was pinched with the effort of keeping him aloft. The elf struggled just as much, judging by his shuffling steps, but he attempted to keep it off his face.

"Sorry, Ellie," Celen said, winding his arm around Killian's neck to wipe a trickle of blood from his hairline. "I wasn't much help in a fight with water beneath us. No earth to raise."

"Not your fault," Elmerah said, looking to Killian. "You, on the other hand, how did you manage to infiltrate the Arthali?"

Though his shoulders were hunched with Celen's weight, Killian beamed and lifted his chin. "When the fight broke out, I saw Celen throw one of the Arthali off the docks. I just made myself look like him."

"But we told you to leave," Alluin argued. "We *saw* you leave with the others."

Killian grinned. "I didn't go far."

Vessa hurried toward them, her features slick with sweat and sagging with fatigue. She stunk of the burnt corpses she'd passed. "Saredoth will survive. We should leave while we still can."

Elmerah glanced back. Isara and a male elf were trying to help Daemon onto a horse, but even in his injured state, he fought them.

Isara, her expression uncharacteristically stern, tugged Daemon's arm around her shoulder then dragged him along past the horse. He stumbled, too weak to fight her much, though he cursed all the way.

"You can't take me onto that bloody ship!" he winced, gasping.

"Quiet now," Vail soothed, trailing behind them. "You'll reopen the wound."

Daemon hung his head, matted blond hair covering his features, and allowed himself to be guided toward the ship.

"Can you climb the ladder?" Isara asked Daemon as they passed.

"I *will* not."

Isara's next words were lost on the wind as she and Daemon made way down the docks, followed by Vail, who glanced again at Alluin as she passed.

Elmerah leaned more heavily on Alluin, the gravity of all that had transpired catching up to her. "Take me to the ship, will you?"

He nodded to the others present, then helped her walk onto the docks. Daemon, Isara, and Vail had already reached the ship, and to Elmerah's surprise, Daemon was willingly climbing the ladder, with Isara scowling up at him from the docks.

Elmerah glanced at Alluin's profile as he silently supported her, curious about his thoughts. He'd been the one guarding her back against the Dreilore, the only one not too consumed in battle to see what had happened from start to finish. What must he think of her now?

He'd never looked at her as a monster, not even from the moment they first met. She hadn't realized such a fear was on her list until that moment. Her list of fears was growing longer by the day.

Number one: Egrin Dinoba.

Number two: losing those she cared for—also a growing list.

Number three: no longer having Alluin to watch her back.

Number—

Well, there were many more fears, but they had reached the ship, and the pressing fear now involved how she would board it. She peered up at the daunting climb. Isara, Vail, and Daemon had all gone up, so at least there were three less people to see her should she fall. A larger ship would have had a plank to embark upon, but it seemed her lack of luck would continue.

"Don't worry," Alluin said as she removed her arm from around his shoulders. "I won't let you fall."

They were just the words she needed to hear . . . in so many ways. Her legs trembling, she grasped the ladder and hoisted herself up. With a steadying inhale of salt air, she took it rung by rung, one step at a time.

Egrin

E grin waited north of the port, down on the coast with a view of the docks above. He stood utterly still, feeling centuries of work crashing down around him, swirling away like the sea foam eddying near his boots.

If he'd been asked a year ago who could thwart him, Isara Saredoth would have been the last person to cross his mind. He'd watched her grow up, always a timid little thing, never arguing with her father or brother. Having realized her particular gifts early on, he'd always wondered at them, as she was not his true kin. In all his years in this realm, he was never once tempted to sully his blood with the weakness of humanity.

Now Isara, with the help of the cursed Volund Sisters, had become a true threat. He'd seen Elmerah's fire. It had shocked him. He wasn't sure he had ever been truly shocked. She was another threat, and with Isara's gifts able to nullify his magic . . .

He couldn't let this happen. He couldn't lose centuries of magic gathered from near and distant continents, almost enough to sustain his *true* power in this realm.

Now that he was so close to regaining his love, he could not lose her again. He *would* have those circlets, and he would devise a way to use Elmerah's power. Once it all was within his grasp, he'd tear his true love free from the realm of death, and all in the land would cower.

There was no room for humanity in the empire he would create with her. A new land of demons, ruled by their king and queen as they once were, so very many centuries ago.

CHAPTER TWENTY-THREE

Rissine

The ship swayed gently far out on the calm sea, lulling Rissine to sleep. She almost felt guilty for maintaining the captain's quarters while the others slept like fish piled into a barrel. She smiled softly. She didn't *really* feel guilty, it was her ship after all. They sailed south, and slightly west in no direction in particular, though they'd eventually reach a chain of small isles if they continued on. For now, this direction would buy them time to decide what would come next.

Flat on her back, she watched her lantern swaying from a hook on the ceiling. Normally she'd douse the wick when it was time for sleep, but tonight . . . tonight she needed light. She'd lived in darkness for far too long.

But Elmerah . . . she let loose a long inhale. Elmerah had seen her lightning in the distance, and she had come for her. Well, she chuckled, she had come for Celen and that Nokken, but when it really mattered, Elmerah had been there, refusing to let her big sister be taken away.

A knock on her cabin door made her jump.

"Come in!" she called out, knowing the visitor was unlikely to be an elf, for none would dare disturb her. Probably Zirin, though the fool should be resting after the injuries he'd sustained.

Her head turned as the door opened, revealing Elmerah. The lantern overhead swayed, for a moment harshly illuminating her burnt hair and red, welted skin. White bandages wrapped her hand clutching the door, winding down her wrists to disappear beneath the sleeves of a fresh tunic.

Rissine looked her over, ending on her face. "You should have the healer tend you. Those welts will scar."

Elmerah entered the cabin and shut the door behind her. "Vail gave me a salve." She tugged at the end of her burnt locks, now barely reaching her shoulders. "Nothing to do for this though."

Rissine sat up, leaning her back against the cabin wall abutting her bed. "You should be resting."

Elmerah walked across the cabin, then plopped down on the bed, elbows on knees, her back to Rissine. "My fire," she began after a moment.

"I saw but a flash of it, but we could all see what it did."

Elmerah's head hung further. "I could barely control it. It overwhelmed me."

"I thought as much, judging by the burns."

Elmerah turned a scowl her way.

Rissine sighed. "I was not being critical, I just don't know what you want me to say." In truth, she didn't understand how Elmerah had summoned so much magic, and why it had burned her.

"I want you to tell me I can control it. In the end—" she hesitated. "It was like a wildfire. I could not have quenched it even had I wanted to. The only thing I could do was set it free."

Rissine watched her back for a moment. It had been so long since her sister had talked to her in this way. After their mother died, Elmerah had shut her emotions away. She'd acted like she blamed Rissine even before she learned that to blame her was justified.

Rissine came to her knees and edged across the bed, swinging her legs over the side to sit beside her sister. Gingerly, she placed a hand upon her shoulder. "I cannot say what will happen. I cannot guarantee that you won't lose control of your magic, but you cannot hide from it, and you cannot run away. To do so would be the surest guarantee that it will overwhelm you."

Elmerah smiled softly, though her red-rimmed eyes drooped with fatigue. "You never were one for comforting words."

"You are strong. You don't need my lies."

Elmerah's expression shut down at that, and Rissine realized she'd said the wrong thing. For it was a single lie that drove Elmerah away in the first place. One she would never forgive.

"I cannot believe you allowed Daemon Saredoth on my ship," she sighed, hoping to quickly change the subject.

Elmerah snorted, a bit of emotion returning to her expression. "He's Isara's brother, and we need Isara on our side." Her shoulders slumped so far forward, Rissine worried she might fall over.

"Lie down," she instructed, rising to help Elmerah down onto the bed.

"I'll return to my cabin," she yawned.

Rissine pressed Elmerah's left shoulder until the right fell to the mattress, then she took her boot-clad feet and lifted them onto the bed. "Stay here, I'll fetch the salve for your burns."

Elmerah didn't answer.

She went for the door, stopping to don her boots along the way. Her laces knotted, Rissine turned back to find Elmerah had wiggled her way up to the single pillow, and had clutched it greedily beneath her head and shoulder.

She reached for the door, but paused to watch as her sister drifted off to sleep. Her heart hurt with how badly she wanted to protect her. It had been the one task her mother had given her that morning, so long ago, when she knew she'd be saying goodbye to her two daughters forever. *Protect your sister. She may lack power now, but give her time. When the time comes, she will burn entire empires to the ground.*

The words now held new meaning to Rissine. At every Arthali's birth, the stars were charted, giving clues to what that witch would become, and what he or she would accomplish throughout their lives.

Her mother had never told them what the stars held for Elmerah, not until that fateful day. Rissine realized now why Elmerah had been kept in the dark. Even as a girl, she wasn't keen on responsibilities, and would have fought her fate with every step.

With a sigh, she left the cabin and shut the door. For tonight, all she could do was fetch the healer's salve and tend her sister's burns.

As her boots echoed down the narrow hall toward the few other cabins, she realized that she didn't mind it. She didn't mind that her sister was more powerful than her, and she didn't mind that she'd found loyal allies who would die for her. Elmerah could burn down every city on the continent for all she cared. She only hoped that her beloved sister would not be reduced to ash in the process.

For that was a fate she could not control, as much as she would most certainly try.

Alluin

Alluin waited in the cabin he shared with Celen, Merwyn, Killian, and two other male elves. Elmerah, Vail, Vessa, and the other females shared another cabin. Daemon was locked in the brig, and Isara refused to be anywhere else but with him. The elves and Celen had lain to rest, while Merwyn sat hunched on his straw mat, gazing at his lap as if deep in thought. Alluin paid him little mind, as he had many thoughts of his own to contend with. Elmerah was supposed to come fetch him after she'd spoken to her sister, but he supposed the talk they needed to have was not one to happen quickly.

With a heavy sigh, he looked to Merwyn. "Are you feeling alright? Will you get sick without your treatments?"

Merwyn jolted as if startled, then turned wide eyes to him. "Treatments were to make me better, but damage is already done. My organs are damaged, but I do not think they will get worse." His gaze drifted back downward. He was silent for a long moment, then asked, "Where do you think Saida is?"

He'd known Saida was the only reason Merwyn had journeyed with Rissine. He'd probably hoped to find her somehow miraculously rescued by Elmerah. "Somewhere with Malon. We can only hope she is safe. Can I ask—" he hesitated. "Can I ask why you care so much for her?"

Merwyn shook his head, still looking down at his lap. "She is in danger. Hotrath will come for her. He will not give up so easily, and he has dark magics to guide him."

Truly, Alluin had not spared many thoughts for the Akkeri's High King since they'd escaped his clutches. "He wants her that badly?"

"He hopes to lift Akkeri curse. He will not give up. Ever."

Alluin laid back atop his straw mat. It wasn't comfortable, but it was better than hard ground. He stared up at the lantern swaying overhead. "Add him to our list of worries, then, but do not worry too much about Saida. Something tells me she is in less danger than any of us. Hotrath may hunt her, but Egrin hunts Elmerah. All near her are in great peril."

"Then why stay with her?"

He turned his head, but could only see Merwyn's hunched back. "What do you mean?"

"Why stay with her, when she puts you in peril? Perhaps better way could be found to defeat Dinoba."

Alluin opened his mouth, then closed it. "She is my—" he cut himself off. *Friend* wasn't the right word. *Friend* didn't cover the trust that had grown between them, nor the depth of their unlikely partnership. "I cannot explain it, not really, but I cannot abandon her, and I believe she feels the same for me. Even if there was a better way to defeat Egrin—which I do not believe there is—she gives me the strength to try."

Merwyn bowed his head further. "Then you understand why I care for Saida. Why I boarded this ship."

He turned his gaze up to his lantern, hoping Elmerah had found solace with her sister, and not a fight. "Yes, I suppose I do understand."

"Will you both shut your gaping mouths?" Celen groaned from a nearby mat. "Some of us incurred heavy damage today during a great display of heroics."

Alluin grinned. "Really? All I can remember is you being held prisoner by those Arthali."

"Held prisoner, *heroically*," Celen countered.

Alluin's grin broadened. He still found Celen a bit insufferable . . . but he wasn't the worst to have around. Not that he'd ever tell him that.

"Good*night*, Celen. Let us hope you prove more *heroic* tomorrow. I'm sure Rissine will give you a task on the ship befitting your station."

"Bloody elves," Celen laughed, "worse than even the sharpest-tongued Arthali."

Still smiling, Alluin closed his eyes. He and Elmerah would survive to see another sunrise, and for now, that was enough.

Saida

Dawn's light found Saida still in terrible pain, but she was alive, and she was riding in the direction of home. It would be a long journey with too few antlioch, but at least they had Brosod to guide them. She rode next to Saida, her eyes keen on the passing sand, scouting the ingredients she needed for her curse. They'd cast it once they reached the edge of the desert, and Saida would know where to find her friend.

Malon rode at her other side, having already taken a long turn walking in the hot sand. He wouldn't allow Saida to do the same, and if she was honest with herself, she likely wasn't capable. Her body ached from the beating Urali had bestowed upon her.

As she watched, Malon's brow furrowed beneath his head wrap. He glanced over his shoulder, his silver eyes locking on something in the distance.

She followed his gaze, then gasped. "The Makali."

Tan-clad figures on foot crested the horizon at their backs, their shapes hazy in the sharp sunlight. She could recognize no faces beneath the head wraps in the distance, but their numbers were vast.

"My clan," Brosod rasped.

"Saida," Malon said cautiously, "you stay here. I'll see what they want."

"I'm coming with you." She turned her antlioch, then pressed her heels into its sides and rode toward the Makali before Malon could stop her. With the circlet at her belt, she should be safe.

Malon's antlioch caught up to her a moment later. The other elves waited behind with Brosod.

"Will you at least let me do the talking?" Malon sighed.

"Maybe, if I like the words you choose."

He laughed tiredly. "This is going to be a very long journey, isn't it?"

She had no time to answer as they reached the Makali together, peering down at those nearest from atop their mounts.

"Why do you follow us?" Malon asked.

Saida recognized the male Makali who stepped forward as one who'd been in Urali's tent the night they first arrived. He held Urali's staff, the blue stones shining brilliantly in the sunlight. He bowed his head. "The magic of the gods flows through you. You have the power to regrow the desert. We did not know what Urali planned, and for such a slight, we are in your service. We will follow where you lead."

Saida looked to Malon, as she had absolutely no idea what to say.

But he was looking further into the Makali ranks. Far back, the crowd was shuffling. The movement came toward the front line until its source was produced.

Two young female Makali warriors held Phaerille between them, her hands bound in front of her with thick twine. Her face was badly bruised, her once-shining hair matted and dull.

The Makali who'd first spoken gestured to Phaerille. "Your traitor. We bring her to you for judgement."

Malon looked down at Phaerille's bruises in distaste. "It seems you have already passed judgement upon her."

Phaerille's gaze was all for Malon, her eyes pleading. "Malon—"

He lifted a hand to cut her off. "You tried to have Saida killed."

"I only—" The Makali holding Phaerille shook her.

Malon looked to Saida. "What would you have me do?"

Beneath her head wrap, Saida's mouth fell agape. He wanted *her* to decide?

"She betrayed you most of all," Malon pressed. "It is your choice."

She looked down to Phaerille, but couldn't quite meet her eyes. Was this what it meant to be a leader? Had her mother, as one of the six members of the High Council, dealt with such decisions every day?

The Makali waited silently for her judgement. Her gaze still on Malon, Phaerille quietly wept.

Saida hands balled into fists in her lap. Her mother had always taught her that leaders must be strong, and fair. Yet she was learning that the High Council had not always been fair. Far from it.

Had Faerune's treatment turned Phaerille into what she'd become?

"Bring her," she decided. "Keep her hands bound, and I do not want to hear a single word from her."

"You would have us lug her all the way across the desert?" Malon asked.

She smiled, though he could not see it. "No, Malon, I would have your army lug her across the desert."

He tugged the lower half of his head wrap loose to

reveal a crooked smile. "You mean, we get to keep them? Surely you jest."

She laughed, feeling emboldened by her decision. If she was to lead, then she would *lead*. "Egrin wrote his fate when he attacked my people and had my mother killed," She cast her gaze across the rows of waiting Makali, "so no, I do not jest. Now is not the time for jokes. Now is the time for war."

EPILOGUE

Days passed by, and slowly, they all could feel it. That shift in the wind, a sick feeling in the gut. More demons were pouring into the realm, more magic being stolen.

Upon the deck of a ship stood an elf and a witch, their sights set on the single death that would lead to a better future. Accompanied by kin and kith, they would find a way . . . together.

Sailing secretly behind them was an Akkeri ship, shrouded in mist. Few Akkeri possessed magic to summon an unearthly fog, but High King Hotrath was not just any Akkeri. He sensed Cindra's circlet very far off. He'd not relinquished hope on attaining the ornament, nor the one who bore it.

Far south at the desert's edge, rode a small party of elves with a mighty army at their heels. An army which had grown as word spread across the sands. Word that the magic of gods had returned to save them all.

And in the greatest city, a demon devised a plan. He could not confront his enemies directly, but he'd been alive long enough to understand mortal nature. He knew without doubt, that the best way to destroy a witch was to turn those she trusted most against her. For her power may be mighty, but deep down, her faith was weak.

Elmerah was the keystone. She had raised his enemies up against him, and she would be the one to make them fall.

ABOUT THE AUTHOR

For news, updates, and information, please visit:

www.saracroethle.com

MORE SERIES BY SARA C. ROETHLE

Tree of Ages

Tree of Ages

The Melted Sea

The Blood Forest

Queen of Wands

The Oaken Throne

Dawn of Magic: Forest of Embers

Dawn of Magic: Sea of Flames

Dawn of Magic: City of Ashes

The Duskhunter Saga

Reign of Night

Trick of Shadows

Blade of Darkness

Heir of Twilight

The Will of Yggdrasil

Fated

Fallen

Fury

Found

Forged

The Thief's Apprentice Series

Clockwork Alchemist

Clocks and Daggers

Under Clock and Key

The Xoe Meyers Series

Xoe

Accidental Ashes

Broken Beasts

Demon Down

Forgotten Fires

Gone Ghost

Minor Magic

Minor Magics: The Demon Code

SNEAK PEEK AT REIGN OF NIGHT, BOOK ONE OF THE DUSKHUNTER SAGA

I wiped the blood from my blade on the dead vampire's loose white shirt. Vampires share a penchant for fine fabrics and lace, don't ask me why. I'm not a scholar, I have no interest in studying the undead. My only purpose is to kill them.

I stood, taking in the stone walls mostly covered with tapestries, the heavy wooden furniture, and the sconces casting firelight across the dead vampire's body. I sheathed my sword across my back, wincing at the protesting bruising lining my shoulder blades. Even through a tough leather cuirass, getting thrown into a wall by a thousand-year-old being took its toll.

I froze at the sound of footsteps behind me, then relaxed as I caught his scent. "Hello Steifan, you're late." This was only our second hunt together, but it didn't take me long to memorize a scent.

"Alright Lyssandra, how do you do that?" He stepped

into the room, then stood at my side, looking down at the corpse. His armor matched mine, bearing the flaming crossed-swords insignia of the Helius Order. His jet black hair, hanging loose to his chin, framed questioning eyes.

"Do what? Kill vampires?"

"Know it's me approaching when I haven't spoken a word."

I shrugged as I unbraided my fiery red hair. "Trade secret." Unfortunately, I couldn't tell him I could recognize his scent. It would lead to other questions. The answers to which would guarantee excommunication from the very order to which I'd sworn fealty. The red hair, an uncommon trait in the Ebon Province, had already caused me enough trouble within the order. Lesser hunters thought me a witch. They were wrong, but the accusation was better than the truth.

"Did you cut out the heart?"

I smiled. "No, that's your punishment for being late." Cut out the heart and burn it. Just to be sure. I turned and strode out of the chamber, leaving Steifan cursing behind me.

I hated cutting out the hearts, though there was one vampire for whom I'd make an exception. I'd hoped tonight's hunt would lead me to him, but it seemed I'd been wrong again. Years of hunting across the continent, and still he eluded me.

Sometimes I could swear he watched me from the shadows, laughing at my ineptitude. Or maybe all that haunted me were the memories of what he'd done. Maybe he no longer cared at all.

I walked through the quiet estate, wondering what had happened to its true owners, though my imagination didn't have to stretch far. The vampire I'd just slain had likely killed them. The blood-drained bodies were probably buried in the wilting gardens.

I pushed open the heavy oak and iron door, taking a deep inhale of cool night air, tinged with the scent of swamp water. I wrinkled my nose at the after-scent. I hated hunting in the mires.

I waited outside until Steifan joined me. We untethered our horses and began our long ride. We wouldn't reach Castle Helius until the following night, if we were lucky and did not run afoul of any beasts. Or the dead vampire's flock.

I'm an experienced hunter, and Steifan had made it far enough to be my trainee, but facing an entire flock would be the death of us.

We rode on through the night until morning's light graced us. The dawn was always a sigh of relief for a hunter. During daylight we could rest easy.

Steifan dismounted first. We weren't far from the road, but in these parts, bandits were less of a worry than the creatures which dwelt deep in the mires. Still atop my mount, I searched for a flat area to sleep for the first time in three nights. Yet another thing I couldn't tell Steifan. Going so long without sleep was . . . unnatural.

Finding a suitable spot, I dismounted, unfurling a

rough woolen blanket from my saddlebag. The covering was more to keep out the light than for warmth. I hated sleeping in daylight.

With our horses tethered to a nearby tree, we both lay down to rest. Steifan was too close to me, but I didn't chastise him. It was only his second hunt, after all. Though most hunters were trained from birth, actually going on a hunt was always unnerving. We come from family lines resistant to vampire trickery, not from lines impervious to the emotional effects of cutting out someone's heart.

"Lyssandra?"

"Call me Lyss," I sighed, hoping whatever he needed to say would be brief. I was desperately in need of sleep.

"What if something sneaks up on us while we rest? Shouldn't one of us stand guard?"

"I'm a light sleeper."

This seemed to comfort him, for soon he began to snore as loud as a bear.

I sighed, tugging my blanket further over my face, willing myself to rest. I focused my senses on our surroundings. The horses gently grazing. A stream running somewhere far off. Birds carrying on a conversation in the oaks overhead.

I had almost drifted off when a new sound joined the cadence. Soft steps. Human. More than one.

If I woke Steifan I'd give myself away. I moved my fingers toward the sword at my side, under the blanket. I had just sealed my grip around the hilt when they charged.

I leapt from the ground, striking at a man who'd been ready to plunge a dagger into my chest. He jumped back out of reach. I knew instantly what he was, what they all were. I could sense them, just like I could sense vampires.

"Human servants!" I shouted, hoping Steifan was already awake behind me.

I glanced back to see him standing with his sword out. The three human servants, two males and a female, circled us. Their clothing was little more than rags, their forms thin, but appearances could be deceiving. Servants were almost as strong as vampires, and almost as fast, though they lacked vampire mind tricks and a thirst for blood.

"Watch my back," I growled to Steifan. I hefted my sword, looking to the man who'd tried to impale me in my sleep. "Well, are you going to avenge your fallen master, or are we going to stare at each other all day?"

They attacked. The man with the dagger fell easily to my blade. The second man went for Steifan, and I could only hope he'd be alright. The woman wielded her blade like she knew how to use it, and her rage-filled eyes were on me. Her brown hair hung limp and loose down to her waist, adding to the feral appearance provided by her tattered clothing.

We charged as one, our blades meeting with a deafening *clang*. Her eyes widened at my strength. I sensed what she was, but it was clear she did not share such gifts.

She let out a guttural cry and charged again. I could hear Steifan fighting the other man behind us, but couldn't look. I had to quickly disable my opponent so I could help him. The woman sliced her sword toward my belly. I spun away, then rammed my blade's tip into her back. I shoved the blade upward, then pulled it out. Before she could drop, I turned toward Steifan.

The man had him on the ground. Steifan's hands patted about him for his sword, lost somewhere in the yellow grass. They were ten paces away, too far for me to reach him in time. But I couldn't let Steifan die so young.

I threw my heavy sword, aimed with precision, and it thunked into the remaining man's back. He toppled over, dead.

Human servants aren't nearly as hardy as their masters, though these had not belonged to the vampire we killed. Servants died with their masters. Kill a vampire, kill its servants. These belonged to someone else in the dead vampire's flock.

With a final glance around to ensure no one else approached, I walked toward Steifan and retrieved my blade.

Steifan stared up at me, his hazel eyes wide. "How did you do that?" he panted.

I knelt to wipe my blade on the man's grimy clothing. "I've been with the order a long time."

"No." He was still sitting in the grass, looking at me all

horrified. "No, I've seen the greatest fighters perform, none moved as fast as you. None could throw a heavy sword like that. A dagger, maybe, but not a sword."

I grimaced, rising as I sheathed my clean blade. It would need to be oiled later to prevent rust. "I don't know what you want me to tell you."

Finally, he stood, his eyes scanning the grass for his sword. "I want you to tell me the truth."

I looked down at the three dead servants, debating my options. What would he say if I told him the truth? Would he tell the Order? My cynicism set in. That would be some way to thank me for saving his life. But if I didn't tell him, would he speak of what happened here today? Would he tell others I moved too fast for a human? Would the elders begin to question what I was?

The Potentate had made it very clear Steifan was to be my trainee until he was ready to hunt on his own. It would take at least a year. Could I really keep my secret from him when our lives might depend on my skills?

I sighed heavily. Better to catch him off guard and know his reaction now. If he seemed too horrified, I could always kill him. I didn't like the idea, but if I thought it necessary, I'd do it to protect myself.

I met his waiting gaze. "I will tell you this, and your secrecy will be my payment for saving your life."

My gut churned. Maybe I should just let him talk, let him tell others his suspicions about me. Then again, if he told them what I was about to divulge, would they even believe it? Not likely, but . . .

"I am a vampire's human servant," I breathed. "Every hunt, I hope that he will be my quarry."

Steifan blinked at me for several heartbeats, then burst out laughing, sounding a bit shrill and hysterical, probably because of the three dead bodies at our feet. It took him a moment to calm himself. "Thanks for that, I needed a laugh, and thanks for saving my life."

He searched around, finally finding his sword. He picked it up and sheathed it, then turned back to me. "Perhaps we'll find better rest at an inn."

I nodded hesitantly, schooling my expression to not give too much away. It was probably for the best that he didn't believe me. He now seemed to have dismissed my speed as a trick of his frantic mind.

I took one last look at the bodies before we moved toward our battle-hardened horses. Poor sots. Most human servants were entirely devout to their masters, they would die for them. But not me. I wasn't sure if it was because hunter blood ran through my veins, or some other trick of fate, but I hadn't been besotted with my *master*. He'd been the one besotted with me.

Though neither of us would die for each other, we'd eventually die together. Taking his life would in effect take my own. I quite literally couldn't live without him.

What price, freedom?

Printed in Great Britain
by Amazon